Let's Date Together

A Companion for the Sexually Adventurous Couple

by Lisa and Jim Morrison

POLYAMORY PRESS

BARCELONA

Let's Date Together
A Companion for the Sexually Adventurous Couple

Copyright © 2019 by Lisa and Jim Morrison

978-1-7336067-0-7 (paperback)
978-1-7336067-1-4 (eBook)

Published by Polyamory Press

Cover design by Julian Luskin
Publishing services by AuthorImprints, California

For Inquires Please Visit

nonmonogamy.com

Table of Contents

INTRODUCTION

HIS VACANT GAZE slowly turned to me. The group fell silent.

"Can anyone tell Bret what to do when the chatter inside your head is louder than your own thoughts?"

"I drink!" Wayne blurted and then laughed his three-pack-a-day cackle.

"Sure, drinking can stop the voices in our head but only temporarily, right?" I said, and then I noticed Bret preoccupied again—the internal stare had set in. I made a note on his record, "check Seroquel dosage."

the Awakening

At the edge of the semi-circle, I saw Annie coyly shift so that her skirt showed more of her chubby teen thighs. I forced my voice to brighten, "Bret, yesterday you told us you had a dog when you were a boy. What was his name?" Annie stopped flirting for a moment, "I have a boxer, Ralf—he's so cute!"

When all else fails, when the group is getting out of control, pets are the universal mood shifter. That's not something I learned in grad school, no, the pet distraction comes from conducting thousands of groups at the psychiatric hospital.

However, today when a group is getting out of control I say, "I like to start with a woman and end with a good pounding by a man." That usually gets their attention and lots of nods from the women. But, I'm getting ahead of myself—let me explain.

As you have probably guessed, I'm a psychotherapist. I work with the most severely mentally ill at a crisis stabilization unit at a public hospital. I conduct two to three group therapy sessions a day with whomever has been admitted. I see suicide attempts and people with bipolar, schizoaffective, and addiction issues, and all forms of anxiety and depression that are severe enough to require hospitalization. I make assessments—dozens a day—and I have become quite good at it. The goal is to determine the patient's mental status at the moment, then, in coordination with the psychiatrists, stabilize them and hopefully give them the tools to manage their illness. Perhaps equally importantly, I work with the families of the patients to educate them in understanding their loved one's condition and help them navigate the complex task of living with an ill family member.

I came to therapy via poetry. From my earliest nerdy days in high school I was reading and writing poetry. And although I put myself through college without financial support from my family, I graduated with the most unemployable degree—poetics. When I met my husband, I fell in love with not just him, but his family, and I decided to follow in my father-in-law's professional footsteps. I received an advanced degree from a university where Freud once lectured, and so my training is in analytical therapy. After internships in community health centers, I moved with my

2

the Awakening

engineer husband to a southern city—blocks away from where we went to college.

Although we appeared to live a life with the trappings of bohemian intellectuals, we actually had a very conventional suburban existence. I raised two children and took a backseat to my husband's career. After 22 years of living in the shadow of my husband, I chose to separate and eventually divorce. There was no single event or crisis that led to the end of my marriage just the slow realization that I would never have a life that didn't revolve around my husband. We had a good sex life, a comfortable home, and a high profile in our community, but I was treading the sea of my own existence.

I had confidence in my professional life and as a mother, but my self-esteem at home was so low that I felt I had no choice but to move out of the family home. I was in my early 40's and assumed I would downsize my life to accommodate the low salary of a psychotherapist. I was resigned to a simple life, but a life of my own. It was then that I met Juan, a Latin dance instructor, and during a bachata, I asked him if he made love like he danced. He did.

Juan rang my bells, but it was clearly a friend-with-benefits arrangement. After my separation, I practiced dating. I went on Match.com, kissed a few frogs, and reconnected with old friends. And then one night at a bar with girlfriends I was introduced to Jim. "You have a lot in common, he's a writer and newly separated after a long marriage. Jim's a character like you—he's lived many lives," our mutual friend told me. "But you should know he is in a relationship with a girl 30 years younger than him, a college student."

You would think my assessment skills would kick in and I would avoid a guy in a questionable relationship, but I didn't. While in college, two of my girlfriends had married their much older professors (you could do that back then without being fired) and they are both still happily married 25 years later. Jim had an irrepressible smile and a quirky sense of humor, and as the night wore on (and with a drink or two in me) I blurted out, "When you are done with the college girl—give me a call—I'll wear you out!" My mother always said my mouth would get me in trouble, and she was right. Trouble, yes, but fun trouble.

4

A few weeks later Jim and I were dating. His affair had ended and although he was going through a difficult divorce (and he was living on a houseboat that looked like a trailer on pontoons and driving a bright-red used smart car), I was falling hard for him. We were spending a lot of time together, but I was concerned that I was just a rebound girl. I feared I was getting too involved.

Jim had an interesting background having grown up in a privileged family where famous people came for family dinners, but like many in his generation, Jim had rebelled. He had studied writing in college and once drove from London to India where he lived a simple existence wholly different from his upbringing. Eventually, Jim found his way back to the U.S. and to a middle-class family of his own. He started a business and had a few patents—his rebellious spirit even came out in his work. From the outside his life looked ideal, but Jim's marriage was all about his children, and after decades of living with someone who had grown to dislike him, he had an affair with the college student. When I met

the Awakening

him, he was the target of gossip and judgment, but he had a strange calm about him. I recognized that he had been emotionally damaged, but he had a quiet confidence and was able to withstand the swirling drama around him.

What I recognized in Jim then, and see now, is that despite being judged by others, he's not afraid to embrace controversial lifestyle choices. When he was a teen, he turned his back on his family's comfortable life and traveled the world as an itinerant backpacker. When he decided it was time to have a family himself, he left his hippy ways behind and moved to a luxurious gated community in the suburbs (much to the chagrin of his crunchy friends). After his divorce, he left his comfort zone again and moved into the houseboat. Like my friend said, Jim has lived many lives—lives that I had only read about as a literature student.

Having said that I understood him and his situation, I did seriously contemplate breaking up because I was afraid of getting hurt. And then in another moment of being more therapist than girlfriend, I told him, "You are fresh out of a long and bad marriage; you need to date more."

Jim didn't skip a beat and replied with his boyish naughty grin, "I agree, but I really like you, I don't want to date anyone else. Why don't we date together?"

"What the hell does that mean?"

"Well, I'm not sure, but I have some ideas. I mean, when you were seeing Juan and me at the same time it made me jealous but also kind of turned on."

And so began our discussion about non-monogamy.

A month later we were at an industry convention in Vegas for Jim's work. Our first night in Vegas we were obliged to go to a sponsor event at the nightclub Tao. I was wearing a knee-length black, Ann Taylor skirt that had a flirtatious flare and a beige long-sleeve silk tunic. I was dressed appropriately for a professional event—certainly not sexy club wear. Intermixed with the industry crowd were the young, dressed to seduce, beautiful partiers—it was very clear who was with the conventioneers and who was there to have fun.

Jim and I had a couple of drinks and danced and flirted with each other when Jim excused himself to go to the bar. There was a long line, and Jim had been gone for maybe 15 minutes when he slid up behind me and playfully danced and teased and ground himself around my backside. I giggled and wiggled back in response.

I could feel his growing member press against me and when his hands went from my bottom to catch a feel of my breasts I pulled back—those weren't Jim's hands! I looked up and saw Jim across the bar watching me, and the look in his eye was sheer rapture. He was transfixed. I slowly turned to come face to face with a handsome impeccably dressed man about the same age and build as Jim. The stranger wore a beautifully tailored shirt that hinted of a workout body and straight black Armani slacks where I could see the healthy bulge I had felt behind me.

The man put a hand on my face and leaned in to kiss me; I kept my gaze on Jim, tilted my head and met the stranger's kiss. He had firm lips and tasted of a dirty martini. I let myself go, closed my eyes, and wrapped a hand around his neck. I was shaken and stirred. I remember thinking, "Well, here goes nothing, I hope this is what Jim meant."

The Awakening

I felt Jim come up behind me and he whispered, "I love watching you. I love you." I reached down and felt the stranger's package and then put my other hand behind me and did the same to Jim. A hand slid up my long skirt to my panties and another on my butt. This time when I opened my eyes I saw one of the gorgeous young nightclub studs staring at me. My skirt was up, my thighs exposed, and a hand was caressing me. The voyeur's shocked gaze traveled right to my genitals, and I felt my legs buckle between the two men.

There was a moment when I thought, "What am I doing?" Not because of the morality (I was comfortable being naughty), but rather it was my fear of losing Jim. Even though we had talked about threesomes with another girl or a guy it seemed different having a spontaneous encounter in a nightclub, and one that Jim didn't arrange; we hadn't talked through all the "rules." I had fallen in love with Jim, and now only a couple of months into our relationship I was making out and groping another man in front of him.

It was the perfect first dalliance. The stranger, Greer, a rep for a manufacturer, was a gentleman and when we declined to go back to his hotel, he gave me one last kiss. Oh my, I still get tingles thinking about it—his stubbly beard brushing my cheeks, the martini tongue, and the way he gently moved a lock of hair from my forehead. I held Jim's hand while Greer kissed me and I could feel Jim's thumbs sweeping over my fingers in the most loving way. Greer slowly pulled away put a hand on Jim's shoulder, "She is a gorgeous, sexy woman—you are a very lucky guy."

There were voices in my head telling me what I was doing was risky and selfish—after all, my whole life to that point was about caring for others from my work to my home life. But, another voice came through, "You are free—make your own choices."

Jim and I sat on a couch in the corner of the club and silently watched the dancers. I was so close to Jim I was half sitting in his lap, his hand on autopilot stroking my thighs. I was on blissful, high alert. My body and mind seemed to dance with the sensation of the line we just crossed. A train of thoughts streaked across my mind. "I'm alive. I'm young. I'm me. I'm back!" The Lisa-mom and the Lisa-wife was resurrecting into a new woman, and oddly a stranger/ sales rep was the man in the right place at the right time. On the way to our hotel, Jim opened the taxi door for me and practically carried me over the room's threshold. When we made love, he narrated what he saw that night with Greer, and his slow storytelling made me feel like I was a character in an Anaïs Nin novella—I had a literary, out-of-body orgasm.

The next morning Jim slept in, and I went to the internet. The first thing I searched for was "threesomes" and imme-diately got a blizzard of porn sites. Interesting, I thought. So I bookmarked a few for later viewing; however, that was not at all what I was looking for. My academic hat was on. I had one overriding question, "If what we did was wrong in the eyes of normative coupling, then why did we feel so excited and seem to be closer than ever?"

I went through a pot of lousy coffee and half the lap-top's battery life, and all I found was negative, negative,

8

the Awakening

negative. From the professional literature that I perused almost all the papers focused on the issues revolving around infidelity—the causes, frequency, and treatments. But I found very little legitimate academic work on consensual non-monogamy. I bookmarked the syllabus for the annual conference on sex therapy—American Association of Sexuality Educators, Counselors & Therapists (AASECT). There was only one paper/lecture on non-monogamy. When I read the abstract, it was obvious the author was starting from the assumption that non-monogamy was not normative behavior and is either practiced by people with pre-existing psychological problems or by people who would be damaged following the practice of non-monogamy.

The professional bias against non-monogamy reminded me of when I was first studying analytical psychotherapy when homosexuality was still listed in the *DSM* (*Diagnostic and Statistical Manual of Mental Disorders*, the standard diagnostic manual for mental illness) and therefore considered to be "treatable." My instinct, in the absence of facts, was that the cultural bias against non-traditional sexual behavior was affecting the professional research on non-monogamy.

My brief experience and intuition were indicating something very different—that non-monogamy was not all bad. There must be more. Therapists are skilled at being non-judgmental—to not just listen to the content of what a patient is saying but to assess the underlying emotion. What I was feeling—as well as Jim—and probably even Greer—wasn't adding up to what I was reading. And so began my quest to not just understand what was happening to Jim

9

and me, but also what was being researched and especially what was not being studied in the professional realm.

Later that same day Jim received a message from a couple on a dating website who were also in Vegas for the weekend. "Let's go and meet for at least a drink," he said. Little did he know I was about to interrogate the poor couple.

Turns out they were not at all what I expected. The couple were not the sleazy, tacky image of swingers I had conjured. Mike and Eva had been married for over two decades, and both were physicians. And let's just say I learned and, um, experienced a lot that night. That was my first physical interaction with a woman. Perhaps the biggest surprise of all, in the heat of the action, I told Jim I wanted to see him with the wife—an incredibly charged experience for me that would have seemed crazy just 24 hours earlier. We went from a boundary-pushing nightclub flirtation to playing for the gold in the Olympics in just 24 hours. By the time we left Vegas, I needed a new computer.

Our ordinary lives continued. Other than heightening our own sex life, not much changed after Vegas, although at times we'd meet someone and I'd wonder if they too were non-monogamous. BV (before Vegas), I would have thought that if someone had swung once then they were then a swinger, but, of course, that isn't true. Even now, although we are highly immersed in the subject of non-monogamy, we aren't swingers any more than people who go to church on the holidays are religious. What did change was our academic and intellectual interest in contemporary relationships and sexuality.

the Awakening

Jim had been writing (trying to write) a novel about the spiritual transformation of an American teen—a tongue-in-cheek Siddhartha for our times. After our trip to Vegas, he wrote a scene where the protagonist of the novel met a non-monogamous couple. When a literary agent read an early draft, she told Jim, "That scene about swinging is the book—write that!" I agreed with the agent. Jim's fascination and excitement about having a committed relationship and still having sexual adventures were obvious in his writing. Jim then wrote a short story based on something he heard from the physicians we had met in Vegas—"We started spooning again after we opened up." I knew we were on to something.

After reading the spooning story (and getting hot and bothered), I asked Jim if he was trying to illuminate the "best-friend paradox." Jim just shrugged, so I continued, "One of the most basic and yet ironic problems with otherwise happy long-term relationships is that at some point most couples become complacent and the sexual dullness can be in converse proportion to how emotionally close they are. Being best-friends is sweet but not sexy. "

Jim was intrigued with my psycho-talk and wanted to hear more. After all, Jim wrote the story because he thought it was fun and sexy—not to illustrate a point. So I decided to write about what I saw was the underlying conundrum of the long-married couple who spoons again after opening up their marriage. I ended up writing a complement to Jim's fiction. That gave us an idea. Jim would write the stories, while I write the commentary from a psychological perspective.

There was a problem—a big problem but a solvable one. We didn't know anything about ethical non-monogamy. Jim thought live research into sexual adventure was the best idea ever—boys will be boys, right? The reality, though, was that I had a professional reputation and family life in our small town; I wasn't willing to come out as open. Along the way, I discovered that there was a nudist and adult resort about 100 miles from our home.

Our first night at the resort Jim and I were in the sports bar talking with a couple when some of their friends joined us. Soon, there was a circle of people around me as I playfully asked questions and flirted. A bemused man turned to Jim.

"Who the hell is she?"

"In the real world, Lisa is a group therapist," Jim explained.

"Well, it sure looks like she is conducting a session now," the man mumbled.

From that comment, we decided to conduct a workshop, "Cocktails and Confessions." The get-togethers were for couples to share their experiences about non-monogamy. Most of the participants were like us in that they were quiet about their sexual practices at home but were eager to meet like-minded people and discuss the discovery of their new activity.

Jim and I didn't conduct therapy sessions. In fact, I am no more a sex therapist than I am a couple's counselor; my practice is limited to severely mentally ill patients who are almost exclusively under the care of a psychiatrist. I admit now that I thought the academic pursuit of sexual practice was beneath me. Similarly, Jim was writing a coming-of-age

the Awakening

spiritual novel and viewed erotica as, well, trashy. But the very fact that sexual pleasure is limited to closed-door activity and hushed discussion is what makes the subject all the more important to us. Jim recounted advice from a creative writing professor, "Don't write something unless you are embarrassed by it."

Pursuing sexual pleasure is selfish and vain—so we are taught. However, we seek gratification all day, every day in the food we eat, the clothes we wear, the entertainment we enjoy, and the friends we socialize with. Humans are driven to pleasure because pleasure and seeking it is what keeps us alive and thriving as a species. Believe me, I know from treating depressed and suicidal patients if one can't experience pleasure (and that could be as simple as a bite of something yummy), the will to live is gone.

Humans have strong sex drives that have nothing to do with reproduction. Sexual desire propels human activity. Embracing non-traditional sexual pleasure for your partner and yourself can be risky, embarrassing, and uncomfortable but for all the reasons we fear sex, that same intensity can awaken us more than the five senses combined. By far.

We conducted workshops that I led with a series of questions I'd propose to the group and then moderate the discussion. It was fun and enlightening for all of us. We had couples who were just curious but not yet active, 20-some-things navigating Tinder dating, long-time open couples who frequent adult cruises and resorts, to couples who had opened up and then stopped for a variety of reasons.

The stories in this book are fictional, but all are based on snippets that we heard along the way—just like the spooning comment. The Commentary, "That's What She Said," and the Q&A, "WTF?" cover in detail many of the questions and answers we learned over the years, but here is the summation.

Make or break.

Sexual non-monogamy is the make-or-break of relationships. Opening up can bring a couple much closer together or push them farther apart.

You can't cure a bad marriage by having sex with others. Period.

You can enliven and enhance a good, but perhaps dulled, relationship through playful sexual adventure. Exclamation!

I learn and grow with the sex Jim and I have with others. My confidence in every aspect of my identity strengthened. I have pursued, but not always succeeded in, seducing people I wanted to make love with and learned a lot from the effort. I have expanded the type of people I am attracted to—younger, older. Most of all I view sex as a form of play with pleasure and delight as the focus, and happiness, relief, and expansiveness as an enduring result.

I have never been happier, and I have come to realize that female sexual agency is one of the last incomplete bastions of gender equality. Women are the key to the sexual non-monogamy phenomena. Obviously, the female in a couple has to participate, but the difference now is that women are actively sexual in a way that used to be the prerogative of men. Men have always had sexual choices that females didn't. But now that women can control their fertility (and don't need to be married to please the church

14

or their parents) and can be financially independent, sex is a woman's choice, as it always has been for men.

I know now that when Jim said "let's date together" what he meant was that he loved me, he wanted to spend his life with me, and he wanted us to experience and explore our life together, with security and with full sexual freedom—something neither of us thought was possible in the past.

In the wake of #MeToo incidents—the egregious acts of assault and harassment, abuse of power as well as the initially consensual encounters gone wrong—I can't help but wonder why sexual pleasure, the undercurrent of consensual sexual activity, is a subject rarely addressed. I'll leave the legal and socio-political issues to others who are more qualified than I. Unfortunately, like most women, I have had my #MeToo occurrences with all the accompanying anger and regret and conflicting emotions. However, as the mother of a teenage daughter, a therapist, and as an open partner, my concern is for the individual rather than the subject in general. My priority is for a person's well-being. So in addition to practical advice about sex, I also quote an original, Socrates: "Know thyself."

When I treat a patient with anxiety, we first identify the physical clues of anxiety. For some, it's a pounding heart rate while for others, it's sweaty palms or dizziness. The signs vary with the patient and with the circumstances. One has to recognize the signs of anxiety to try to mitigate the effects, then we can use the tools and tricks to fend off an attack. The treatment is proportionately much more successful the sooner one recognizes the anxiety building.

So, here is some good news. The better and more accurately a woman recognizes the signs of her sexual arousal or conversely her hesitancy, repulsion, or reluctance, the easier it is to enjoy and heighten a sexual experience or to make the decision to stop, slow, or modify a sexual encounter. There are times when women go along with sex even when it is not pleasurable to them. Let's use #MeToo not just to end sexual assault and harassment, but to put an end to female sexual acquiesce. Sometimes therapy is stating the obvious, so here I go again—sex is pleasure. A woman's orgasm has absolutely nothing to do with procreation. If it doesn't feel right physically or emotionally, speak up; be clear.

And here is even better news: the path to a woman's self-knowledge is play, play, play. Masturbating. Teasing and games with a willing partner. Reading and watching erotica. Exploring your body and erotic mind. Finding triggers—good and bad. Talking about sex with your partner and friends. Think of it as coming out as a sexual being. And even more good news—the learning never stops! As any open woman knows they have turn-ons and turn-offs that change and evolve. As one workshop participant said, "I even surprise myself!"

As much fun as it is to explore one's sexual turn-ons, for a female the signs of arousal are not always obvious, to her or to others. But, what about men you ask? Men are relatively easy—we all know an erection is a spontaneous and a visible response. But the magic and beauty and mystery of the sexual female is her subtle and sometimes masked and evolving signs of arousal. When a woman is aware of her

the Awakening

body's reaction to sexual interest, she has power over her flirting, signals, and communication. When a woman feels her interest and arousal build, she is in better control of her actions. She can better make an informed decision.

The human mating ritual is full of nonverbal cues, and that's fun and exciting. But a woman's consent should not be a cue. "Yes" and "No" come from knowing thyself.

Jim and I have had almost exclusively positive experiences with non-monogamy. We have met wonderful people and made new friends that we feel close to emotionally and physically. But please don't confuse our fascination and excitement about ethical non-monogamy with the promotion of it. Opening up a marriage to sex with others can be a tricky business. We do hope this is a companion for happy couples—couples in untroubled relationships—who are looking to free up their imaginations, tap into their fantasies, and enliven their sex lives: the last frontier of fun and pleasure for adults.

CHAPTER ONE

Oz

EVERYTHING WAS DIFFERENT. I mean everything. Maybe it was better that way; we were so out of our element that we couldn't compare anything to our home life in suburban Arlington, Virginia. It's a funny story how we got to a single day that rocked our world, but you can assume we did it on a lark and without a bit of planning. Good thing—we probably never would have come if we knew what we were in for, especially when we think of Isabella. God bless that woman, I do love her like crazy. But if she knew we were going to be having sex in public in a city of 65,000 naked people well, of course, she would have thought I was out of my mind.

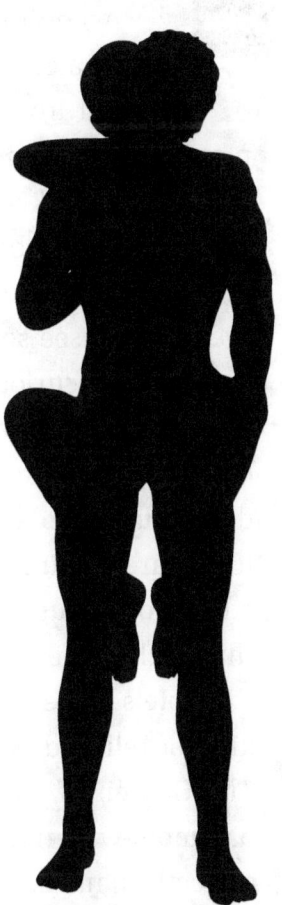

Ok, so I guess I should tell you how we got to the nude city and the public sex. Isabella and I were on our summer vacation in France. It was our second time, and we just loved touring romantic, enchanting, love-affirming Paris and the countryside charm of Provence with its stately chateaus, tempting vineyards and rolling, flowered, painting-inspiring hillsides. This time, we went to the South of France, and we were a little bolder than then our first, itinerary-designed trip.

We rented a car and stopped wherever we liked, stayed where we could, and moved on. A little off the typical tourist-track of the chic French Riviera was a charming Mediterranean town, Bouchon—a city dating back to the Ancient Greeks from 500 BC. According to the brochures, Bouchon was one of the oldest towns in France. The village had ruins and forts and winding stone streets along a canal with movie-setting barges. And so it was in the tourist office—the regional government tourist office—where we learned about the "ciudad naturiste," or the "nude city."

According to the brochure, the French government designated the ciudad a nudist colony in 1973. The rather absurd irony that the government had founded the damn place and the pamphlet was on the rack between a vineyard tour and a boardwalk with kid rides made the idea of going there seem almost blasé. Isabella looked at me like I was her naughty little boy. "Go ahead," she said, "ask them if we can visit it. I know you are dying to see some French boobies." I didn't bother to pretend that I wasn't curious.

The matronly tourist office volunteer showed me where it was on the map but explained that we couldn't just go into the ciudad naturiste, one must have a special pass. But, she explained, if you are staying at a hotel in the village you automatically get admission. It just so happened that we didn't have a place to stay that night. The lovely lady made a few phone calls for us. All the hotels were full including the Jardin de Hédonisme. I was kind of relieved because staying in a nude city at a place called The Garden of Hedonism might have pushed my sweet subur-ban-mom-wife from "maybe" to "no." Turns out Hédonisme was perfectly named, but I'm getting ahead of myself. On a French version of Airbnb, we reserved a studio apartment in a building called Thebes—the original condo of the ciudad. The condition, though, was that we had to rent the apartment for a minimum of two days. We stayed five. By the time we left, we had reserved a week for the following summer.

At the community's gate was a sign that Isabella and Google translated to, "Welcome to Our Naturist Ciudad—Live Like Us—Undress Yourself." Underneath was the seal of the French government. I took a picture of the sign even though there was a prohibitive image of a camera with a slash through it. That was the last time we took or even saw anyone take a photo in the Ciudad, but, believe me, there were about a billion times I wanted to.

The gate lifted; we drove in and passed a strip of shops. So far nothing unusual, a typical French town with a boulangerie with fresh baguettes piled high, a wine shop, a post office. A car passed, then a man on a bicycle wearing a swimsuit. We turned left at the Hotel Demi and there we saw our first nudists. I'm not sure if the car stopped or it drove by itself, but there was no way that I was in control.

Not an old, naked, balls-to-his-knees geezer, nor a saggy-boobed geriatric you fear seeing at a nudist colony. No. In front of us was a young woman, all-over bronze tan with nipple rings that were connected with a chain hanging between her bouncing breasts. Something jeweled dangled from her shaved genitals and, are you ready for this? Holding her hand was a young, maybe 6-year-old naked boy.

"Oh, my God," Isabella said. "I mean what the hell?"

Fortunately, before I had a chance to respond, although of course there was nothing I could possibly have said, we drove around a traffic circle and passed a pedestrian pathway. There we saw a parade of every possible combination of naked and near-naked man, woman, child, grandparent, teen, and middle-aged nudist. Isabella's silence was deafening—mine was screaming.

We snapped back to reality as we approached another round-about and saw our building, Thebes D. The gigantic, concrete, horseshoe-shaped building was a few football fields in diameter and must have been a super-futuristic design in the 1970s. Today, however, the architecture seemed kind of silly. Feeling way, way over-dressed, we unpacked the car and climbed the stairs to our second floor, bare like a college dorm, studio. There was a small balcony, and I went right to it. There was a view—I found my spot.

22

Below the apartment was a series of long open terraces each with some furniture and towels strewn about—not a bathing suit in sight. Beyond the balconies were pathways that led to the beach and the azure blue Mediterranean Sea, and the parade of people. Although a procession of nudists was a fantasy come true, I was momentarily distracted by the Mediterranean Sea, a lifelong fascination, almost fetish of mine. The sea that borders France, Spain, Italy and stretches to Turkey and North Africa—in total bordering 21 countries—held an ado-lescent allure for me almost as strong as women's bodies. And I chuckled to myself because I felt proud for having a thought that didn't involve sex.

Isabella took a shower while I unpacked and I have to admit her continued silence had me worried. Isabella was an adventur-ous woman but since the kids arrived her role as mom came first. She was still fun-loving and sexy, but when she went silent, I knew I had crossed a line.

The shower stopped, I pulled myself away from staring out the window and braced for her to let me have it. She opened the bathroom door with a towel wrapped like a turban on her head, stark naked, and announced, "Okay, I'm dressed. Let's go out, I need a drink!"

I ran over and gave her a lift-off-the-ground hug, "You're amazing! Baby."

Isabella settled on a bikini bottom but still topless, I went full Monty but kept my bathing suit in a bag along with our towels and some money. Later I would learn that the bag should have also had rubbers (for him and her—yeah, you read that right) but again, I am getting ahead of myself. When we reached the first floor a door opened, music and laughter were followed by a naked man, ridiculously tanned a deep brown, completely devoid of body hair and the longest uncircumcised penis I had ever seen (not that I had seen that many).

23

"Bonjour. Ça va?" he said in that smooth French way that makes the most innocent words sound seductive. "Très bien, et vous?" Isabella said, her eyes trying to stay on the ruggedly handsome man's face. But as he turned to walk in front of us, I saw Isabella sneak a peek at his package, and her eyes followed as his small round bottom bobbed and led the way.

We were both silent as the man strolled in front of us. "Baby, your French is suddenly so good, you must be inspired. Any other French words come to mind?" The rakish god turned onto a pathway, his long pendulum undulating beside him. Isabella gave me a coy look and in a sultry tone said, "Oh là là…"

To be with Isabella as she walked topless in public was thrilling and erotic, and a little scary. Of course, I saw Isabella naked all the time, but to view her and having others see her exposed rocked my world. Isabella's nursed-a-baby breasts were still firm, and when her nipples were erect, the girls turned up. And erect they were. The problem was, I was starting to form an erection of my own. The warm Mediterranean breeze teased the boys. The sight of Isabella topless among naked bodies was all a bit much for me to maintain control. "Barbara Bush, Barbara Bush, Barbara Bush," I chanted to myself and, sure enough, my impending boner began to subside.

We passed the hotel Le Jardin d'Eve and a billboard that read, "La Savon Party." A blast of Euro-techno-pop filled the air and, sure enough, foamy bubbles wafted from behind a wall. I made a mental note to investigate The Savon Party—hopefully it wasn't a children's bathtub on steroids.

A few feet beyond the hotel complex, and like a living post-card, the Mediterranean beach appeared. Kids dug in the sand, deeply-tanned bodies bronzing, teens playing paddle ball, a steady stream of strolling beachcombers and all, or mostly all, naked. We stood and stared like we had just stumbled onto a secret. Two barely adolescent but naked girls were throwing a frisbee. I saw them and quickly turned the other way. It had never occurred to me that teens, pre-teens would be nude and I was very, very uncomfortable. "Um, babe, I, uh," and before I could formulate the words Isabella took me by the hand, "Holy shit, everyone is naked, even the kids, of all ages. We better get that drink now, I mean, I'm not sure about this…"

We found two lounge chairs in front of a seaside restaurant and tried to focus on the menu instead of the naked people. We must have been obvious Yanks with our pale, white skin and stumbling through the French menu because the woman sitting next to us asked if we needed help—in English.

Monique was a 60-some-year-old French woman, chubby with a no-line, dark tan, and speaking a comfortable French-tinged English. She recommended the local blush wine, rosé, and a plate of tapas. We did just as she said. Monique explained that in the summer in the South of France, and in this region in particular, the rosé was the drink to have. We looked around and nearly every table had a whole bottle of rosé, just as she said. And it

24

was served with ice in the glass. So much for the French as wine snobs. Iced tea with a kick; it was the perfect antidote to our shock.

Monique explained that she spent her winters in Florida and was still getting accustomed to our culture, so she understood what we were going through. Monique had been coming to Bouchon since she was a teenager when she would vacation with her parents, which, in and of itself, begged a storm of questions. Although Monique knew nudity was unusual to Americans, for her it was not only normal but actually a relief.

"My closest relationships are with people I've met from the ciu-dad. There's something about the place that allows one to be yourself, more open, and so the people you meet are more authentic, you know?" She drank some rosé and nibbled an artful piece of paté on toast, "It is what we call 'libertine,' very hard for me to explain but the nudity and open sexuality are an extension of a life we embrace as fulfilling."

I could have listened to her ramble on all day with her French accent and description of the libertine philosophy. She spoke about the French joie de vivre, choosing words like an artist describing an esoteric painting. Monique was so comfortable in her older, fleshy body that pretty quickly I forgot that she was naked. "Now, what is this open sexuality business?" Isabella asked in a tone that was concerned but curious.

"Well, my husband and I have other lovers when we are here. In fact, I met him on this beach 28 years ago when I was here with my boyfriend of the time. Have you been to the Savon Party? You really must go, it's a lot of fun, and you will get an idea of the 'libertine' lifestyle."

Turns out savon in French is soap by which they mean bub-bles. "There is a machine pumping bubbles onto a dance floor which is near an outdoor pool—it goes on until 19:00 so after your wine and tapas you'll still have time to experience it. C'est très bien, really."

Isabella didn't let go, though, and grilled Monique on open sexuality and the libertine lifestyle, but mostly got in response Monique's philosophy about living an authentic life, accepting ourselves and our natural biology. I could see Isabella nodding in polite agreement, but I had no idea if she thought Monique's free-sex rap was crazy or cool.

When Isabella turned to me and asked if I wanted to go to the Savon Party, I did an internal fist pump but pretended to be indifferent, "Sure, I mean, if you want to. I'm okay to just check it out."

26

It was a total bullshit response, and I knew it and so did Isabella. I would have taken out the garbage and folded the laundry for a year to go to a party with naked people having sex in a giant bubble bath, but I feigned mild interest. Such is the game we married folk play.

The rosé bottle empty, we headed off the beach and got in line for the Savon Party. I paid the €20 cover, and the cashier handed me a bag and pointed to the towels Isabella and I were wearing and our flip-flops, "Everything in zee sac, s'il vous plaît." She then handed me a plastic wallet about the size of our passports but with a neck strap and the logo of a swinger website stamped on it, "For zee Euros." There were two rubbers inside the wallet with the same logo.

They weren't kidding. Everything off or you can't go in. Isabella figured it was a way of keeping creepy voyeurs out. Isabella also translated a sign hanging by the cashier—"Couples Only." So, there weren't any people who were not willing to be naked and no single men allowed. I didn't quite understand why that would matter, but Isabella did; she felt it lessened the potential creepo factor.

We passed underneath a shower as if we were cattle being sprayed for mites and walked around the corner of a high wall and... Bonjour! Bonjour! Bonjour! Welcome to libertine!

I'm not sure what hit first. Was it the sounds of people moaning, the sight of naked people dancing, well, actually grinding, in a sea of bubbles, or was it the tangles of people on outdoor beds in pre-, active and post-sex entanglements? Was it the beautiful young bodies, the men strolling and sporting full erections like they were giving directions, women of all ages kissing and fondling each other, or, the weirdest of all, groups of people in full social interaction talking and laughing while engaged in some sexual act or another?

We stayed right by the entrance holding, no, *gripping* hands like we were at a horror flick. I don't know who was holding on to whom but as much as I love seeing naked women—and some damn fine naked women—this scene was beyond anything, I mean anything, even porn-anything, I had seen, or frankly ever imagined.

We walked a few feet into the party and turned toward the sound of a woman crying out. On a bed-sized lounge chair was a woman laying on her back. She was not young, maybe 50, and although she was totally naked what I noticed was her hairstyle; a conventional, short, professional women's cut that would have made her look like a corporate executive–if she wasn't naked and having sex in public.

On top of her was a man vigorously thrusting into her, his bare ass dancing above her. She had both hands on his chest, looking him in the eyes. Another man was squatted next to them, his hand on one of her breasts. The man on top was almost in a push-up position sliding in and out of her, the woman crying out with each pump of his hips. The woman turned to kiss the man squatted next to her and she looked straight at me and then at

27

Isabella. The women fixated on each other as the woman rose her hips with each stroke, kissing the squatting man, and peering into Isabella's eyes. The man on top slowed his rhythm, stopped all movement, and then grunted like a wild animal and collapsed on top of her. Isabella's grip on my hand squeezed so hard I almost stopped watching.

If the pleasure police had shut down the party and made us all go home, just having seen Isabella watch that woman and her two men was enough for me. I was so turned on by Isabella being naked and watching people—real people, not strippers or porn stars—having sex in the open. And add to it that my wife was vicariously involved via a staring contest—seriously I was charged up just watching Isabella watching the action. Chanting "Barbara Bush" like a Buddhist monk on meth wasn't going to stop my package from growing.

28

"Forget that rosé wine nonsense. I need a real drink," I said, not sure if Isabella could hear me or even wanted to. I led her to the bar in front of a conversation pool with a platform in the center where people were sitting and doing things. Yes, sexy things. Fortunately, the bar was a standard setup, the bartenders dressed in T-shirts and shorts. Although surrounded by naked bodies, I still found myself checking out the servers. Go figure.

I pointed to a red, bubbly drink in a large tumbler that the naked, Amazon goddess next to me was sipping and I held up two fingers. The bartender yelled back, "Deux Aperol Spritz, no?" I nodded.

"This is insane," Isabella said. But what was different about the way she said it was the way she was holding me at the bar. Isabella's arm was around my torso hugging me close, much closer than she would have done at a regular bar. Isabella was moving her thumb back and forth on my side in an absentminded love-caress, a little gesture she used to do to me after we had sex—before, kids, mortgage, and our non-stop activity-driven lives.

Giant, delicious, cold, bright red drinks in hand, we walked around the rest of the party scene. Beyond the pool area was another bar, a DJ, and the savon machine. Bubbles streamed from a giant tube above the dance floor, and a throng of maybe 50 people were dancing—slipping and sliding among each other's naked bodies. And let me tell you, I'm pretty damn sure they didn't all know each other.

A few smaller groups on the dance floor in 2s,3s,4s, etc. were engaged in oral or full-on intercourse. "Fucking crazy," I yelled to Isabella who smiled at my lame joke when a woman covered in bubbles walked by us. The woman smiled at Isabella and then approached her, took Isabella's hand and used it to slowly move some bubbles from her own ample chest to Isabella's. The woman said something in French to Isabella then kissed her on each cheek and kept on walking. Isabella blushed like a schoolgirl at a middle school dance and whispered, well, *shouted* to me above the music, "I think that was the woman we watched earlier with the two men."

At this point I really didn't know what was going on. We had watched people have sex, we were surrounded by naked and some super-hot naked bodies, and I was pretty sure Isabella just had her first almost bisexual experience.

"Let's rinse those bubbles off of you," I said as I approached some outdoor showers, but Isabella took me by the hand and guided us into the conversation pool. There were maybe 20 people in and around the oversized hot tub. The drinks and sun and blush/rush from the naked people were getting to me. I was definitely feeling it and Isabella gave me that giggly smile that tells me my lightweight, lover-wife was buzzed, too.

Isabella had picked a spot along the pool's edge that was perfect for watching the action—that's my wife, she was getting bold in her naked drunkenness and I loved it. On the pool's island were several couples, two of whom got my attention right away. The two women, 30ish, with fit, young looking bodies and small, firm breasts were making out like they had just reunited after a long absence. I mean they were all over each other. Their men were behind them, stroking the women's backs and, I'm sure, other body parts. The women were fondling each other as they were kissing and, in turn, I was fondling Isabella. I swear, I didn't even think about it, my hand was between her legs as if we were in bed at home watching a sexy movie.

30

Although we were in the water, I could tell Isabella was very wet. We both looked straight ahead and I continued to touch her under the surface, but let me remind you—in public. Oh man, I couldn't believe it. We were watching the hottest girl-on-girl sex I had ever seen, ok, the only live bi-female scene I had witnessed, and at the same time playing with my beautiful, buzzed wife—in public.

A couple took the spot next to Isabella, and we nodded hello, but I boldly kept my hand on Isabella's vulva as we talked with the couple. They were Dutch and their English was nearly accent-free. This was their fifth time to the ciudad and they told us they attended the Savon party regularly. As we talked, the man lifted himself to the side of the pool and with his wife still in the water and facing both him and us, she started to play with his growing cock.

The Dutch woman toyed with her husband's cock while chatting with us, occasionally giving it a kiss, a lick or a full mouth BJ, and it seemed totally normal! Not to mention, Isabella is now rotating her hips slowly against my hand under the water and still talking to and watching the couple. At one point the woman asked Isabella if she wanted to help her with her husband and she held his dick like she was handing Isabella an appetizer. Isabella shrugged her off and looked over at me, and without hesitation, I said, "Go ahead, baby, I'd love to watch if you want to try."

Isabella pushed her crotch hard into my hand, leaned into me, "I don't know, I mean I guess it couldn't hurt...," and damn if her hand didn't go around the man's cock. If the pool were deeper, I would have drowned. Isabella was now bent over in the pool, my fingers deep inside her wet pussy while she stroked the Dutchman's penis in concert with his wife. I was so hard my cock periscoped to the surface.

I felt an opening, so to speak, so I turned and positioned myself behind Isabella and entered her from behind while she and the wife played with the man's cock. The Dutch woman leaned over to see my hips moving behind Isabella, and she moved her hands to tease Isabella's nipples. I heard noises across the pool and saw that the two bi women in the center pedestal were now in a position similar to ours, still facing each other and kissing but their men fucking them from behind.

Hearing the young foursome pushed me to pump harder. My hand went around Isabella's side and brushed against a hand—I suppose it was the Dutch wife's hand, but I couldn't tell. Maybe it was the husband's. Isabella was really moaning, looking the Dutchman in his eyes and then as if on cue, she went down on him, she took his whole cock in her mouth. I slowed to watch her and then thrust deep inside her, lifting her up to the water's edge.

The husband was saying something in Dutch under his breath. The wife was all over Isabella. I was on the brink of coming inside Isabella on the side of the public pool, the young lesbo scene was hitting a crescendo, and just as I was about to come, I reached around to touch Isabella's clit and found fingers already there. Mystery fingers—the man's, his wife? No, I realized it was

31

Isabella's own hand, so I lightly ran my thumb over her fingers the way she had done to me earlier at the bar.

Isabella screamed. I mean she actually screamed. A strange man's cock in her mouth, his wife holding Isabella from the front, me thrusting deep inside her. Isabella twitched a few times, and I looked over at the bi girls, one of whom was now between the legs of the other, her long hair streaming down her shoulders to her perky tanned breasts. I held Isabella like a life raft in a storm and I came inside her, shooting a load that could have won a pole-vaulting contest. I watched Isabella holding onto the man's thighs while the wife kissed her and I throbbed in my glorious wife.

The Dutchman stumbled up to rinse off and his wife—still an arm around Isabella—kissed me, on the lips, slow and tender, open-mouth in front of Isabella. Of all the craziness we saw and experienced, that kiss haunts me to this day. I have often thought about that day and that kiss. I can only tell you that I learned that balmy French Riviera afternoon that a kiss is as amorphous as love. I love my wife, but I also love my children, my parents, our dog, a good steak and the Redskins. A kiss can be affectionate, passionate, loving, casual. The after-sex kiss with the Dutchman's wife was an "I like you" more than "I am turned on" kiss; it was a moment of sweet, authentic expression. And maybe it haunts me because my best friend in college was from a famous family. Born famous he spent his life wondering if people honestly liked him or did they have an agenda? The kiss from a stranger who I just had sex with at a Savon party was true, intimate, and haunting.

After the couple left, I handed the drink to Isabella and was almost afraid to look her in the eye. We pulled ourselves out of the pool and sat on the deck. Isabella seemed to be as unsure of herself as I was. I whispered in her ear, "You ok?"

32

Isabella turned, held my face in her hands, looked at me for a long time, her gorgeous naked body half in my lap, and she slowly said, "I love you more than ever." I was relieved and emotional, a post-sex-but-getting-hard-again semi-erection evolved as tears welled.

I kissed Isabella on her neck and then her cheek. Isabella stopped me and said in her work tone, "Oh no, don't get started again, boy scout. First things first. Time to feed me and then we have to talk. I mean this was intense, and we need to process it."

Oh shit, I thought. "Process it" was the death of fun. I feared we would have to review our entire marriage and discuss our true feelings. "Well," I thought, "lightning struck once, and I'll be happy with that. Party over. Back to reality."

33

Isabella read my expression, "Hey, this is serious. Communication about non-monogamous acts is essential."
My dick was now entirely in Bush-ville.

"If we are going to get through this we need to share and support each other." Isabella was now in full-on mom voice and I was about to cry, but this time for different reasons. "We have a lot riding on this, you have to look at the big picture." I nodded and looked down like I just got caught eating the last cookie. "And you listen to me..." She took my face and made me look at her straight-on even though one of the bi women was getting spanked and yelling just behind me, and I wanted to look in the worst way.

"Yes, of course, honey, we'll process everything, I promise," I said in full husband defeat.

"And for this to be real, to matter, we need to tell each other every thought, every feeling, every detail..." Isabella said and I saw her look soften, "while I'm giving you the best BJ of your life."

CHAPTER TWO

The Flirt

IT STARTED AS pillow talk. But it was mostly me doing the talking. Elaine was unusually quiet and distant. We had come home from a wedding, we were a little drunk, and I was gossiping about family when Elaine blurted out, "You know that rock and roll looking guy? I think he is one of Danny's cousins, well anyway; he kinda hit on me. Well, more than kinda."

I knew just who she was talking about. After all, who goes to an indoor wedding wearing dark sunglasses and a leather jacket?

"I was sitting at the cousin table talking with Danny's niece. You know the one who wants to go to NYU? Anyway, that guy, Cliff, sat down and started talking to me. He came on pretty strong. I'm embarrassed now, I mean, we didn't do anything but when he began to talk, I was kind of shocked. I didn't stop him, I mean, I definitely should have."

Elaine paused, and I resisted filling the silence. She stretched a thigh across my legs and snuggled close to me, a hand on my chest. I stroked her hair and told her that I loved her.

In a voice so soft I had to strain to hear her, Elaine told me how Cliff sat behind her, close enough that their chairs and, maybe even their bodies, were touching. He slumped so that as he talked, she could feel his breath on her neck. They were both facing the dance floor, and in an accent that Elaine described as sounding like a raspy, smoky, New York cabbie, Cliff told her what he would do to her if only she would dance with him.

"I'd have to feel you, trace the lines of your neck until my fingers reached the arch of your shoulder." And then Elaine said she felt his calloused hand brush her neck. An image of his hand trilling a guitar string swept over her followed by a shudder from her neck to far below.

36

"I froze. I should have told him to stop, but I just couldn't believe this was happening at a wedding reception. Out of the corner of my eye, I could see his long, knobby, Mick Jagger fingers stroking his thigh. I tried to ignore him, but when someone passed by, Cliff leaned in closer and whispered that his lips would follow his fingers across my neck so he could smell and taste how turned on I was."

Elaine seemed to hold me tighter and tighter as she talked. I didn't say a word but inside my thoughts jumbled with my emotions. I was both worried for Elaine's safety and pissed at the asshole. Even more disturbing, I was aroused. When Elaine asked if she should go on, I moved her hand to the growing bulge in my boxers, and I told her I wanted to hear every detail.

Elaine's voice grew stronger and more playful, and she slipped her hand under the band of my underwear, "I like what's going on here. Hmmm. Cliff said he wanted to press me to feel my thighs against his. He wanted to hold my ass tight. He wanted me to feel how hard he was against my thigh. And that's when I glanced down and saw the outline of his cock through his tight jeans. He shifted his legs to give me a better look, and his cock grew. For a second I was afraid, of him and what he was doing. I was afraid of getting caught and of his growing cock. But he kept talking. I couldn't look away." Elaine was practically squeezing my cock as she talked about Cliff's.

"He said he would slide his hands inch by inch, up the sides of my dress to my breasts, slowly as not to catch the attention of the other dancers. He wanted to squeeze and feel my chest swell in his palms. Cliff said he would turn our bodies away from the crowd where he could pinch my nipples hard and, holding my ass with one hand, he would slide a finger into me with his other. I couldn't stop him from talking. Maybe I didn't want him to stop. All the people around us, his bluesy rasp, his scent like old cracked leather. I wanted to tell him to shut up, but I wanted to hear more."

37

She now had my boxers off, and I was close to the edge. I asked her if Cliff turned her on, my voice breaking with anxious anticipation.

"I didn't want to be but, yeah, I was squirming, squeezing my legs together. His face was craggy like he had been up partying all night for years—I couldn't look away. I could feel myself getting wet." And Elaine took my hand and brought it to her panties, "Wet, like this."

I almost came when she did that, and then I moved her hand under mine.

"Feel yourself," I said, and the tension between us was like the first awkward time we made love. My hand was shaking as our fingers mingled. I told her that I wished that I could have watched her and Cliff. I moved her hand so we were both stroking her pussy together. I told her I wanted her to describe what she would do to Cliff.

She opened her legs, and we both played with her stiff little clit.

Her breathing shifted.

"He was so dark and moody. He creeped me out, but I was strangely turned on. I wanted to hurt him. To punish him. He was so cocky. The fucker."

Elaine shoved two fingers inside her pussy as she cursed. "I wanted to tease him, to shove him onto the wedding table. I wanted to hold his scrawny, muscular arms down. I wanted to lean over him, my shirt unbuttoned so he could see my bra, the outlines of my tits. I wanted him to smell my perfume but also my eau-de-me, that dewy scent I get when I'm turned on. I want him to smell that—to know that I wanted him but that he couldn't have me. I'd unbutton my blouse so he could see my sheer demi-bra and then I'd shake off my heels and put my foot against his hard-on. My foot pressing against those worn, tight jeans. Pushing against his cock, feeling it with my naked toes clenched, up and down, teasing him, making him throb, and then I'd push hard until he groaned."

I moved in front of Elaine and watched as she moved a hand to tug her nipples while she was talking. She was gasping her words, arching her back.

"I wanted to take my tits out and bring them right up to his snarling mouth, my nipples just brushing his rough yet somehow feminine lips while my foot pushed against that long skinny cock." And she sighed, loud, hips high in the air, nipples squeezed. "Oh, fuck, yeah! That cock."

She came, shaking hard on the bed, and pulled me close, taking my shaft in her mouth and getting me off with a vigor I had never felt from her before.

We fell silent and then asleep in each other's arms. The next morning we slept late. Elaine quickly dressed in a long skirt, the

38

one she wears when she feels bloated and wants to be invisible. We were awkward and quiet. Maybe Elaine felt as I did—had we crossed a line we couldn't retreat from? We rushed off to work avoiding eye contact.

Around mid-morning Elaine texted me, "Are you okay? I'm kind of freaking out…"

I wrote back, "No, damn it, I'm not okay. I can't concentrate. I'm so fucking horny; I can't wait to get you alone tonight."

No response. I waited. I re-read my text. I was frantically second guessing what I had written to her. I gripped the phone so tight that when it vibrated with Elaine's next text, I felt it through my whole body. "Lunch?" and then my phone vibrated again, "panties off…"

CHAPTER THREE

The Text

PLAY DATES FOR adults. That's the way Missy likes to think of them. I think of them as date nights with legs like an annuity that just keeps paying long after the initial investment. Even though we were at Hedo in Jamaica where crazy sex can happen anywhere day or night, a date has the potential for a higher return. I'm not risk-averse, but if I get a hot tip, I go for it. The more insider information, the better.

Ari and Sara came vetted by the Carters. The Carters were not only good looking but socially compatible with us, so we trusted their recommendation. We are high-profile people in our town, which is why we go to Hedo and never date couples in our hometown. The Carters are similarly cautious but from another city; a referral from them implied discretion. It also indicated a similar cultural status. Sounds snobby but at least I admit my arrogance.

The fact is, it's just easier and better for everybody if the playing field is somewhat even. We are successful and don't want to feel like we can't talk freely about our lives, the trips we take or other details that expose our economic status. Missy and I are apolitical, and not religious. The friends we are most comfortable being with tend to share the same worldview.

Now we have had experiences with couples at Hedo and at Desire in Cancun that weren't dates, but were random fun hook-ups by the pool, on the beach, or in the club. But a rendezvous with drinks, dinner, maybe some music is different; we like couple-to-couple dates. We like getting to know people. It's a cliché, but almost all of our new friends have come from the lifestyle.

Referral in hand, I exchanged a few texts with Ari, and we set up a date for the next evening. But as fate would have it we recognized each other at the gym, so we had a pre-date mini-encounter. And we hit it off right away.

42

Ari was an Israeli who went to college in California where he met Sara, so he had been in the States for nearly twenty years. He was boyishly handsome and had that quiet confidence I have known in other Israelis; that sense that they don't need to be macho but if need be, they know how to handle themselves. Sara was tall, thin, and more reserved than Ari. Her hair was short and pulled back in a ponytail but with a few locks floating free on her face. She smiled but had a slightly worried look on her face. And although she was thin and her bottom looked cute in yoga pants, she was not uber fit. And I liked her. Two things. One I like moody, intense women and two, I am not into those workout moms. They look like men to me and it telegraphs to me they spend a lot of time in the gym, which I find shallow. Again, I might sound snobby, but I am being honest.

By the way, ironically, my wife doesn't fit my model woman criteria. Missy is not moody and intense, which is a good thing because as you probably already have figured out, I am both intense and have been known to have the occasional mood swing. Missy, on the other hand, is open and lighthearted and funny and amazingly almost always happy. She is also the smartest person I have ever met. Period. Missy is my counterpoint, my rock. I love her. I am, in fact, still after 18 years of marriage in awe of her. I don't mind admitting that I am pretty much lost without her. From the moment I met her I have felt that she was out of my league not just in her beauty, without the gym obsession, but as a person.

We have met lots of couples in the lifestyle, and they come from every walk of life, but the one common feature is that they are in love. In the vanilla world, men, when among their gender, complain about their wives—it's a certainty. But, you rarely hear men in the lifestyle complain about their wives. We, the husbands of libertine women, are lucky, and we know and cherish it: that is the most common sentiment.

43

Being crazy in love with your spouse and being in the lifestyle means seeing them being passionate with another person—man and/or woman. There's a look Missy gets when she likes someone. Her head cocks to the side when she is speaking with them, and her body shifts like she is resisting a tingle in her groin—that's the way she looked at Ari. Missy was flirty and playful with him. She sensed his confidence, so she was sarcastic verging on insulting from that first moment in the gym. I knew right away they were a good fit.

That evening I got a text from Ari confirming the plans for the following night. I was just heading out for a sunset run, so I asked Missy to use my phone and respond to him. The date was set.

When I got back to the room, Missy was dressed in what she called her "slut wear." Clothes she would only wear when we were at a lifestyle resort and a complete contrast to the formless professional clothes she wore back home. She wanted to go to the club and see if there was any action. I loved when she took control like that, so we headed out as soon as I showered and changed.

At the club, we danced and fooled around on the dance floor. We ran into a few people we knew and played a bit with them. Missy was in a particularly frisky mood. She even got up on one of the stripper poles and danced with a couple of young hotties, kissing and grinding in a great show for us grateful, proud men. As the evening wore on, we decided to go out to the beach, and there we made love under the pure, starry Jamaican sky.

When she was on top and slowly, lovingly riding me, she told me how she flirted with Ari in the texts. She told me how she was going to tease him by making him watch Sara and her together first, then seduce him after. I asked her what she liked about him. She leaned over to kiss me, moving a little faster, and told me she that when they were in the gym, Ari wiped the sweat off his shoulders and arms with a towel. His slow firm movements and the smell of his sweat turned her on and then she got a peek of his stomach when he stretched. He had a sexy torso, thick and firm. She paused, sat up playing with her nipples. "That firm gut is going to fuck me good tomorrow. I want him to pound me!" And I came with the rhythm of the waves crashing at our feet, watching my sexy, smiling, out-of-my-league wife.

The next day we spent the morning kayaking and the afternoon by the nude pool. We started years ago like most people at the prude pool, but that was several years and many self-imposed rules ago. While sipping aged Appleton rum, watching some sexy action in the infamous cave, I got a few texts from Ari. I handed the phone to Missy so she could respond to him. She told me she confirmed drinks at the piano bar with dinner to follow. As fate would have it, we never made it to dinner.

The flirting at the piano bar went as expected. Missy and Ari hit it off and were touching and kissing each other from the first drink. There were giggles and guffaws, and occasionally Missy

44

punched him like a middle-school crush and then giggled some more. Sara, on the other hand, was more interested in getting to know me. I didn't bother trying to charm her, not that I'm very good at that anyway; it was kind of nice to just be my blunt self.

Sara was an academic on staff at a liberal arts college. Her passion was the education of the student as an intellectual, a critical thinker; her contention was that grad school was for career training. We got into an intense debate on the future of campus-based education. And although she was probably the most conservative dressed at the bar that night she did have on a skirt with a high slit and her long naked legs were driving me wild.

In an attempt to turn Sara's attention to sex I asked her opinion of the philosophy of ethical hedonism. After all, we were at a resort dedicated to hedonism, and chances are I was going to have sex with her that night. But the strategy backfired when she launched into the history of hedonism dating to Socrates' students; then she espoused on the various schools of discourse to present-day philosophy. Her seriousness was a real turn on to me because I believed in the inverse proportion rule of passion—the more sober a woman was, the greater her passion when she let go in the throws of sexual delirium.

By contrast, Missy and Ari were nearly naked and groping each other's genitals on the piano bar's stools. Eventually, Missy turned her attention to Sara, and she suggested we all go back to the room for some homemade limoncello and a girl-girl show.

When we got to the room, Sara seemed to loosen up with Missy, and when they kissed, the uptight Sara closed her eyes and got lost in Missy's arms. My favorite moment was when Ari and I were on a couch watching them, and Missy was standing behind Sara, caressing her and kissing her neck, and Sara was moaning in raw pleasure to Missy's touch. Sara closed her eyes and gave into Missy's attention. And that brought me to attention, for sure.

Eventually, the ladies joined us on the couch. Sara kissed her husband first then me—a soft, tentative kiss. I put hands on either side of her face and held her face close to mine. I asked her if I could kiss her again. Sara paused, holding my gaze then looked down and slowly nodded yes. Her reluctance was both mysterious and exciting. Did she not like me? Was she nervous? Was she jealous of her husband who was around the bases, in the dugout, and into the locker room already with Missy? While I was cautiously asking Sara to kiss, Ari was already going down on Missy and asking her if she was ready for some butt play.

Sara's resistance was all the more exciting because she was slowly saying yes, um, maybe, yes. I went from kissing her to running my hands through her hair and lightly touching the back of her neck, down her shoulders, her long thin arms to her elegant, unadulterated, educated hands. Missy was riding Ari like a cowboy on a bronco, and she leaned over to kiss Sara. Sara responded more enthusiastically to Missy, so I backed off to let Sara focus on her. I moved onto the couch next to Sara and told her I wanted to enter her from behind so she could continue to kiss and fondle Missy.

Ari picked Missy up like she was a case of wine from the trunk of a low sports car. Ari placed her on the couch, so she was facing Sara. Ari entered Missy from behind just as I was doing to Sara.

Sara moved against my torso as she got deeper into the pleasure of the moment. I felt an orgasm building in me and tried to resist. But then I saw Sara reach for Missy's beautiful full breasts, and that sent me over the edge. I started to buck with an orgasm and Sara quickly moved, so I was out of her pussy. She rolled over and in a voice a full octave lower than I had heard before said, "Come on me! Come on my face!" I tugged on my cock and blew a load right across her face as she opened her mouth and took me

46

to her throat. I came hard into her mouth, harder than even with my Missy.

Missy and Ari had stopped, well, almost stopped to watch the Sara show. But not for long. As I was recovering from the orgasm of a lifetime, Ari climbed on top of Missy and entered her just the way she described the night before when she was riding me on the beach. Ari held Missy's legs wide open and thrust into her.

Sara laid down next to Missy and moaned to me. "That is just what I want. Fuck me, Take me! Tear me up!" Sara said in a voice that sounded like it came from another woman, from a distant place and time. Just hearing the uptight Sara use such harsh words turned me on as much as the sex. "Pull my hair! That's why I wore a ponytail tonight." I was glad I had taken a half a Viagra.

47

Missy started to scream calling out Ari's name, urging him on. Sara wrapped her legs around me, digging her heels into my back as I fucked her missionary with her finger on her pussy. And as I was working us both up to an orgasm, Sara called out, "Fuck her Ari! Fuck Missy good!" I pulled Sara's hair, and she tried to bite me, and she thrust herself into me so hard I held on the best I could.

The next day I sent the Carters a thank-you note for their referral.

A couple of months later I was on a business trip, alone in a hotel room. I was naked on the bed and thinking about our encounter with Sara and Ari. I reached for my phone and found the history of the texts between Ari and Missy.

"8:30 at the piano bar. Wear a tight T-shirt so I can see the muscles of your arms," Missy wrote.

"Ok, then. I want you to wear a long skirt, no panties so I can slide my hands all the way to your ass."

"I'm wet now, you Israeli bad boy. Come sweaty."

"Wait for me. Don't orgasm until we meet. I'll do the same. You'll have me, all of me. Maybe." Ari wrote.

"Oh, you're gonna take me. You won't be able to resist but go ahead and try."

I was now hard and pointing straight to the ceiling of the hotel room. I loved that Missy had been so direct with Ari and that she knew I was going to read the texts one day. I called her and told her to get into bed. I read her the texts. Missy told me how she loved Ari's strong hips, his athletic, raw, macho smell. Then Missy confessed that she kept his sweaty T-shirt, and she was wearing it in bed. I shot across my chest onto my neck. We came a thousand miles apart. Investment paid. Dividend spent.

CHAPTER FOUR

I REMEMBER THE first time I saw my future husband notice me. My lips pursed and turned up. My eyes cast down and head tilted. We were flirting. There was a recognition in his eyes—I saw my own reflection, but better. It was for a flash, the real me, the ideal me, and, at a nerdy, smirking 19 years old with messy red hair and a book of poetry tucked under my arm, who I had hoped to become. Several college degrees later, two kids and two businesses in, it was the thing that I missed the most—the adoration of m e , and thepromise of the discovery and adventure of all of our potential together. We lost the spark—and the flirt that fanned the flame of our desire for one another. What eventually replaced that moment, many of them in the beginning, were obligations, and an effort to create a

What's in a flirt?

(a-that's-what-she-said-commentary)

life together. We both did this voluntarily and with love. But with difficult and ambitious goals, routine was favored—we became a reliable and comfortable vehicle—our marriage became an efficient machine.

Our machine was average, and not unlike many upper middle class, traditional marriages. We shared the same values, had similar backgrounds, and had compatible goals for our lives. Routine replaced the unexpected. Familiarity and intimacy replaced the potential of discovery. Desire waned, the machine hummed, and stability reigned. There was little new but so much to do.

We were determined, though, like many couples, to not let the fire die. We had sex—it was scheduled—and we enjoyed it. Date nights were tried. And we talked and talked. But I still missed it—the quality without a name— the quality I couldn't quite put my finger on. Was it freedom, potential, or adventure? I didn't know.

In my first marriage, this inexpressible quality only became more elusive. Sexual adventure, or non-monogamy, as an anecdote the emotional complacency and dulling of passion and desire for one another, would have seemed absurd then. It was difficult enough to fit in sex and a date night! Besides, flirting with others, or flirting with the idea of having sex with others, was an idea that contradicted a core assumption about marriage—*that we were to be forever and exclusively sexually desirable of only one another.* The question of how flirting and opening up could fan the flame of desire for one's own spouse was just inconceivable at the time.

It was only after leaving my first marriage, stumbling into sexual adventure with Jim, and talking with so many couples, we learned that open couples were highly invested in one another's experience of erotic pleasure (sometimes more so than their own pleasure). We were even more surprised by

What's In a Flirt?

the observation that couples experienced a greater sense of sexual passion and desire for one another as a result of having sex with others. Most interesting was that this unusual marriage practice was a stabilizing force in a happy marriage, helping to fortify commitment to one another through the experience of shared pleasure. For couples who could temporarily suspend the idea of sexual monogamy in marriage, this became an anecdote to the emotional complacency and waning sexual desire couples naturally experience. The erotic passion and pleasures generated were, in a sense, a welcome reward: sexual adventure was a playtime or recess from the inevitable demands of marriage or family life. The husband in "The Text" states it plainly: "playdates for adults." They, like many couples, make sex a priority and then use the memories of their encounters to tease and flirt with one another. Sexual adventure has a way of reminding us that we desire what other people want; and when someone desires our spouse sexually, we can be shaken out of what we may have taken for granted or have become dull to. The flirt, for open couples, is an ongoing activity and enlivens their sexual attraction to one another.

What is in a flirt? Flirting is fun. It is a behavior that conveys attraction and elicits a confirmation of our own desirability. Think of flirting as a cloaked question—a glance, a wink, a risqué comment—that asks, "I'm cute, clever, sexy, aren't I?" But flirting, once one married or paired off, is a behavior within a couple that naturally wanes. As a matter of decorum, flirting is curtailed or hidden when it occurs with others outside the pair. Some couples have a "safe flirt" every once in a while, but it is rarely acknowledged except when it becomes a problem of jealousy.

The need, however, to confirm our attractiveness or desirability does not die off with marriage. Just look at the culturally acceptable and elaborate rites some women employ to get this need met—they transform flirting into an elaborate ritual of grooming, dressing up, and preening, but stop just short of actually flirting with another. Women will ask for confirmation of their sexual desirability and attractiveness from same-sex friends. "How do I look? Is this too revealing? Do you think he will notice?"

At the beginning of a relationship, it is fair to say that a romantic pair does not need to flirt with others—their own romantic dance, their seduction, is powerful and consuming. But even in long-term loving relationships, passion wanes, emotional complacency develops, and flirting with one another can all but disappear. Familiarity does not necessarily breed contempt, but it certainly dulls the senses of our novelty seeking brains and can lull our lust into an extended slumber. And like the couple described in "Oz," mature and responsible adults who have accepted the demands and wear of marriage and have learned to curb their sexual expectations, sexual boredom sets in. Although the incredible and new environment does a lot to re-energize this couple sexually, I bet that husband would have danced a treble jig for months if taking her top off in public was the one and only thing Isabella did. Oz, of course, is a fictional place, but the illusion to the original allegory reminds us that our imagination, shared, is the first and best place to re-enliven sex and re-energize the erotic bond.

What's In a Flirt?

In "The Flirt," when Elaine shares with her husband her lusty flirt and strange attraction to Cliff, she is defying convention, and stirring up powerful emotions including fear and anxiety. Her flirt narrative is done to demonstrate to herself and her husband that she is still hot, sexy, and keenly desirable. Shared with her husband, the flirt rattles his emotions, shakes up routine and, ultimately, reminds him, through the eyes of another man, that she is an erotically desirable woman. Passions are stirred, and they both awaken from their teeth brushing and flossing routine. The ritual of seduction is reawakened.

Even couples who never have engaged in non-monogamous sexual activity or interpret flirting with others negatively understand the power of the flirt. Couples will often repeat the story of their own initial encounter and flirt in an effort, I believe, to convey the fire and desire that once existed. Some believe the repetition of the "how we met" story contains some sort of magic or forbearance of what was to come—perhaps marriage or the inevitability of their couplings. Actually, I believe it is a recollection of the erotic passion and fun that once came naturally and easily in the beginning. It is a reminiscence of a shared emotional state—the state of excitement and passion that can only fully exist when "the other" is not entirely known. Asking the question, "Am I desirable?" entails risk, generates anxiety, and feeds into the tension and sexual excitement. There is a risk of rejection, the challenge of converting ambivalence, and the thrill of success.

Sexually non-monogamous couples and other sexual adventurers recreate the initial excitement they experienced in their early relationship in encounters—whether online, in a club, or at a resort. Though non-monogamous activities like swinging are sometimes cartoonishly portrayed as an indiscriminate orgy of bodies, the initial dating rituals are similar, if not exact, to those of typical dating situations. Couples put on their best clothes and faces, meet and greet, flirt, charm, evaluate, and maybe hook up (ask anyone, it is never a sure thing). Of course, the primary difference is that these sexually charged situations are carried out together or in tandem by the couple, and the goal is sex or sexual excitement and perhaps friendship, not a romantic relationship—they already have that.

This is a book for happy couples, probably in egalitarian relationships that already have a high degree of emotional sharing, closeness, and intimacy. Experts call this relationship style "best friend." And this book is for couples who are seeking to make shared sexual pleasure a priority. A lot is asked of marriage, and a lot is missed in marriage. Had my first husband and I been better able to balance responsibilities and pleasures, sexual adventure could have been broached, and flirting together may have expanded and enhanced our sexual lives. Flirting, seduction, and pleasure are important. When a couple can share and re-experience lost or forgotten positive, even euphoric, emotional states together, it is good for the relationship.

Remember, though, sexual adventure doesn't fix bad relationships or marriages. If your relationship is troubled, or if you are with someone who is dominating, manipulative, secretive, cheating, compulsive, or controlling; flirting, much less opening up, is a bad idea. Non-monogamy will

What's In a Flirt?

probably destroy a bad marriage or relationship. For those in more honest, equal and emotionally open relationships, you can take a cue from Elaine. Women, share your fantasies and your flirts with your partner, not your girlfriends. Ask for what you want sexually. Men, if you look at porn, do it with your wife or partner, not by yourself. Ask her about her sexual fantasies. Tell her what is on your mind during sex, or what you really want to do. If your talk leads to some hot action, enjoy; it's your adult playtime. When putting aside your fears and sexual secrecy for a minute, the door to sexual adventure can swing open. Hold hands and take a step in.

CHAPTER FIVE

Tattoo

TATTOOS, I DON'T get them. I don't have any, never will.

My aversion to tattoos may be from being Jewish. You know, we have a rather unpleasant history with them. Or it might be because I am a physician, and I am intimate with human bodies every day and tattoos strike me as somehow disrespectful. Whatever the reason or emotion when I see some-one with a tattoo (and my wife Maureen agrees), well, we just shake our heads in disbelief.

However.

A young woman, naked or nearly naked with tattoos moves my blood to where logic has no home. Keeps me up at night, pun intended.

My initiation was suicide, suicidegirls.com. I stumbled onto the site one night and nearly destroyed my pajamas. The girls there had a girl-next-door look; they were not models or traditionally beautiful, but the girls on the site are college-age youth-ful and have the bodies young women have.

The attraction there should need no explanation. But the one thing they all had in common was a plethora of tattoos.

We have been in the lifestyle for years and being in health care, Maureen and I are very open about sex, but I was nevertheless hiding my attraction to tattooed girls from Mo. We have to have some secrets, don't we? But my fetish came out one night when we were looking at porn together and the browser bar autofilled, suicidegirls.com. Fortunately, Mo found it amusing and ironic, but not repulsive. As a therapist, Mo has come to accept human behavior in all its flavors—not to mention she has her own kinks. Let's just say her strap-on has a name, Marquis, and I'll leave it at that.

58

Fast forward to our anniversary dinner. Chez Sylvie's is the nicest, most expensive, elegant, quiet restaurant in town and when Mo showed me our anniversary present, I wanted to shout and swing from the chandeliers. The first envelope had a brochure for an elegant hotel in Amsterdam and a receipt for two flight tickets. We had been talking about a romantic and sexy trip to Amsterdam for years and the fact that she got the tickets, meaning she labored to arrange our absurdly busy schedules, was really exciting. Not chandelier swinging excitement, but definitely a great gift. But...

The next envelope had folded sheets of copy paper in it. I unfolded them and stared in disbelief. The papers were printouts from a Dutch escort site with 20 to 30 pages of girls' pictures and profiles. The name of the escort site: SuicideGirls.nl. Hello chandeliers!

When I asked Mo if she was really okay with us using a sex worker, her response was, "Don't kid yourself, sweetheart, Marquis is coming with us." And she paused and added, "In your suitcase."

"You know you are whistling, don't you?" Mo chided me as I washed the dishes the night after the anniversary dinner. "Holy hell, darling," I said, "I am on cloud nine. I feel like I have a crush on a girl who just agreed to go out with me." And that night I began my research. I favorited profiles, and then Mo could concur or veto. We settled on a few ladies, and there was one in particular that really got me going. Ingrid was a green-eyed blonde of medium height and build and had young, full, pale breasts framed by colorful dragon tail tattoos. Mo liked her, too, and called me to the bed where she put on Marquis and arranged the laptop between us. As we laid on our sides facing each other and Ingrid, we stroked ourselves to pillow-biting orgasms.

For the next month, I played the best tennis of my life. Facebook went unvisited. Patients and colleagues told me I looked different "Did you lose weight? New haircut? You look 10 years younger, Doc." If I wasn't perusing the site, I was emailing the agency and eventually even some of the potential girls. To my great dismay, Ingrid wasn't available the days we were in Amsterdam, but I comforted myself with a funky alternative—a short Ukrainian, Naomi, who had tattoos of train tracks along her thick muscular legs. It turned out Naomi wasn't bi. I moved on, ever the optimist.

Fortunately, the agency was amused by my obsession, and they even gave me a nickname. Mo was again amused but was praying her psychiatrist colleagues never got wind of it. "How in the world would I ever explain that I got my husband a tattooed sex worker for our anniversary and he's known in Holland as Dr. Suicide?"

And then, days before the flight, I got an email from Jordi at the agency, "Dr. Suicide, we have some news for you. We have encountered a problem. But I will write to you soon." The depth of my disappointment—more like depression—scared me. I checked the site, and it returned an error. I fervently checked my emails. My tennis game went to shit. It's a good thing I married a psychologist.

On the plane to Amsterdam, I checked my phone one more time before takeoff, "Update" was all the subject line read. And, hiding the phone in my lap, I opened the email. "We're back" and a link to their new and improved site. I bought the in-flight Wi-Fi.

There were a few new girls, and then I noticed a profile for Heather. She was Canadian, bi, and a grad student studying abroad in the Netherlands, but the pic had a "Coming Soon" label. I texted Jordi (by now I had his WhatsApp number) and asked about Heather. "Hahaha Doctor Suicide, yes, she is perfect for you and your wife," and attached were photos of a funky, emo brunette covered in tattoos. Her body was curvy and full—and despite how much she hid behind her tattoos, black ugly hipster glasses, chopped hair, and faux snarl— her total cuteness won through.

60

I showed the pics to Mo, and she agreed; we had a winner. I wrote Jordi and asked to schedule her the day after we arrived. That way if we liked her, we might see her again before we left. Hey, I didn't get through medical school without strategic planning.

Jordi confirmed—I put my seat back, popped an Ambien and woke up the next morning in Amsterdam. So much more than marijuana coffee shops and girls in windows; Amsterdam stuns with beauty and charm. Twelve years before, when attending a conference in nearby Brussels, we snuck away from the lectures and sales reps for a day of sightseeing in Amsterdam. What I remembered most was being surprised by how many people spoke English and that I drank beer made by Trappist monks.

This time with my awareness heightened by the prospect of a threesome with Maureen and Heather—I saw Amsterdam in a new way. Our hotel was on a canal with funky houseboats lining its shores and a walking bridge with bikes tied to the iron railings. The rows of townhouses with varied, intricate edifices and intersecting windy narrow streets evoked a romantic swell that had Maureen and me strolling hand in hand and kissing under lamp posts like new lovers.

We meandered and sampled beer and bar food—amazing french fries and fried bits of fish and other mysterious morsels—until the jet lag set in and we headed back to our hotel. The next day we killed time in a museum, had a nap, then prepared for our time with Heather. We did some personal grooming and dressed for our date. I ordered a fruit-and-cheese plate and a bottle of champagne from room service and then we nervously— well, I nervously—paced awaiting Heather's arrival.

Right on time, a knock at the door and Heather came breezing into our suite. Yes, a suite is part of the strategy because there's more furniture to work with. She gave me a kiss on both cheeks—the same for Maureen—went to the window and looked out onto the canal and then checked out the room with its giant bed and sleek furniture.

Heather seemed genuinely excited to meet us. Apparently, I had a quite a reputation at the agency. Despite her rough look, Heather was very engaging and had that stereotypical Canadian positive, easy-going manner. She smiled and laughed easy. She loved telling us about her adopted city including that she goes to her "appointments" on a bicycle. She was one year into her MBA in international studies. We genuinely liked her. Of course, we were dying to ask her what the hell she was doing as an escort, but we held our tongues.

Mid-conversation and as casually as removing a coat, Heather started to undress. "Stop!" Mo barked, and I thought, well, there goes the sex, Mo must have gotten cold feet. And then Mo said in a more quiet voice, "I want my husband to undress you."

Heather broke into a giggle and, "Oh, I like you," and Heather came to Mo and kissed her on the lips like an old lover. Mo sat in a chair in the middle of the room, and I approached Heather. I was nervous, my steady surgical hands shaking. I lifted her sweater off and as her arms went up I, got a peek of her exposed belly. I bent and lifted her shirt and kissed the spot I had just revealed. Her skin was soft and taut, her stomach sporting a little pooch. I continued to kiss her torso lifting her shirt as I went up her body. And then I saw the underside of her braless breasts. I held the shirt in place still covering her nipples, and I ran my fingers along the beautiful pale skin of her breasts. Young, full, rising breasts. I moved my hands to cup her chest over her shirt and brushed my lips and the tip of my nose along the long curves of her breasts.

Along her right side, the steep curve of her side—was a tattoo. Black and white, like a Japanese pencil drawing. The design was both intricate and spare, a thinly drawn image from an ancient garden. It was a beautiful tattoo. I leaned back to admire the work, and with a hand, I read the art like brail. The image had a lot of white space between the twisting vines and delicate leaves. I traced them first with a finger and then my tongue.

With a low "hmmm" from Heather I removed her shirt, her nipples were high and soft and slightly erect. As I teased around her nipples, my hands moved to her ample ass that was covered by loose, ripped jeans. When I squeezed her ass Heather's "hmm" got louder. "I found a spot, a zone," I said to myself. I paused to look over at Mo, who was still clothed but with her hand inside her pants and the sight caused a twitch in my pants. "Kiss her," Mo said, her bark diminished now to a breathy command.

62

Heather closed her eyes and tilted her head to the side, I brought a hand to her neck and pulled her to me. Our lips barely touched and in the same way, I explored her under breasts, Heather slowly swept her lips across mine. She made small kisses around my mouth. She took her time and drew on my face with her lips that sent me to my own "hmmmms." Her kisses were so sensual and well, loving, I closed my eyes and gave in to her. When our lips finally engaged in a full kiss, Heather's pants were somehow off and around her ankles. My hands glided along her thighs, and I was surprised how thick and muscular her upper legs were. Where her torso was soft and fleshy, her thighs were hard and defined.

Heather was now naked except for boy-short panties that perfectly complemented her masculine legs. Heather slowly turned around, and there were the tattoos I had seen in the pics Jordi had emailed me. On her lower back a large, colorful winged tattoo curved along the border of her panties. Down the back of her thighs were brightly colored tattoos that looked like Bali masks—beautiful and fierce. I removed her panties and, to my surprise, her exquisite full bottom was completely tattoo free.

The tattoos on her lower back and on her thighs that stopped at the crease of her bottom made her ass even more brilliant in contrasting with the inked areas surrounding it. I was so mesmerized I didn't notice Mo standing next to me in a lacy negligee. "My turn. I want you in the seat," and Mo motioned to the chair now by the side of the bed. When I sat down, Mo whispered to Heather, and the two approached me and pulled out two neckties Mo had hidden under the chair. Before I knew it, my hands were bound to the side of the chair. The two women undressed me and took turns fondling me to full attention. The Viagra I took when Heather and Mo were kissing was engaging, and the girls seemed euphoric with my lonely erection.

Then Mo told Heather to get on the bed face down so we could see that beautiful ass. Mo attached Marquis, the strap-on, while still wearing her negligee. Marquis was powerful looking as he protruded from beneath Mo's short-short lingerie. Mo put some lube on Marquis and stroked her cock with long smooth movements. Heather had turned to watch Mo who said, "I'm going to fuck you, sweetheart, are you ready for me?" and then before she could answer, Mo grabbed Heather by her ankles and pulled her toward the edge of the bed.

"On your knees!" Mo said in a voice I barely recognized. Heather did as she was told. The tattoos along her thighs led to her ass high in the air; her vagina was suspended between her strong legs. Mo felt along Heather's ass, her fingers moving to Heather's clit and then inside her. "I want your cock in me," Heather said, and Mo forcefully grabbed Heather by the hips and guided the dildo into Heather. There were gasps and Mo slapped Heather's ass and moved her hips, fucking Heather at the same time.

Heather let out a cry, and Mo spanked her again. When Heather demanded, "Yes, fuck me with your big cock!" Mo grabbed her hair and pulled Heather's head back fucking her harder and harder. "Oh, yeah, Jesus you're hot!" Heather purred, and Mo pulled her hair again. Both women were moaning, and I was straining to release my arms. I was so erect I thought I would come without touching myself.

Mo slowed down and between the women's legs I could see fingers moving on Heather's clit. "Are you going to come for me?" Mo said, and she grabbed Heather's ass taking in handfuls and squeezing and then spanking her. Mo thrust faster, and Heather started to "ahhhh" in a high voice and then she screamed, "Don't stop. Fuck me harder!"

And Heather went silent, her back arched. Mo slowed down, but Heather swung her head from side to side gasping for words and Mo quickly pulled Heather toward her and Heather grabbed the sheets into her fists. Heather twisted from her toes to her head, and she let out a snarl and yelled, "I'm coming! Holy shit! Yes! Fuck me!" Heather reached around and held Mo in place, the strap-on cock still inside. Moans and slow, jerky movements continued until they uncoupled and collapsed onto the bed together.

The two women kissed, and it was Heather this time who took control. She pushed Mo onto her back, and Heather started to go down on Mo's strap-on. Heather's glorious ass, surrounded by colorful snarling tattoos, and her red, wet, pussy were pointing straight at me. My cock felt like it was defying physics and was pointing away from me like a crazed compass needle. Heather took the dildo off of Mo and went down on her like a hungry animal. Mo grabbed her head and started to make her coming sounds, a low murmur that I knew was building to a long orgasm. But instead of her usual build-up, Mo let out a sudden scream, "I'm, I'm, I'm." And her hips went up, her toes curled, and she grabbed Heather's head between her legs moving it with her hands until she let out a loud gasp. Mo's thighs clenched Heather's face between her legs, Mo's shoulders came off the bed in a jerk forward motion. Twice. Three times and then a final thigh squeeze of Heather's face.

Mo's thighs slowly parted, and the two women laid side by side panting and sighing. "Ahem. Ahem!" I called, now ready to join the action before I exploded. Both girls turned to look at me and broke out laughing. I guessed I would have laughed at the sight of me naked, tied up in a chair with an unrequited, Viagra-prolonging hard-on. They whispered to each other and left the bed and moved onto the floor. Slinky and silly the two naked women crawled over to my chair and with my straining member

65

at full throttle, they kissed softly and slowly with the tip of my cock a millimeter from their lips. When Heather's cheek brushed against my straining pole, I let out a groan.

I had never been so teased and so turned on. The sight of my beautiful, amazing wife having aggressive sex with the tattooed Heather and then the two of them kissing passionately in front of me while I was bound and tied up on Viagra—well, the one thing I knew was that when someone touched my man, I was going to shoot the moon.

The women pretended to lick my shaft, their tongues almost touching it, their hands caressing each other. "Girls, someone has just has to utter my name and I'm going to paint the ceiling," and no sooner had I said that then Mo knowingly nodded to Heather.

66

Heather stood up, her back to me and she lowered her pussy until it was just touching the top of my cock. I practically yelled, "Oh, baby, I want to fuck you, get me a rubber 'cuz I'm about to come." And Mo, to my total surprise, shook her head, "I want you to come inside her," and before I could object, Heather lowered herself on my aching cock. I held her fleshy sides and watched as the tattooed girl raised and lowered herself on me all the time kissing Mo. I lasted longer than I thought. Mo bent down and tongued Heather's clit, and Heather responded by moving to her own rhythm. I grabbed her hips, and while watching her tattooed back squirming in front of me, I let go with a massive orgasm in her. Without the condom, I felt every pulse and cell in her and on me. Heather pumped every drop out of me, and I swear I saw the wings on her back fly.

The next day Mo and I went for a canal tour of Old Amsterdam. I had snuck a bottle of champagne onto the boat, and Mo bravely pulled the cork so no one would notice. Lightheaded from the night before and the champagne we stumbled off the boat, and as we got close to our hotel, Mo pulled me in the direction of a side street. I was looking at a bikini-ed girl in a window when I realized Mo was guiding me into an adjacent storefront. "You pick the design, and I'll pick the spot," Mo said and pointed to the images of tattoos on the walls. Mo hiked up her skirt and stroked the inside of her thigh.

CHAPTER SIX

My Little Secret

USUALLY WHEN I go out to dinner with another couple, especially a couple I haven't met before, I dress conservatively; this time was no different. Even my panties were pretty tame—silk and lace trim—not some crotchless thong that I might wear back in the room with Jim. And my bra was not traditionally sexy, but Jim loved it. It was a plain cotton, unstructured, bikini top that my kinky man called my training bra.

But what I was wearing under my Talbots skirt and over my panties was my secret. The harness for a strap-on. My little secret. I didn't want anyone, not even Jim, to know—at least not yet. My secret.

I could feel the straps as we walked through the lobby. When we politely hugged Brett and Stacy, the straps dug into me and flushed me with my secret. I wanted Stacy to know, to brush up against her so she could feel the outlines of the straps. I wanted her to feel what might come later.

Stacy had a pretty young mom face, roundish with almond eyes and brown skin. I guessed she was Thai or Philipino, but her accent was all Chicago. She was not too tall—about my height—and her short skirt showed slender, tapered legs. I had a bunk-mate in summer camp who was Thai who was my first girl-crush so Stacy triggered a fantasy gene deep inside me.

Brett was cute, almost pretty. He had a kind, clean propor-tional face with small features. He looked like a pediatrician who moms had a crush on. He wore a golf shirt tucked into slacks and I would have written him off as too pretty to be sexy, but the tattoo on his under forearm hinted at him being more than vanilla.

70

The conversation was the usual—polite and fun and a little awkward. We were talking about our lives, but we were also sizing each other up. Was there an attraction? Was everyone on board? Was everyone safe? Did we like each other? Did we want to go to the next step? We were sizing up the others as well as our partner's willingness in a fun, mysterious dance.

By the second round of cocktails, the lights in the Hyatt bar had dimmed, and our conversation was getting more graphic as we recalled experiences and fantasies in the lifestyle. Almost absentmindedly I slid my hand under the table over Stacy's leg looking for her hand. I had noticed her hands right away when we first met—elegant, sexy hands.

I wanted to feel her soft thigh with her hand together with mine. She was tentative at first, and I liked that, so I backed off. In a few moments, she found my hand again under the table and delicately caressed my fingers. Backing off then coming back was so sexy. Jim and Brett were comparing travel plans, but my heart rate had picked up and I could barely hear the men. I moved our hands over to my skirt and just as Stacy's fingers met the inside of my thigh, I felt the pull of the strap-on.

I was suddenly panicked as if caught playing with myself in the dorm. I was afraid Stacy would think I was crazy and too kinky, but I wanted her to know anyway. I wanted her to catch me. I shifted, and her hand went higher. I could feel how wet my panties were. I was so close to being caught. Back off. But don't. Feel me. I tensed. Another inch. My little secret. Come closer. Closer to my secret.

I guided her hand to the strap around my upper thigh. She didn't pull away. I traced our fingers along the strap to the harness and held it there. My heart was beating so fast I was sure it was visible through my shirt. Stacy turned and looked me in the eye, held my gaze and announced to me and the boys that we were going to the ladies room. I leapt to my feet and quickly pulled down my skirt. The boys were all eyes. Now we had their attention. To really get them going, I held Stacy's hand as we walked through the bar.

71

Inside the bathroom I locked the door and started to say, "I hope you don't think it's too forwa. . ." but Stacy put a finger over my mouth then brought her lips to mine. I love the feel of a woman's lips and Stacy's were full and soft and tasted of a heavy, sultry red wine. I brought my hand to her face as our tongues met and I could smell her perfume, light and rosy, stirred and mixed with her body heat. Stacy pushed me against the bathroom wall and reached under my skirt. I let out a moan pulling her close, my lips buried into the crease of her neck.

"You're so wet," Stacy said in a guttural whisper. "What are you going to do with that harness? Are you going to fuck me?" Her fingers pressed my clit through my panties. I gasped and bit her shoulder. The tension of the moment and the straps and the long build-up had me so aroused, I was shaking. I pressed and then rotated my clit into her hand, "I want you to fuck me from behind while I suck Jim off." My legs started to buckle, and I felt an orgasm build. She pulled my panties aside and slid a finger inside me. The straps of the harness pulled around my vulva like an S&M restraint. "I'm going to play with my clit as you fuck me like a man." She said and bit me back, and I came, holding her hand on my pussy, standing up in a flood of wetness against the bathroom wall.

Even though I had already come in her arms in a dry-hump-through-my jeans-in-the back-seat-of-a-high-schooler's-car, desperate, kind of way, we kissed again, like it was for the first time, gently like we were starting from the beginning of a seduction. And when I moved my hand under Stacy's shirt, she suggested we go straight to the room. "Oh, I like the way you think," I said moving to straighten myself up a bit. "I've got a key, I'll text Jim," I said and took out my phone. "We are going to the room. Come if you like. We already started without you," and I sent it knowing Jim would get an instant hard-on then take a screenshot of the text for his library.

72

We got into the elevator with a young, clean-cut guy who was in workout clothes—a film of sweat on his thick, muscular legs. I absentmindedly slid my hand into Stacy's then realized we had to play it cool, and I pulled my hand back. Stacy grabbed my hand again and then pulled me into a deep kiss. The elevator seemed to take off like a fighter jet making me dizzy with excitement. "Holy shit!" the guy blurted, "This is the best elevator ever—I may pull the emergency stop." The elevator stopped at our floor, and Stacy reached for the guy, "Wanna see more? We are going to put on a show for our husbands." And she pulled all of us out of the elevator. The shocked but grinning jock was being pulled along like a little boy in a toy store.

We entered the large bright room with its faux-Victorian decor, and with a shaking hand I texted Jim, "Heads up—we met a sweaty young guy in the elevator!" I turned around and Stacy was taking the guy's shirt off. He stood tall but still, with his hands at his side. He had a knowing grin on his face as he watched Stacy's face in rapt attention as she admired his body. She called me over, and we ran our hands over his bald, taut chest. "Sit down over there, take your cock out, but don't touch it. We'll be right back. Oh, and what's your name?" When he opened his mouth, Stacy ran her fingers up his throat and covered his lips. "Never mind, we'll call you Damian," Stacy said and pointed to a chair across from the bed. He dutifully obeyed but with a look like he thought he was still in control.

73

In the bathroom, Stacy stripped down to a little teddy she had on under clothes. I started to undress, but she took over. She removed my shirt and bra, fondling my breasts and kissing my nipples playfully. Then she took off the harness, my panties, and the Talbot's skirt. She handed me the harness and the pink, thick, firm, but slightly flexible dildo on the bathroom counter. "Assemble that thing, and then I want you to put the skirt back on," she said in a cute, mischievous way.

I loved the way she took control. She had a sweet mom voice that made the commands even sexier. My thoughts raced from the sex I was about to have with Stacy to the sexy elevator boy to imagining Jim and Bret walking in on us.

Damian was sitting in the chair completely naked with a perfectly straight, twitching, jock cock straining high in the air. He was sitting on his hands. The grin on his face replaced with a serious focused peering gaze. Stacy came over to his chair and started a little dance, running her hands over me, her ass inches from his tool. "You know, Damian, we just met in the bar, and I took this little slut into the bathroom and fingered her to a dripping orgasm." She turned around and brought her breasts to his face and then pretended to slide down and go down on him. "Do you like that Damian?" Damian silently nodded. "Do you want to watch her fuck me, Damian? Don't touch yourself." Stacy said her tongue a millimeter from the tip of his straining cock.

I was so horny my pussy throbbed against the strap on under my skirt. It was my turn to take over. I turned Stacy around and pushed her onto the bed. I took off her panties to the prettiest shaved pussy I have ever seen. Perfectly shaped with pouty lips hiding her clit. I wanted to go down on her, but it was my turn to tease. "Show Damian your pussy," I barked. "Spread your legs wide. I want to see your clit." Stacy pushed her thighs wide open then pulled her vulva's lips apart.

74

"Play with your pussy, Stacy, show Damian what you do when you are alone." I lifted my skirt, put some lube on the strap-on, and turned around so Damian could see my secret. "Holy shit!" Damian said, his hips fucking the air, his eyes wide and his lips parted.

I pulled Stacy toward me and placed the head of the strap-on dildo in front of her open pussy. I slid my cock into Stacy, and she let out a loud call. "Yes! Fuck me! Damian, are you watching?" I heard the door open, and I pulled out and then thrust into her. Stacy called out again, "Oh yeah, baby, fuck me!" I heard our husbands undressing. I moved my hips in short movements, "Jim, do you see Damian there? That beautiful cock wants to fuck us!? Stacy was watching Damian and holding onto my ass, screaming, "Oh yeah, that's so good!" Stacy pulled me on top of her. I could feel the harness against my pussy, and I ground my hips to get it to my clit. We kissed while I drove my cock deep into her. She moaned and panted. "Are all of you watching?" I called out. "Do you want to show us how excited you are? Show us. Are you all hard? Are there a room full of cocks wanting us?" I said in a teasing voice in between thrusts

Stacy wrapped her legs around me and with a free hand reached between us, and began to rub her clit. I looked to the side of the bed, and there were three stiff cocks begging us. I caught Jim's eye and he smiled with the "I'm so proud that's my wife" look. Stacy brought one of my nipples into her mouth; I could feel her hand moving between us. I pulled out and teased her opening with the dildo. And then I slowly slid into her and shifted so I could push it in even further. "Oh my fucking god!" I pumped the dildo into her with hard thrusts. Stacy yelled, and her legs pointed straight out alongside of me. Her thigh's soft skin caressing me as she stiffened then twitched. "Damian, I'm coming. I'm coming! Damian watch us!"

75

We held each other, kissed, panted, and kissed. We got up—passing our husbands and Damian. Silent, wide-eyed, their cocks pointed at us like artillery waiting for the signal. I promised the crew they were next as Stacy and I walked into the bathroom, holding hands, and between my legs, proudly pointing the way—my secret revealed.

CHAPTER seven

Walls and Borders

WHEN SOFT IS hotter than full on. When a look, a glance, keeps you up at night. When the orgy Olympics are a blur but the flirt is what rocks worlds.

They had come to watch. Their first time. We met them at the sports bar restaurant inside the resort and liked them right away. Bohemian by choice. The conversation flitted from travel spots to music festivals to cooking. What wasn't mentioned, and we didn't find out until much later, were the similarities in our lifestyles—we had non-traditional careers but had managed to achieve some success nevertheless.

Sonya had red hair—thick and a little messy—with freckles on lightly tanned skin and green eyes that, I swear if you covered her mouth, you could see the smile in them. And her mouth. Her lips. They formed curves like a hand-polished sculpture and colored to rouge that no lipstick could ever mimic. Dark red. Toward the peaked center her lips faded to a translucent pink to the thin edges of her mouth. And when she smiled, bright white teeth illuminated her beautiful face. And she smiled a lot, and was easy to laugh. When she listened, she turned her head, and I felt like the room was, well, the world was just her and me.

I have the occasional bi moment but I never really felt it for Daryl. That didn't matter because Samantha dug him. His dirty blonde hair was lighter than his beard, but she really liked his beard. Full and real, but she could tell he kept it trimmed and clean. And although he was thin Sam could tell from his forearms he was in good shape. He was an organic food broker

78

and that telegraphed good health and strength from lots of squats and crate lifting—"an organic workout," Sam commented. He also had an easy smile and a casualness about him that Sam read for confidence. Later she would nickname him "MC" for "model cock," but that was later—although not much later.

When Sonya stood up to get napkins from the waitress, I caught a glance at her body. Well, we all did. Wow, I wasn't expecting that. She was tall. Maybe taller than me. Long, lean legs and when she walked, her muscles tweaked. A college volleyball star turned furniture restorer her man informed us. And that's when my cock grew, and my hopes faded. I am not a jock. I mean not at all. I haven't been in a gym since high school. I'm an artist. Yep, an actual, real, working artist. Painting since a child, I now make a surprisingly decent living doing what most people, heck even I, think is kind of weird. I take existing paintings and paint over, around, and within them. Go figure.

Now unlike some artists, I don't speak art speak, even though I have an MFA from Penn, and if you want to hear about the underlying meaning of a Kandinsky, I could bore you to death.

But when it comes to my work, I just paint and leave the art commentary to others. But let's be clear, I am not a stud at all. Sam is always trying to build my confidence by telling me I'm cute, even (and I hate the term) adorable. I have unresolved curly hair and a baby face that complements a nice layer of baby fat everywhere else. And I swear I keep forgetting to shave, so I always have a few days stubble like I have been in my studio pulling a series of all-nighters. If women are attracted to me, they tend to look like they also just pulled an all-nighter—in a library. So, yeah, I reckoned Sonya was never going to go for me.

Sam, on the other hand, everybody liked. The kids in her Waldorf school third-grade class ironically called her the terminator because she could solve any problem with her perky, light-hearted, but assured, energy. She was short with a boyish body, funny cropped hair, and a cute face with a slight pug nose that just made you want to go, "awwww." Women, in particular, went for her and frankly, that's what got us some awesome threesomes. But Sonya was nearly a foot taller than Sam so, again, I didn't think anything would come of it.

And they were newbies. Like most in our late-20s generation, I guessed they had had plenty of kinky times. Sonya told us about some multi and bi experiences she had in high school and college, but they had never been non-monogamous since they had been together as a couple. They were, however, interested and had talked a lot about it. It seemed to me like Sonya was more into the idea than Darryl—and that was typical. The men almost always wanted to have sex with other women but often were not ready to see their partners with other men.

Like I said, we liked them. I really liked Sonya, but they were there to watch, maybe have some sexy time together, but they were not ready to go full swap. Eventually, we drifted off, and Sam and I ran into some folks we had fooled around with in the past. We went to a playroom and had a great quickie. Fun and sexy, just what we had hoped for.

About an hour later we went back to the bar where we saw Sonya and Darryl on the dance floor. My heart skipped a beat, and I started scheming. This was going to have to be a Sam play if I had any chance, so I suggested she join them on the dance floor. Sam was reticent because she felt they had pretty clear boundaries, and she didn't want to impose. I, of course, wholeheartedly agreed but my internal thoughts were totally the opposite. I played it cool. I turned so I couldn't see them on the dance floor even though every cell in my body wanted to watch Sonya. Plan B. Shots of tequila—for Sam.

It worked. Sam pulled me to the dance floor. I looked all over for Darryl and Sonya, but we were too late. Then across the crowded floor through a gaggle of half-naked bodies, I saw an ankle resting on a jeaned knee. I moved to the left, and the ankle led to long legs that I knew were Sonya's. Darryl and Sonya were on one of the couches ringing the dance floor. I pretended to see a friend and guided Sam toward them and then in an act of sheer brilliance, I turned away from Sonya, spinning Sam around so she could discover the couple for herself.

Darryl's hand was under Sonya's skirt, and Sonya had Darryl's cock out and in her hand. Sam did a quick calculation. Sonya had a big hand with long slender fingers, Sam noticed these things, and if they were wrapped around Darryl's cock and so much of it was still visible—well, he must be huge.

I no longer needed to scheme, it was Sam who was now taking the lead. She moved so we were right in front of them on the edge of the dance floor. She turned me, so I was facing Sonya and Sam squatted down, took out my cock, and wrapped her beautiful little lips around it.

Darryl caught on and went to Sonya's feet, lifted her skirt, pushed aside her panties, and went down on her while stroking those beautiful thighs. Sonya lowered her eyelids and slowly raised them straight to my gaze. Her tongue slid across her lips. She let out a slight moan. Eyes still locked on mine as she wrapped her legs around Darryl, Sonya's muscles bulging around him. Her eyelids went down again in beautiful slow motion; Sam reached for my spot just below my balls, and I started to buckle. Sonya's eyes came back to mine, with a smile and a gasp that I could hear over the music, right to my cock.

Sonya grabbed Darryl's head between her legs guiding him. I did the same to Sam moving her head over my cock. Sonya pushed Darryl away from her crotch and pulled him up and took that beautiful cock in her mouth and drove his hands to her pussy.

I lifted Sam and bent her over, plunging my strained cock into her soaking pussy. Sonya took Darryl's cock in her hand and fixed her gaze on Sam; Darryl fingered her with one hand deep inside and the other on her clit and she started to shake. I held out no more and pounded Sam like I hadn't in years. I came deep inside her watching Sonya, her athlete's legs wide and in the air. The music went into the background, and I could hear every note of Sonya coming. I held Sam down as I filled her and filled her. Sonya pulled down her blouse, her nipples pointing straight up and Darryl came all over her chest. Sonya lowered her eyelids one more time, and ever-so-slowly opened them. Her green eyes fixed on me, her lips pursed to a kiss.

And then. . .

We woke up to them fucking right next to us in the bed the four of us had slept in. Darryl was on his knees fucking Sonya from behind. I slid my hand underneath Sonya; her clit grew between my fingers as Darryl's cock thrust into her. Sam folded over me so she could kiss, no, make out with Sonya. Sensuous, gentle, eyes-open kissing. Sonya's clit was sliding between my fingers. There was a hand on my cock.

The morning after. Yes, after our sex from a distance we ended up spending the night together. They followed us to our home and when giving them a tour of my studio, Sonya asked if we ever made love on the bed Sam dubbed my all-nighter retreat bed. Sonya told me how the smell of paint reminded her of her furniture workshop but that the aroma from oil paint was much sexier than varnish. We had a grown-up sleepover among the canvasses and brushes and easels. Step by step the walls came down.

82

Mostly we checked with the gatekeeper of the moment, like when Sonya and I asked Darryl if it was okay I go down on her. And each time a border was crossed, the passion heightened.

The first time I went down on Sonya I treated Sonya's clit like I was savoring a beaujolais nouveau. I kissed and tongued around her clean, sweet lips; I ran my fingers slowly along the thighs I had been lusting after. When she would push her hips up to me, I would back off and then circle her vulva, my tongue painting the valleys around her clit, teasing her. When her hips would lower, I would bury my face into her soft skin taking her whole clit, her lips, and all of her pussy into my mouth. I pulled all of her deep into me, and she moaned that she liked it. I sucked her like a little cock until my tongue found her opening. She squirmed. Her spot right at the opening of her vagina. I released her from my mouth and focused my tongue on the spot of my discovery. Lightly my mouth kissed her there and then I moved my tongue like I was motioning for her to come to me. Come to me. Come to me.

Boundaries. The final frontier (no, not anal, this isn't a Ted movie).

Perhaps I'm soft at heart. My first touching of Sonya had me shaking with anticipation, but Samantha had another, bigger, thicker line to cross. After waking up to Darryl fucking Sonya, Sam was so worked up she came just playing with herself and kissing Sonya. But then she propped herself up on pillows, opened her legs, and declared she wanted Darryl's model cock in her. ""Now!" Darryl looked at Sonya and, in a gesture, she acceded by handing him a condom. He handed it back to her and told her to put it on him. Sam watched with a hand still on her own pussy and the other entwined in my hand.

Sonya guided Darryl's thick cock into Samantha. Sam's hand tightened its grip on me. Darryl held Sam's cute thighs in his hands, and we all watched as he slowly entered her all the way and held there. Sam declared that was just what she wanted. Sonya propped up Sam's butt and put a pillow under Sam, so Darryl had a better angle. She knew. Darryl pulled out and reentered, and Sam yelled out, yes, that's it—that's the place at the back of her cervix, and off he went, holding her legs wide open as he pumped her. Sam was calling out, caressing Darryl's chest, running her fingers through his beard. She looked at me, then Sonya. From wide to closed and I realized what "eyes wide shut" meant. The two girls kissed the best they could with Darryl thrusting on top. Sonya's big hands on Sam's tiny breasts.

I moved behind Sonya, her hair cascading down her back. I put on a condom, bent over and whispered into her ear, "I'm going to fuck you now. I'm not asking; I'm telling you," and I placed my cock at the edge of her opening. Sonya pushed against me as I entered her small wet pussy. Sonya was telling Sam and Darryl what I was doing, and Sam wrapped her legs around Darryl and pulled him in tight, she was screaming that she loved that thick cock in her. I could feel fingers around Sonya's clit, and then my cock and I heard Darryl grunt and pull out, pull off the condom in

83

one quick movement and stroke himself to orgasm right on Sam's stomach.

I pulled out of Sonya, and the two girls took off my condom and both mouthed my cock while kissing each other. As I felt my orgasm approach, Sam took me for herself and Sonya ever-so-cautiously, with that same look she gave me on the dance floor, like a curtsy, lowered her eyelids. In a moment that suspended time, she bathed me with a look both innocent and wanting. In a delicate turn, her mouth rose and parted with the tip of her tongue silently calling me, and she brought her lips to mine. The full, sweet lips I had been pining for.

And for the first time.

We kissed.

CHAPTER EIGHT

Crossing the Line

CAITLIN AND I held hands as we walked to their room. Mr. Confident here was nervous. I wasn't sure why, because Caitlin was awesome; we hit it off right away. Her husband and my wife were just as comfortable with each other. It was a good match.

Lately, we had been striking out on dates, no-shows, newbies chickening out, people who didn't look like their pics, or one or both of us just didn't feel it. But Caitlin and her husband were a "go" from the start.

My wife Denise was fooling around and giving shit to Caitlin's husband like they were brother and sister—that's when I know Denise digs a guy—when she can elbow him in the ribs and playfully insult him. And Caitlin and I were in our own little world while the other two were jibing each other. It started. We clicked almost immediately when we met at the bar. Caitlin saw the two of them being silly and said to me, "They're awfully cute together but let's show them how it's done." And she put her hand on my chest, unsnapped my shirt—right there in the bar—and kissed my shoulders and chest.

She got me. I was sporting a hard-on before the first drink ever arrived. The more Denise and Caitlin's husband, Marty, fooled around, the more Caitlin and I kissed and caressed and told each other what we were going to do back in the room. She was awesome, and I felt like a rock star. A dad, husband, working Joe, rock star!

When we got to the room, Denise and Marty kissed and got familiar, but Caitlin pulled me to the bed, and we started right in. I pushed her down on her back, lifted her skirt, pulled aside her panties and went down on her—boots on and in the air. She ruffled my hair and twisted her hips and pulled me into her. She was full into it, holding my head and scratching my shoulders. I got onto the bed and on my knees and put one, then two fingers into her. I reached deep inside her. I love fingering a woman; my mechanic's hands are used to manipulating in tight spots. I flicked her nubby G-spot while she reached for my other hand and eagerly sucked my fingers as she would later do to my cock.

86

I found that little ball just behind her G-spot and her hips started to go wild. "Yes, damn it, oh God that's the spot." I kept fingering that little gland, and then in and out until she tensed up and then damn if she didn't squirt like an ejaculating teen. Hottest darn thing I've ever seen. I had never seen a woman who squirted before, except on my computer of course.

And that was just the beginning. Caitlin pulled me up and kissed me like I just got back from the war. Denise was going down on Marty, but they stopped to watch us. I'm telling you, even I wish I could have seen us. Our connection was electric.

We destroyed that hotel room. I must have gone through a half dozen rubbers. I caught glimpses of Denise and heard that familiar moan and even an orgasm shudder, but I gotta tell you, Caitlin and I were playing in the Super Bowl while they were just in the regular season. If I had to pick a moment that really got me, and this sounds kinda goofy, but when Caitlin walked into in the shower with me at the end of the night and kissed and washed every part of me, well, I darn near fell apart.

And that's why I was nervous, I guess, because I plain, old, really liked Caitlin. It had never happened before. Denise and I had been swinging off and on for years, and when it was good, it was just sexy fun. But I never liked a gal like this.

When Denise and I got home and we collapsed into bed, my head was spinning with thoughts of Caitlin. "Honey," I said my voice cracking, "Are you okay with what happened tonight? I mean, I'm a little freaked out. I think I may have crossed a line, I, um, really fell for her. That's never hap-pened before." I was curled up in her arms like a baby. "I don't think we should see them again, cuz I want to too much—you know?"

87

Denise didn't say a word as I rambled on like a drunk soldier. Her silence was making me more nervous, so I stopped talking, and we just laid there. Denise finally pushed me out of her arms and looked at me for a long moment. "I love you, you hulking softie. What's the big deal? I mean what did she do to make you such a mess?" I said something about us being compatible and she gave me a little slap. "No, you knucklehead! What did she do? What did the two of you do?"

She reached for my turtle-hiding-in-his-shell cock and gave it a little tug. "Tell me," she said again. I was tentative at first and said, "You know, we kissed." Denise gave my Johnson a tug, "Tell me, or I'm gonna pull this guy right out of you. How did you make that hot, little bitch squirt? I want to hear it." And she went under the covers and started to lick under my dick which she knows is my ticket—I'd give her the house, the truck, and all my tools—thank you, god, just keep licking around the boys.

Clueless as I can be, I finally got it. I told Denise how I grabbed Caitlin's sweet little ass and pulled her to me. Denise picked up the pace, stroking my tool like a master, so I kept going. "I tongued her clit from side-to-side and she squeezed my face between those athletic fleshy thighs."

I could feel Denise rubbing her cunny against my leg so on I went, "Her twat tasted so good. She pushed that bald little cunny into my face, and I slid a finger into her. She was totally, fucking, wet." Denise was now fingering herself and moaning, "Keep going, you big, nasty, bad boy." And Denise climbed on top and lowered herself onto my dick.

88

"You liked that sexy little bitch, didn't you?" Denise rode me hard as I told her how Caitlin bucked and squirmed and moaned. Denise grabbed a vibe from the drawer and rubbed it against her clit as she fucked me. I love her on top.

"I teased that sweet cunny of hers while she sucked my fingers like they were the best cock she ever had." And I kid you not ,Denise and I came together. Another first. We had been lovers since high school and, this time, we came at the same time like in a good porno.

We held each other, we panted, we tasted sweat, we kissed and told ourselves how much we loved each other. And just as we were going to sleep, spooning like we used to, long before kids. Denise whispered, "Next week I'm gonna do Caitlin, and maybe I'll tell you all about it. Big boy."

CHAPTER nine

Reluctance

I WASN'T HORNY. I wasn't attracted to him. Or her. But when I saw the look on Brock's face, I knew it was worth it. He's my man. Brock would do anything for me, and I was OK with this because Brock wanted it so much—it made him so damned excited. I hadn't seen that look on Brock's face, well, since our first years together. You know those times when you're first in love, and you catch your man checking you out as if you were the goddess he never thought he could have?

That's the way he looked that night: our first swinging encounter. Brock was flirting with the wife, Sandy, and yes that was cute, and I have to admit the way she responded to him was just fucking adorable. Of course, I thought I'd be jealous, but that was the last thing on my mind. The idea of Brock having more-than-sexual feelings for Sandy seemed absurd. I mean, Sandy was cute, but there's not a chance in the world he would ever fall for her. In fact, when we were at the table with Sandy and Mitch, her husband, Brock gazed at me with more adoration than either of us expressed to each other since at least child number one or for sure child number two—that adorable little terror of a Brock clone.

Sandy and Mitch were both gracious and engaging. They had invited us to their home where we sat by the pool at a table with a nice spread of wine and nibbles. Sandy was a nurse, and Mitch a physical therapist, but their shared passion was wine. They were amateur vintners, and whenever they could, they traveled the world touring vineyards. They had been to Italy several times (their favorite), and Sandy was terribly cute speaking Italian with her Midwestern accent. But Sandy and Mitch had also been to South Africa and Portugal and, of course, French and Californian vineyards. Next, they were going to Argentina, and God bless her, Sandy was learning Spanish so she could talk with the vintners in Argentina.

90

Looks-wise they were attractive enough. They were mild workout people—fine with me. Sandy had short blonde hair and a comfortable nurse's smile. The few extra pounds she was carrying were kind of cute on her. Mitch was in a little better shape. He looked like a college athlete who had not renewed his gym membership but still had the hints of a jock's physique. And let's not kid ourselves here—I think Brock and I might have been a notch better looking than them, but we are certainly showing some wear, too.

Brock and I had found ourselves in a sexual rut. We started to crawl out of our ditch by talking about sex, the lack of it, and what we could do to transform the affection we still had for each other into sexy time. Mostly it came down to scheduling—not an erotic conversation at all. We decided to plan date nights—ugh, boring! I got some sexy lingerie—OK, that helped for a night or two. We looked at porn together, which wasn't my thing, but I knew Brock did so why not look together? Mostly it just meant having a laptop in bed as our virtual ménage-à-trois—another ugh.

On one of our date nights we went to a strip bar—definitely not my thing. I wanted to tell the girls to quit dancing and go to college. But I have to admit when we got home that night, Brock took me like a teenager, and I had a more-than-clit orgasm. And I whistled while making the morning coffee. Yeah, he was that good!

And although I didn't realize it at the time but now looking back on it, that first lap dance was when I began to discover how aroused I got when I saw how turned on Brock was with another woman. And then, some friends confided in us that they were swingers and that it was the best thing to have happened to their marriage. Seemed ridiculous to me.

But, that's when Brock and I started talking about opening our relationship. At first, I was turned off by the idea. I mean, I love Brock and pretty much never looked at other men; it was like I had turned that part of me off when the kids invaded our lives. But I knew Brock was a healthy, typical man and no matter how much lingerie I bought, he was still fantasizing about other women.

One day, confessing to a girlfriend about the disparity in our sex life my swinging girlfriend summed it up for me, "Look, you can ignore or fight off what Brock is feeling or join in. It's that simple. Men are men. So why not do it with them? I mean, if you went along with it, wouldn't he love you even more? Wouldn't he be totally indebted to you for allowing him to indulge his fantasies?" She got me thinking. It became apparent to me—ignore our desires and most married people will end up cheating. Or, I could acknowledge and even embrace Brock's libido, and he will thank me forever. And notice that I didn't consider my desires—that would come later.

So there we were with Sandy and Mitch, an attractive middle-aged couple by the pool of their suburban home, and I'm watching

Brock flirt with a woman who I assumed he was going to have sex with. And then in the middle of a discussion about the difference between American zinfandel and Italian Primitivo wine I stood up and said, "Why don't we go into the pool?" And I took off my clothes—full on naked—right there in front of everyone.

I would give up my minivan and twice-a-week housekeeper for the look on Brock's face. I mean, come on. I wasn't a prude when he met me, but yeah, we had both gotten rather conservative and more so with each child. Anyhow, I stripped down and strolled into the pool, and Brock nearly came right there. And to tell you the truth, I felt better because I had taken control of the situation.

92

The conversation ceased and then they all followed me into the water. Brock and Sandy started kissing right away.

Mitch swam up to me; his big ole' dick already hard. And even though he was packing a nice piece of equipment, I told Mitch to hold me so we could watch Brock and Sandy. And you know what? I was totally turned on watching my man with Sandy. No shit. Even with the lap dance experience that I guess I didn't understand at the time, the sight of my Brock excited as a little boy and that pretty blonde, putty in his arms, well damn, if that didn't make me wetter in places the pool water didn't reach.

I felt Mitch's big schlong press against my lower back, so I wiggled a little to give the poor guy some attention. But I couldn't take my eyes off Brock and Sandy. I realized that I just wanted to go over and play with the two of them. So I did. Well, first I grabbed Mitch's tool and gave it a few tugs. Damn, that was a sweet-feeling cock. I had forgotten the variety of penises out there in the world, and it was definitely exciting handling Mitch's. But, after a little exploration of my own, I pulled Mitch by his rudder and waded over to the two lovebirds.

Brock stopped when he saw us and turned to me, "You okay, I mean with this?"

"Yeah, baby," I said surprising myself, "let's make this hottie come."

Seriously, you would have thought Brock saw a ghost; his eyes went so wide I think he almost passed out right there in the pool. But then my man took over. He picked Sandy up by her chubby little ass and placed her on the side of the pool. She gasped like a helpless little girl. Brock stood on a pool step, slid his thick little cock into her, and she grabbed onto him for dear life. And are you ready for this? I fingered her clit while he fucked her. I ran my hands over her soft wet breasts and then back to her clit, and she moaned to my touch. Damn, she was a horny little chubster. I loved the way she felt; soft and familiar, yet new.

93

I felt Mitch's monster cock press against my ass, so I ground against that big boy, filling the space between my bottom cheeks. Brock pounded Sandy's coochie like he hadn't had any in years. Holy shit I loved watching him. A finger went to my clit, and I honestly don't know if it was Mitch's, the wife's, or even Brock.s. And just as Sandy crescendoed to screaming like a schoolgirl, I started to build up to coming myself. My mouth was on Sandy's puckered nipples and my-oh-my, those nips felt good. I forgot where I was, lost in the menagerie.

Somehow Mitch's tool, now even bigger than before, was in one of my hands and Sandy's clit between my other fingers. I could feel Brock's manhood still moving into Sandy and sliding along my fingertips with Sandy's thin clit between my digits. Sandy's soft breasts slapped my face and all the while I watched Brock fuck the shit out of the moaning blondie. I squirmed around the hand on my clit, stroked Mitch like I was angry at him, went on my toes, and then my knees gave way. I came in a rush of spasms to the sounds of Sandy's screeching orgasm.

Just as I was coming back to normal vision, I heard Brock howl, and he pulled out of Sandy, rose up, turned to me, and I took him in my mouth in a torrent of an orgasm. Sandy was totally mesmerized by Brock, watching my swarthy husband with fascination and a hint of fear. And I fell in love with that crazy man all over again.

Strangely enough, all I wanted to do was get home so I could fuck the shit out of my naughty, Sandy-satisfying, husband. Yep, that's just what I did. Three a.m., babysitter sent home, kids asleep, and with memories of Sandy's nipples, Mitch's big cock, and Brock's squirting dick–I pushed Brock down on our bed, climbed on top, grabbed the bedposts, and rode my husband till we both came for the second time that night. We fell asleep in each other's arms. Just a little more in love than the night before.

CHAPTER TEN

LET'S GET THIS out of the way—love and commitment are more important than sex or the pursuit of sexual pleasures. Hard to believe I would say so—but this is what is true for me, and apparently so, for most happy sexually non-monogamous couples. I'd also like to say that love and commitment are most evident, not at the beginning of a romantic relationship or when a couple is having fun, but when the tough times hit—and there will be tough times in a long relationship. Love and commitment are the glue that allows us to both enjoy and weather the beauties and struggles of life with a sense of underlying security and well-being no matter what happens.

What Does Jealousy Have to Do With It?

Sexual non-monogamy can seem contradictory to love

(a-THAT'S-WHAT-SHE-SAID-COMMENTARY)

and commitment, and, especially, to the idea of marriage. Before opening up, I pretty much believed that sexual monogamy was the load-bearing wall in the house of marriage or romantic commitment. I knew that the wall was imperfect and was sometimes breached, but that in general, it was a basic tenet. Even after opening up, I think that the concept of non-monogamy remained ill-defined in my mind. I had thought of non-monogamy as basically "cheating." In my mind, it was associated with illicit or extra-marital affairs, or some weird, new age or pseudo-religious practice. And, even if it was not "cheating" per se, I figured that the concept of non-monogamy was made up by guys and mostly benefited guys—those dogs! In other words, I could not understand that basic trust and honesty could co-exist in marriage without sexual monogamy. And the idea that monogamy could be negotiated never crossed my mind.

I also didn't know that monogamy embodied three different concepts: sexual, emotional, and practical. Traditional swingers, by and large, retain all emotional and practical monogamy. Sexual activities are non-monogamous but "regulated" as to not run the risk of developing romantic relationships with others. Polyamorists deconstruct the notion of dyadic monogamy entirely—any number of sexual, emotional, and practical activities and relationships can be shared with more than two persons in poly relationships. Other forms of consensual non-monogamy, such as "being open," are negotiated and can vary in style and structure. For instance, some open couples pursue sexual interests separately but have agreement not to develop romantic relationships. Others may have both extradyadic sexual and romantic relationships.

My beliefs about non-monogamy, of course, were shaped and distorted by a culture that both exalts male sexual freedom and female sexual virtue. But more importantly, my ideas about non-monogamy were distorted by my own experiences. My first husband had two brief sexual affairs. So sex and lying were closely associated in my mind. I had also given men a free pass or two when it came to monogamy because of the cultural bias that led me to believe that a man's sex drive was stronger than a woman's. Although his affairs did not land the deadly blow to our marriage—and I never interpreted his affairs as an indictment that something was wrong with our sex—the affairs certainly helped shape my early beliefs about non-monogamy, and by association, swinging, polyamory, and other nontraditional relationships.

For happy couples, opening up requires an exceptional capacity for honesty, sensitivity, open communication and, for women, especially, personal agency—which is the power and strength to make and enact decisions for oneself. People who decide to open up probably do not grant sex in and of itself as a sacred act (though they may distinguish lovemaking from recreational sex), as the mental gymnastics to justify sex for just fun and pleasure with others would require some serious and compromising mental contortions. When the topic of non-monogamy is broached or stumbled upon as it was for Jim and me, the liberal couple must have open communication and a pretty sophisticated understanding of one another's emotions. They also will need to understand what consent really means and how difficult it can be to talk about sex and desire. Excellent emotional communication skills are critical if the happy couple decides to explore non-monogamy further.

Jealousy was my biggest concern when Jim and I first stumbled upon non-monogamy and, of course, I quickly learned that it is most people's major concern, besides STIs and privacy, for most couples considering opening up. At first, I thought that most non-monogamous couples somehow banished this seemingly destructive emotion from their psyches in service of the thrills of new sexual stimulation. I eventually discovered that jealousy, well managed, was an emotion intrinsic to the whole process of opening up, and instrumental in making the sex more exciting, especially for long-committed couples who were securely and happily attached.

So, if it is not banished, how could jealousy make sex more exciting for couples? For one, jealousy is activating—because it is the natural alarm bell for potential loss. It signals our brain to do something. It prods us to act, makes us stand up and take notice. The emotion shakes the couple out of any emotional detachment or complacency. Couples will often describe a heightened desire for one another, and sexual fire after an illicit affair is had, and the couple reconciles—makeup sex. I don't advocate for illicit affairs, but they serve as an example of how these contradictory actions and the resulting emotions can stir up sexual desire. During swinging, for instance, the alarm bell sounds in the background, stoking up arousal, and desire, but remains managed because of the overriding sense of security within the couple's relationship.

Now, that doesn't mean that jealousy in consensual non-monogamy never becomes overwhelming—say when one partner feels left out, or another seems just a little too into it, and an unpleasant emotional cord is struck. That is when the sensitivity to one another is paramount, and

What Does Jealousy Have to Do With It?

the process of addressing difficult emotions and problems quickly is important. If one person feels humiliated by being left out or by their partner's grand enthusiasm when they are not so into it, it can create a huge emotional barrier to sexual adventure. Sophisticated open couples stay in tune with one another or repair any emotional riffs quickly.

In "Crossing the Line," Mr. Confident is feeling anxious with his wife. It's because the novelty of the new lover has him excited and worried, and he feels guilty. If he were single, we'd say he had a crush. But because he is married and is emotionally open, he confesses his fear, lessening his anxiety, and relieving some of the pressure of the crush. Falling in love can indeed happen when we are attracted to someone. However, it is well understood that falling in love is a process of building of intimacy and trust through sharing secrets. Happy and wise couples reserve secrets and emotional intimacy for the couple. Although in the case of polyamory, emotional intimacy is consented to explicitly— all channels are open and negotiated in polyamory, sexual, emotional and practical. Mr. Confident's wife also takes the opportunity to use his anxiety and guilt to tease him. She ramps him up physically and emotionally, adding tension, and creating sexual drama through the use of emotions that we don't typically associate with sex.

For sex to be exceptionally good, strong feelings need to be included. People normally associate sex with love and happiness. And for a good reason. Love and happiness aid in the impulse to care for one another. But feelings of love and happiness are often the result of good sex, not necessarily the emotions that fuel hot sex. Fewer, especially in the context of traditional marriage, consider the darker emotions—jealousy, anger, fear, surprise, guilt, and anxiety. These, too, can add flavor and texture to sex. In fact, these darker emotions can enhance sex, resulting in intense and euphoric sexual experiences. Defying political correctness, "Tattoo" addresses the contradictory emotions that fuel erotic excitement. The husband is repulsed and offended by tattoos but is strangely, and at least initially, secretly, turned on by them. That is because what is forbidden stands at odds with the innate human capacity and drive toward curiosity. In other words, "what we are told we can't have, we want more." And if what is forbidden is tied to our sexual arousal, the erotic pull becomes more intense. In the case of "Tattoo," like with many sexually adventurous couples, the forbidden and the secrets are not hidden from one another, they are shared. The couple benefits from this sharing and the sexual activity. (Please note that this story addresses the sex trade, some of which, unfortunately, is largely exploitative. There is a portion of the sex trade that is not—in places where it is legal and regulated. Though this story is purely fiction, we strongly discourage any sex exchange that is illegal, involves minors, or exploits any socially or economically vulnerable persons.)

Think of a sexual encounter in a place where there was a chance you were going to be seen or caught. Was it better, or more exciting, than your typical sexual experience? Yes? It was the fear, just enough, not too much, of getting caught, and the anxiety, that fueled and flavored the encounter. Games, like in "My Little Secret," are common among sexually adventurous couples—and they are games

What Does Jealousy Have to Do With It?

that play on fear using risk, anticipation, and just a touch of the forbidden.

Jealousy, at a fundamental level, also creates a psychological distance and, coupled with the activity of swinging or other open arrangements, allows us to view our spouse from the eyes of another—temporarily. As another party eyes our loved one, we are reminded by example and the interest of a new person that our spouse is interesting, attractive, new, and desirable. And in "Reluctance," another phenomenon is illuminated—that one can take pure pleasure in enjoying the sexual pleasure of their adored spouse. The security of their marriage and desire to please one another overrides any temporary fear of loss or momentary lack of sexual interest in the encounter. Sexual pleasure is not just about satisfying one's own needs at the moment, it can be about observing and enjoying the pleasure of the person we love the most.

Couples therapists will always ask a troubled couple to describe their first meeting, and how and why they were attracted to one another. This is because, among other reasons, the therapist is trying to assist the couple in emotionally re-engaging with one another through reviewing a time that was full of excitement and hope. Couples (even happy couples), for a variety of reasons, become emotionally disengaged over time as the responsibilities of life and marriage rub the novel and exciting edges away. Couples miss the novelty and excitement. Jealousy can remind them not only to care but why they should care through an emotionally loaded manipulation of perspective. Happy non-monogamous couples have discovered that they can recharge their sexual enthusiasm for one another through opening up. The activity generates strong emotions, including jealousy, that are typically squashed in the context of marriage. But in swinging and other types of sexual adventure, the dangerous emotions are embraced and amplified.

Jealousy, in fact, has a lot to do with sex, sexual adventure, and love and commitment— jealousy along with all of our basic emotions. The sexually adventurous couple needs to know themselves—and also be sensitive to and flexible with their partner's emotions. Emotional maturity is key to a long happy marriage or relationship, and a key to enjoying sexual adventures together.

CHAPTER ELEVEN

The Unicorn

I LIKED DANI—a lot. And I was attracted to her from the first moment we met at the ashram. But it wasn't until I saw her naked lying on her stomach, going down on my wife, that I saw her beauty. Her shape, her movement. Her full round ass high on the bed and wiggling in the air as she made love to my Cleo. When she lifted her head, those dark exotic eyes piercing my soul, curly, wavy black hair framing her face and that mouth, oh my, lips almost too big, wet with Cleo's pleasure; she blew me a kiss. A slow motion, full pucker kiss followed by the hint of her tongue sweeping her top lip. Her beautiful ass beyond and elegant, bent at the knees, feet suspended like flags waving above a passing schooner.

Like most couples in swinging the female is bi, or at least a little bi, and the dream of most couples is to find a single girl that will be with a couple and who is also bi. We all search but rarely find the rare

female play partner—the single female that apparently doesn't exist—the Unicorn.

That was our second time together. More relaxed. The passion built slowly and waved in crescendos. Time was taken to savor. We knew from the first encounter together that we liked each other, were attracted to each other. That initial assessment and awkwardness out of the way, the evening unfolded like a gourmet meal where we knew the chef would be amazing, but the menu was a surprise.

We met at our place, a vacation rental in Encinitas, a beautiful coastal town south of Los Angeles famous for its spiritual/new age vibe. The apartment had the comfort of home, but not our home. The living room was big enough to make love on the sectional, but when the action shifted, we had the bedroom with the four-poster bed. The balcony stretched across the front of the living room and the bedroom, and hung over the mountainside with the breeze and sound and smell of the dark, turbulent, moody Pacific below.

We had first met a few days before at a sunrise meditation at Yogananda's extraordinary temple—a two-hour drive, but a million miles from our Los Angeles home. When the mediation ended, and our eyes opened, the sunlight grew behind us and illuminated the Pacific, the serene gardens, the whitewashed and golden temple around us. Cleo and I stood and centered ourselves from the morning *Darshan* when Dani appeared in front of us. In a glowing silence, she bowed with her palms lightly pressed together, and then she hugged us both. The hug was long and warm and like a standing massage. We got her phone number.

That night, meeting number two, Dani had walked up the winding hill from the ashram. When she got to the apartment, her hair was a frizzy mess, and when I kissed her, I tasted her spicy sweat, the smell of the ashram's incense in her hair mingled into

104

my consciousness. She was barefoot. And let me tell you, there's something about a girl walking barefoot that telescopes a raw, carefree, nothing-to-hide attitude. She had a Guatemalan messenger bag slung over her shoulder that had leaves poking out and emanated a smoky, soil scent. Her pants were cotton, cuffed at the ankle, loose, but they still managed to highlight the curves of her high bottom. The dimming evening light gave glancing hints of her braless breasts draped by a sheer, silk, Asian printed blouse.

I put a hand on her side, silky and curvy to touch and I kissed her cheek. The feel of her side just above her hips, her smell, and taste—yeah, it came to me then, that's why I wanted to see her again. I had almost forgotten since the week before. She moved her face so my lips went from her cheek to her mouth and she gave me a full, head-tilt kiss. The door open, not all the way into the apartment, have-to-have-you-now kiss.

Cleo came behind me and with a hand on my back reached between us and took Dani's hand in hers. The two women kissed lightly, then more fully, and I lowered my attention to Dani's neck. It was so soft to the touch—smooth, young, infused with her salty sweat. A hand was on my left ass cheek. An orphaned hand whose owner was unknown.

Cleo pulled us into the apartment, closed the door, and went back to passionately kissing Dani. Cleo turned to kiss me and then Dani moved to nibble Cleo's earlobes in an act that was sweet and intimate—like old lovers do. We kissed each other in a three-way tango. I could smell and taste Dani on Cleo's lips—her flavor even more erotic coming from Cleo. Dani's lips brushed mine and over to Cleo and back to mine. My hands may have moved to Cleo's breasts, but I could have stayed there kissing the two women and never got any farther.

Dani shifted the focus to Cleo, kissing her playfully on her lips. I loved the way Cleo kissed Dani. She moved her lips around

Dani's mouth like she was reciting poetry. It was different from the way she kissed a man. Cleo teased Dani's lips, tasting her like a ripe strawberry. Then a nibble, a small bite, she'd pull back, and I could see her tongue just piercing the crease of her lips and then she'd reeled Dani into her until their mouths interlocked and I could see the action of their passion from the impressions of their cheeks.

Dani's hand had moved to my crotch while still kissing Cleo. Cleo's hand met hers, and the two of them caressed me through my thin drawstring pants. I almost wished they had forgotten me because their passion for each other was so organic I didn't want to complicate the moment. I broke away from their hands and came behind Dani. I cupped her bottom—high and firm and full and fleshy and soft like the cotton that covered it.

106

Dani leaned back into my arms and Cleo moved her lips down Dani's face and neck to the crease of her open shirt. She kissed and licked between her breasts. unbuttoning a button with her teeth. I felt the shirt loosen on Dani, so I pulled her blouse open so Cleo could expose her breasts. Another button released, and I pulled again, and Dani's nipples came out with someone emitting an audible sigh.

Cleo toyed with Dani's nipples as she had done to her lips. She kissed them then ran her tongue, her lips, her nose around her breasts stopping to taste the underside of each upturned breast. Dani's breathing changed as she reached for Cleo's breasts but Cleo held her arms back. Cleo turned her head so we could kiss while Dani savored her chest.

Dani's hips and butt rotated on my bulge. Cleo was cupping her breasts and moving her tongue over her stomach. A hand was back on my cock, and I felt Dani's pants fall to the floor. Cleo knelt in front of Dani and kissed her right on her clit. I could smell Dani's pussy raw and earthy. With her naked ass cheeks in my hands, I could hear Cleo lapping at her pussy and Dani began her calling. A sweet wail, each call long and plaintive.

Still behind her, I reached under Dani's thighs and picked her up, so she was almost sitting in my straining arms. I pulled her legs wide apart, and Cleo dove her tongue deep into Dani's pussy. Dani went stiff in my arms and silenced her trilling and then let out a long cry. Cleo's face burrowed deep into Dani's crotch. A shiver, a coo, and Dani's body went limp in my arms as I gently let her down. The three of us kissed and caressed in an afterglow of affection.

Cleo broke away to get a drink; Dani went to the bathroom, and I silently thanked my personal trainer. As I watched Dani walk away, I could still feel, taste, smell her presence.

Her walk, barefoot and naked from the blouse down, highlighting her playful butt, gave me chills. Her scent was as if the candle and essential oil aisle had mingled with the root vegetable bin from Whole Foods.

There is something about the taste and smell and look of a woman in her unadorned state that screams, "I'll be free in every way." Free from makeup and shoes and expensive perfume and tight, revealing clothes. I have always been turned on by backpacker/hippy girls. It's not what they wear or look like, it is what they don't wear. The appearance projects "I don't need to seduce you with my clothes, my eau de toilette, my lipstick, and mascara" and subconsciously tells me she is in control of her sexuality and not playing by typical rules, and that's exciting, thrilling, and liberating.

I walked out to the balcony, the chill sea air cleansing my palette like a sherbet intermezzo. I also needed to shift focus so my cock could recede just a little from its longtime erection. When I came back into the flat "Mezzanine" was playing—a song that I had Shazamed from a lingerie shop in Beverly Hills. Dani was alone in the kitchen washing the greens; I loved that she made herself at home. I also loved that she was still wearing that sheer blouse unbuttoned to her navel and naked below.

Cleo came into the kitchen barely dressed in a red satin teddy. The teddy stopped just above the last curves of her naked ass cheeks. She gave Dani a kiss and the washing slowed while the kiss lingered. My erection twitched back up at the site of the two women so casually affectionate. As I entered the room, I was hit by a tsunami of herbal scent. The leafy surprise from Dani's bag was deep, dark green basil with soil clumped to the base of its leaves.

108

Dani chopped the basil and put it into a wooden bowl while Cleo readied a pot of water to cook some funny shaped pasta. Dani peeled and then smashed and then chopped a whole bulb of purple-skinned garlic, still green at its tips. She giggled and held one of her garlicky fingers for Cleo to taste. Cleo took her finger and ran her tongue up and down it like the prelude to blow job. Dani watched her with a coy smile that drew me across the room.

I came behind the two women, a hand on each ass cheek and they both turned to kiss me—a garlicky, basil-infused triathlon kiss. Cleo moved to my ear and whispered while slapping my ass, "Sangria. Focus man. Sangria."

I cleaned the cutting board and chopped an apple, orange, and lemon tossing them into a pitcher. I ran my fingers over the cutting board coating them in fruity citrus and held my fingers up hoping the girls would do the same lick job on me. Instead, Cleo motioned for Dani to join her in removing my pants. "Now, don't you need to touch your balls? I know you love playing with them. Now would be a good time to get those juicy hands down there." I did as I was told—coating my boys in fruit juice.

Both girls got on their knees, backs against the kitchen island, and lightly licked my balls. "Yums" and "coos" came from below. Cleo knows the way to tease my balls that sends me galactic and Dani learned like a champ. The action moved between them kissing each other and then to my shaft. I had a hand on each of their heads, clinging to handfuls of hair. Dani took my cock into her mouth, and Cleo went back to my balls and my erection build up climaxed in a knee-weakening shudder.

Water was boiling and as hot as the double, citrus-infused blow job was, watching Dani drizzling olive oil into the pesto bowl as Cleo stirred the crushed basil, garlic, and parmesan were somehow sensual in a way I never thought pesto making could be. I held a glass of sangria to Cleo's lips, and when a little red wine dribbled on her chin, Cleo licked it off which turned into a kiss and then some sangria for Cleo, who dipped her finger in the glass and painted my lips, which turned into more kissing.

Cleo added the pasta into the pesto bowl, "Aren't they sexy? Little flower-shaped noodles," she said toying with one in her fingers. ""Giglis they are called—Italian for lily." And she put one on her tongue so Dani could kiss it from her.

We stood in the kitchen and ate the pasta out of the mixing bowl with our fingers. We fed each other, bit each other, dangled giglis from our mouths and kissed-ate the dangled bits off of each other's faces. We laughed and giggled and had the most playful meal I have experienced since tossing my food across the room from a high chair.

Another round of sangria and Cleo suggested we move to the bedroom. She took Dani by the hand and whispered into her ear as she turned back to tease me. They removed each other's remaining clothes and stood side by side at the foot of the bed. In unison, they motioned for me to come with their index fingers and devilish grins. They parted as I approached and told me to lay down between them. Face down. The lights dimmed, and candles were lit. I strained to watch the beautiful naked women, but they pushed my head down and told me to close my eyes.

The silence was so long I almost dozed off until I felt a warm, soft feeling between my ass cheeks. The warmth flowed down my crack to the base of my balls. The scent of jasmine came over me, and I remembered that I had bought Cleo some massage oil because the name was so sensual, ylang-ylang.

The warm oil flowed up from my lower back to my shoulders in a drizzle that would have made the pesto jealous. I heard the window open and the Pacific breeze rush over my naked, oiled back. And then hands started at the base of my cheeks up my back to my head—firm semicircular movements of multiple hands. Down my side, kneading my legs, and ending with a collage of fingers rubbing my feet and between my toes. After several laps from head to toe, Dani gently but firmly rolled me onto my back.

110

I laid still, semi-hard as the two girls talked in hushed tones. They came on either side of me, propped my head on a pillow, and repositioned me so I could see the floor-to-ceiling mirror next to the bed. Dani took my soft cock in one hand and just held it. Slight pressure but almost no movement. Cleo teased my balls, and I began to grow in Dani's hand. I watched them in the mirror and saw Cleo's hand on Dani's back and then a peak of her fingertips appeared between Dani's legs right at the opening of her lips. That sight, logged into memory, brought me to full hard.

Dani nodded to Cleo and Cleo swung a leg over me in reverse cowgirl, so she was facing away from me, my hands on her smooth back. Dani now slightly stroked me and guided my cock into Cleo. When I was all the way in Cleo then Dani moved to face Cleo. I looked in the mirror and could see Cleo sitting on my thighs, my cock deep inside her, and Dani sitting legs spread, her thighs draped over my calves in front of Cleo. Dani's gaze was fixed on Cleo.

Cleo started to move up and down on my cock but Dani grabbed her by the outside of her thighs and held her in place. My cock strained, and my hips moved up to go deeper, but Dani kept us in place. Then she lowered Cleo on me. Dani moved her hands to Cleo's face and looked her in the eyes; Cleo blinked, and Dani said to keep her eyes open. I tried to go farther inside of Cleo, but Dani held her tight so the only movement I could muster was in my cock itself. The more I had to hold still the more I felt.

Dani held Cleo's face looking her in the eyes for what seemed like an hour. The sound of the waves crashing filled the room, the wind the only movement. Dani slowly moved her hands down Cleo's neck to her shoulders. She traced her shoulders like a bow on a violin. The intensity of my desire and the resistance to my movement transferred all my feeling into my cock. Cleo's pussy moved just a little, and my cock felt every cell of her.

Dani touched Cleo's nipples with just the tips of her fingers, barely making contact. Cleo lifted up and threw her head back, moaned, her eyes closed. Dani pulled her face back and forced Cleo to watch her.

Dani circled Cleo's areola and this time Cleo moved on my cock, and I saw her hands on Dani's breasts. A flush of pleasure and relief stormed through me with just that small movement. Dani continued her slow exploration of Cleo's breasts but still managed to control Cleo's limited movement.

"Keep watching me," Dani said, and she began stroking her own shoulders, moving her hands down to her breasts.

"Watch me," Dani said her voice shaking, "move slow. Feel his cock on the walls of your yoni." Cleo clenched her thighs, her face straining as she held me in place. Dani spread her legs wide and took her own clit between her fingers pulling it out and squeezing it. "My clit is so big. Watch me. Look me in the eyes. Don't move. Hold him inside you. Feel him." Dani's nipples were long and hard and almost purple. Cleo stiffened then rocked, and I could feel her pussy muscles squeeze my cock. Cleo gasped still staring at Dani, who was barely audible, almost talking to herself, "My clit is throbbing."

Cleo moved, and her pussy opened, and I could feel my cock almost slide out and then she pushed down on me and the walls of her pussy pulsed then released. Dani moaned, "I want to come. I'm close. Watch me." Cleo rose high, so the tip of my cock was at the very edge of her lips. "Stop," Dani said her mouth inches from Cleo's and then Cleo slid down with incredible control pushing hard against me—my cock hitting the back of her pussy. Cleo ground into me and let out a scream. The walls of her pussy grabbed my cock, and I could feel contractions. "Don't look away! I'm coming with you!" Dani called out, and Cleo grabbed Dani's face as they shook to a loud orgasm together.

Dani held Cleo as she continued to move on my lap in the aftershocks of orgasm. I was so close to coming myself, but was even more rapt with the ecstasy of my beautiful Cleo and the exotic Dani. Dani kissed her neck in small, tender pecks and stroked her arms in the most loving way.

Cleo finally dismounted and went to the bathroom. Dani saw my dick twitching in the open air and moved in front of me. I sat up, so we were facing each other. "Watch me. Look me in the eye. I'm going to come again—with you," Dani said. And she rolled her clit between the fingers of one hand and slid one, then two, fingers into her pussy. She leaned back but still kept her gaze on me. I held my cock as she fingered herself. I tried to control my stroking, withholding just a little longer. Dani moved her fingers in opposing motion—slow and firm. Her voice rose to the call of a wailing chant, her gaze straining to stay on me. I could hear the sounds of her wetness. She fell back on the bed, and I followed, so I was propped on top of her, my dripping, engorged cock hovering over. All the time staring into her misty eyes.

Dani opened her eyelids wide, pulled her fingers out of her pussy and both hands surrounded her clit, and she called out, "Now. Come on me!" I stroked my cock hard and with only a few movements I shot sperm from her hip to her shoulder, and she let out a deep, guttural moan and wrapped her legs around me in an orgasmic clasp as I collapsed on top of her. She held me tight, pushing her pelvis into me, and I swear I could feel her wet clit pulsing against me.

113

Cleo joined us on the bed with damp, cool washcloths and the pitcher of sangria. We cleaned and stroked and kissed and giggled, our passions melding into each other.

A light filled the room, and I realized I had fallen asleep. Cleo was wrapped around me tighter than I had ever felt her. I looked around and didn't see Dani and my mind raced to what may have happened to her when I heard a whistle and then the smells of cinnamon, cloves, and cardamom reached me—the familiar scent of spicy chai. I relaxed into Cleo's arms until I heard tiny bells and saw the bangles on her ankles as Dani's bare feet danced to the bedside.

CHAPTER TWELVE

MMF

WHEN WE GO through the profiles, I am always surprised by who she finds attractive. Generally, I can predict the women she is attracted to. Pretty much any woman I think is good looking, Leanne will agree with me. Where we differ is when Leanne points out an older, short-haired, butchy female that she thinks is hot but whom I would never look twice at. That blows me away. But when it comes to men—forget about it. In the beginning, I was totally wrong about the men she would be attracted to. Now I'm getting an idea, but I'm still often off-target and surprised.

First of all, there is a difference between good looking and fuckable. Young guys, like under 30, are a non-starter. No matter how good looking they are, and even if she says, "Oh my God, he is gorgeous!" If they are young; she is turned off. That's right; a beautiful, young, perfectly fit model-handsome male is off the table for her.

I've tried to get to the bottom of it—obviously, this is a subject I'm very interested in. Leanne has a few reasons, but deep down she has a visceral rejection to sex with men under 30. My theory is that the younger ones are all stumbling fingers, moving too fast, just don't-get-it-yet lovers. Full disclosure, with Señor Cuervo in the house she has made out with and groped a few under 30s but that's as far as it's gotten.

Leanne may be a young-looking, fair-skinned 42, but her target man is, at least, mid-40s to under 65, and please God have some salt-and-pepper hair. Unless you are totally bald, then all sorts of rules go out the window. So her trigger? Broad shoulders. Seriously. He could have a big old gut or skinny like a rocker, but broad shoulders do it for her. Was it her first crush or her first lover, the first guy she masturbated to? Not sure. But she can tell from a profile picture if the T-shirt is filled out to her liking.

116

And then there are hands. She can talk about a man's hands like I can talk about boobs. Manly fingers that are thick but clean without being manicured, sturdy but not too callused; a set of hands can get her wet before we ever get undressed.

One more thing—OK, there are probably more factors than one—but this is important, the safety with confidence deal. I'll never get this one. I mean, I understand it intellectually but I sure as hell can't tell from a description. She'll look at a profile, read the couples write-up and say, "no, he's too cocky" or "he's too passive." But when the right one comes along, she'll say, "Yeah, he's got it, that quiet confidence that can rock my world." And let me tell you, he can be an older looking guy that isn't someone I would call handsome, but she knows when her world will be rocked, and nothing gets me more excited than when that moment comes.

Now that we have all this out of the way, let's get to what we want to know about: cock size. It's not what you think. Big and thick is not a deal made or broken. Let's skip ahead. In the heat of the moment, we are in full on swap, and she is totally into being fucked—a big cock is great—she loves it. But getting there, a big cock is not the ticket. To my best understanding, from her experience, a guy with a big dick can't always get fully erect or stay there. And then there is something about a guy with a big dick being, well, this is perhaps too easy, but too cocky.

To Leanne finding a man with strong, kind hands, broad shoulders, quiet confidence, and salt-and-pepper hair—we have a date. If his average dick grows to a monster (a grower not a shower) and stays there—bonus. We have a screaming good time.

Now, I'll be honest, when we first dipped our toes in this swinging business, I just wanted to have a threesome with my wife and another woman. Original, right? We had been together most of our adult lives, married most of those years, had a kid, sex was good, life was fine. But, you know, I wanted more than to watch porn and go to strip clubs then afterward fantasize about other women while fucking my wife.

117

One day I heard a podcast about a guy who had a threesome with his wife and another guy, and I couldn't believe how turned on I was. I thought—that's my ticket to lesbian heaven! I'll propose a three-way—with a man. Then I'll get my turn. The strategy worked better than I could've imagined!

I started by bringing it up when we watched porn together. I found a video of two couples having sex, pretty softcore, but then the two men focused on one of the women. As we were watching it and I was playing with Leanne, I was saying, "Imagine I am kissing you, and you are caressing the chest and shoulders of another man. Caressing his back. Now I'm fucking you and you're stroking his cock." She loved it. We had rocking sex that night. We watched videos and talked like that during sex and even out of the bed for a couple of weeks.

In the meantime, I started researching swinger websites and ambitiously set up a profile. I couldn't believe the people on the sites. I guess I assumed slimy, Leisure Larry types would be the most prevalent customer. Creepy guys with gold chains and porn mustaches, and overweight women with giant, sloppy boobs. But what was shocking was how normal people looked. I'd say most were 30 to 50, generally attractive and, well, professional looking.

I later learned that certain sites attract certain crowds, and I had stumbled onto a site that fit us. A lot of the couples were frankly out of our league looks-wise, or at least that's what I thought. One of the features of the site was a travel link, where people could post when they were visiting our city. A tourist was attractive because I figured that an out-of-towner would be safe, and it wouldn't be awkward running into them at the grocery store the next morning. I went through the site and tagged couples and single men to show Leanne. It was a blast. I felt like I was single and on a dating site. Even more fun was getting messages from other couples on the site—what a rush! But, I had a small hurdle—Leanne. How was I going to get her on board with this scheme? She responded to the fantasy talk but this was playing in the real world. I thought, "Well, it's like dating right? What would I do if I was dating her?"

Get her drunk.

Give her a massage.

Go down on her.

And when I took out the computer and showed her the swinger site, she slapped me. Then she blushed and said, "Hmm, he's kinda cute. . ."

She totally got into it. She loved rejecting the couples and the guys I picked. And I loved when she thought a guy was hot or a girl—yes, there is a God. She even commented on how sexy some of the women were. I swear if there were a jewelry store in our bedroom, I would have dropped a fortune right then.

I still played it cool, never pressing her. Just teasing with the profiles and keeping it all on the fantasy level. But what she didn't know was that the next day I contacted a guy that was visiting over the weekend. Leanne had picked him out as a good-looking and safe guy, so I made a mental note and wrote to him. His name was Russell, and he was on a week-long business trip.

He was a few years older than us, single, and staying at the Hilton on the Bay. All good signs. I know this may sound weird, but another thing I liked about him was he wrote back promptly, wrote in complete sentences, answered all my questions, and asked some of his own. I explained to him that it was our first time and that we were nervous, and there was a good chance we would meet for a drink and nothing would happen. His response was perfect. He said, "Let's meet for a drink my first day in town with the understanding nothing will happen. If we hit it off, we'll make plans for the next night." He was good. Just our speed.

119

I couldn't concentrate all day; I rehearsed what I was going to say to Leanne a thousand times. I tried to be casual, my voice cracked, I barely got the words out, "So, ah Sunday night, we have a date with that fellow visiting you know from the website, we're meeting at the Hilton Bar, just a drink, you know, the guy from Boston. . ."

"A date? What?" she said, cutting off my messy ramble. "This is really important to you, isn't it?" I nodded like a boy asking his mom to watch one more show before bedtime. "OK, whatever you say. Let's meet him. And, if we are going to bother meeting him and he's not a total creeper, we don't have to make plans for the next night—nice thought, but if I'm going to do this, a day isn't going to make any difference."

To tell you the truth, I wasn't prepared for her to say yes. I fell silent then said, "Um, okay. Cool. I'll let him know. Wanna watch something on Netflix?" And then, I have to admit, I was nervous. Nervous and excited. Maybe I wanted just to fantasize about this; maybe I wasn't ready.

As the day approached, Leanne did address the rules of the date. She had been thinking about the encounter and that made me feel better. If she had agreed to meet him and then never brought it up again, I would have been concerned that she wasn't really into it or maybe worse, too into it.

"So you do want to see me with another man? For real?"

"Look," I said, "What's the worst that can happen? You like him and I get jealous. He leaves town and we never see him again? How about this, let's make a rule. After we meet him, only I communicate with him. That way I know what is going on."

"Ok, good idea, only you write or text him. Fine. Then I have some rules." She said as if she had been rehearsing. "If at any time—any time—even in the middle of whatever we are doing. I change my mind, I tell you, and you end it. I don't want to be in control. You have to be the one to speak up. Ok?"

I nodded.

"Next rule—nothing in my tush! Fingers—nothing! While we are at it—nothing of his in my vag either. Well," her voice goes to a whisper, "maybe a tongue. . ."

"Oh yeah, this is already hot." I thought, "She's thinking about a guy going down on her, and she's telling me about it."

"So let's go through this," Leanne says, wearing only her bra and panties sitting cross-legged in front of me. "I'm going to be undressed by another man. He is going to see me naked. He's going to touch my nipples, my ass, my pussy. He's going to lick my nipples. You with me so far? Is he going to kiss my breasts, my stomach? You still with me? Is he going to go down on me? You ok over there? Now, is he going to kiss me? On the lips?" I took her hand and put it on my throbbing cock, and that was the end of

120

the rules because we had a quick, no foreplay, fuck like we were back in college and getting it on before the roommate came back.

Friday afternoon I texted Leanne at work, "Let's meet at home to get ready and then we'll head over to the Hilton at 8. I'll bring dinner home." She texted back, "So weird!" and my heart sank. Was she backing out? And then, "I don't know what to think about this," and then "I'm wet. . ."

When I got home, I heard Leanne in the shower, so I unpacked the take-out food, made a couple of plates, and brought them into the bedroom. When I walked in, I saw Leanne, one foot up on the tub. She was shaving her privates.

Carefully.

For him.

Rinse, lotion, makeup, hair styled, perfume on—all for him.

And, the perfume was different from her usual scent. A rich, flowery tone that was spicy and immediately smelled sexy to me. She put on the lace panties I got her on Valentine's Day. No bra and a pale white shirt that in the right light will show the outlines of her sweet breasts. It was like I was peering into a secret world, watching her get ready for a date. Sure, I had seen her get ready a thousand times and carefully prepare for a night out with girl-friends. But, wow! This was different because she was preparing herself for another man to see her, touch her, smell her, make love to her.

Was this the way she prepared for the dates with me when we were first together? Was that why I was mesmerized watching her now? Or was it because I got a glimpse into her erotic preparation? Her personal foreplay? We hadn't met the guy yet, and already I'm seeing my beautiful wife in a new way.

We talked about the kids on the drive over to the hotel in an attempt to distract ourselves. When I spotted Russell standing at a high-top table near the bar, I thought, "Oh no, this isn't going to fly." He looked older than his picture and not what I would call handsome, but then again, what did I know? I thought Leanne wasn't going to go for him. He was almost too plain looking. Fortunately, though, we found Russell very easy to talk with, and we quickly felt comfortable. His story of how he came to be a single man swinging was both interesting and oddly comforting.

Russell told us that after he was divorced, he didn't have much luck dating. Because he had done some swinging with his ex-wife, he changed their couple status to a single man profile. Russell figured that he would never get any responses. But, to his surprise, Russell was able to have a few experiences with couples as a single guy. He even sees one couple in his hometown about once a month and has found living alone with the occasional tryst with a couple a great way to have sexual excitement in his life without the awkwardness of dating.

122

I still wasn't sure what Leanne was thinking. A few times I looked over at her and her expression was a wry smile, and for the life of me, I just couldn't read her. So I thought maybe another drink. I went to the bar, and it seemed like forever getting the bartender's attention even though the place wasn't crowded. I was getting worried that I had left Leanne with this strange guy and without me being there the conversation might get awkward, and she would be upset that I had been so long.

As I turned to walk back with the drinks, I nearly crashed right into a group of conventioneers. Not because I was nervous or distracted but because I was in shock. What I saw was Leanne, her hand around Russell's neck, and they were locked in a kiss.

I froze. I couldn't believe it. It was the hottest thing I had ever seen. And damn if she hadn't taken control. Didn't wait for me. I didn't want to interrupt them, so I stood still and watched as long as I could. I stepped back so I wouldn't be too obvious. Leanne's eyes were closed, and I could see her mouth exploring his. The kiss was gentle and then more intense.

Russel stood next to Leanne and turned slightly toward her as if he didn't want to approach directly. His hands rested lightly on Leanne's shoulder and hip like a slow dance with a cousin at a family affair. His tentative confidence both comforted me and allowed Leanne the room to be the seducer.

Leanne had one hand lightly on Russel's side. She was barely touching him, not moving—as if she wasn't sure if she wanted any further exploration of his body. Leanne's other hand was caressing the back of his neck, tracing the lines of his shoulder to the bottom of his ear. That caress was the sexiest thing I'd ever seen. Sexier even than the kiss itself. The abandon of her fingers along the muscles of his wide shoulders, trigger shoulders to Leanne, got me so hard I had to resist touching myself right there in the lobby.

123

I adjusted myself so I wouldn't faint, and just then Leanne opened her eyes and looked right at me. Her caressing hand stopped, and the kiss slowed, but their lips stayed touching. Our eyes held each other, and when I saw her hand stop, I realized she might misconstrue my shocked expression as disapproval, so I smiled, slightly, and pursed my lips in approval. Her eyelids lowered in super slow motion. The sweetest, sexiest eyelid lowering ever. I will play that eyelid lowering in my fantasies for the rest of my life. Leanne's hand started again around his neck and moved to his shoulder, and then the still hand on his side slid ever-so-slightly toward the top curve of his butt. The kiss went deeper.

I moved the best I could under the engorged circumstances I was in, placed the drinks on the table and came behind Leanne as she pulled out of a gentle, lip-savoring kiss but still embracing Russell. I kissed Leanne and whispered that I loved her. She sighed and reached to feel my hard-on.

Why are elevators so damn bright? And why the hell are strangers allowed in our elevator? Weirdest elevator ride ever! The three of us were all giggles and flirting, and just as the door closed two conventioneers in suits barged in. We stopped, hands to our sides, our smiles dropped to serious expressions. Kids-caught-by-the-parents guilty. The two men tried not to stare at us, but they couldn't help it, and our sudden silence betrayed even more weirdness. When the elevator got to Russell's floor, we tripped over each other getting out, and before the door closed, Leanne broke the silence with a giggle that spread all the way until we got to the room.

124

Once inside, Leanne went to the bathroom, and now it was just Russell and me in a standard size hotel room dominated by a king size bed that, considering our awkwardness, looked like the biggest bed in the world. Do I get undressed? Do I sit on the bed? Do I check out the view? Yikes, I just wanted Leanne to get out of the bathroom. But, I knew better. Leanne wasn't in a rush—the bathroom was her temple and parlor. Russell and I were stuck for a spell in the waiting room.

I scanned the room. Russell had the standard corporate issue Tumi luggage, complimentary *USA Today* newspaper from an airline club, a matching Tumi briefcase, and a laptop charging on the desk. Nothing unusual here to talk but about then I spotted the clock radio next to the bed and blurted out, "Music! I'll find some music. . ." and I plopped down on the edge of the bed and plugged in my phone.

Russell seemed as relieved as me and went down the hall for ice. When he came back, I was still fooling with the music, and he arranged the ice and glasses and the bottles from the minibar and all the snack options. I turned off the main lights and tried different lamps until I got the right combination of mood and visibility. Just then Leanne came into the room.

First, I saw Russell reaction to her and then I saw why. Oh, yeah! Leanne was wearing a turquoise, satin teddy that she must have had stashed in her purse. Short enough to see her beautiful thighs and low cut enough to get a glimpse of her bust. Her hair was brushed out and a little wild like she had already been having sex.

"Beautiful. You are a beautiful woman. So sexy." Russell said, his voice now deeper and raspy with anticipation. Leanne smiled and thanked him coyly. She twirled around, "You two make me feel like the sexiest woman, God this is fun!" And as she twirled her teddy moved, and her cheeks peeked out. I was so excited; it was like I was seeing Leanne for the first time.

A Norah Jones song that Leanne liked to make love to was playing and she swayed to the music as Russell moved toward her. They started to kiss, and Leanne motioned for me to join them. I wasn't sure what was going to happen next, so I came alongside of her and Russell. Leanne shifted back and forth kissing Russell then me. One of her hands was on Russell's neck and one hand on mine. It went like that for a while, and she whispered to me, "Don't make me lead this."

I moved behind Leanne and whispered to her loud enough that they could both hear, "Undress him, honey, unbutton his shirt." And as she did that ,I took my pants off and pressed my boxered hard-on against her back. Leanne fumbled a bit with the buttons but then slid off his dress shirt. She stepped back, pushing against me to look at Russell's chest. I could see his hands wandering over her body, and I wondered if he felt how wet I'm sure Leanne was.

Russell was perfectly smooth, hairless, tan, and slightly muscled. She leaned down to kiss his chest with a light peck, then with small kisses moved all over his chest, and I could hear her inhaling his scent. I knew how important a man's smell was to

125

her, and the right one can really get her going. As I watched her kisses, I saw her right hand on his crotch. Oh, damn! She didn't need me directing her now.

Her hand was stroking his cock right through his pants as she ran her lips from his chest to his mouth. She moved her other hand behind her and grabbed my cock so now she was feeling a cock in both hands. Another Norah Jones song came on with a faster rhythm and Leanne shifted so I was next to her again.

She took my hand and put it over hers and said, "Do you like me touching him? He feels so good." I remembered how much she loves the feel and look of a man's hands. My hands. Our hands together.

126

And now my hand was on hers as it toured Russell's body. My trepidation about being so close to another man made me initially resist, but as I felt her hand, her beautiful hand, glide over his body, my legs touching her thighs, the satin of her teddy against my skin, I gave in. It was unbelievably erotic.

I made love to her fingers as she touched him. I traced the backs of her hand. Leanne kissed Russell's neck, and I could hear her sniff him. Leanne moved her hand—our hands—down ever so slowly until I could feel her fingers curve around his cock through his pants. I instinctively backed off and then put my hand back on hers and squeezed her hand against Russell's twitching member. Leanne let out a deep gasp. "Take his pants off," I said as I reached down to feel her dripping pussy but instead I brushed against Russell's fingers already on her panties. And then it was me who gasped.

I stepped back to watch her remove his pants and then I decided to go to the bathroom.

It was a strange feeling being in the bathroom knowing my wife was alone with a rock-hard man while she was taking his pants off, kissing him, making love to him. I wondered what I would walk back to see. Would she be going down on him? He going down on her? Would they be totally naked? Would she decide her rules were out the window, and they were full-on fucking? And suddenly I was jealous. I didn't feel jealous when we were all in the same room together. I wasn't jealous at all—just turned on. But now with them aroused, nearly naked, and alone, I panicked.

Leanne must have picked up on my vibe because when I came into the room, they were at opposite ends of the table making drinks. Leanne still wore her teddy. Russell had on briefs but had his shirt back on although unbuttoned. I was the one closest to naked.

It was a nice pause, drinks, a bite or two, a few laughs. Russell told us about an experience he had at a club with his ex-wife and another woman. I'm sure Leanne noticed as did I that Russell didn't speak poorly of his ex. Instead, he got excited talking about how she loved the touch of a woman; the way his ex-wife moaned and squirmed was different when she was being pleasured by a woman. As he spoke about his ex, Leanne went over to where he was sitting on the bed and took his shirt off and then his underwear. "Keep talking," she said, "I want to hear about the two women," and she delicately touched his cock, running her fingers along his growing length all while nibbling his chest and abdomen.

Russell continued to talk in gasps but seemed uncomfortable, so Leanne pushed him down on the bed. He was laying on his back with his dick sticking straight up. She laid next to him, running her hands along his body while glancingly touching his cock, "Ok, now," she said, "just relax, let me. . ." and then she went full on for his cock with one hand grasping his shaft and the other tickling his balls. "Oh, yeah," he said. "You're perfect."

127

I loved watching her playing with the man's cock. I came over to the other side of the bed so she could see me watching her. Our eyes met, and I mouthed that I loved her. As I took off my boxers and stroked myself watching them, she kissed Russell, who now had his hands under her teddy.

In one movement, Russell picked Leanne up and laid her on the bed. He came behind her and pulled off her teddy, leaving her topless with only a tiny satin thong. Russell kneeled next to her on the bed and licked and nibbled Leanne's nipples while his other hand traced the outside of her thong. Leanne's hand was running under his butt to his balls, to his cock as he was caressing her. She started to moan as his fingers slid under the thong, her hips pushing up to his hand.

128

Russell then straddled her, his cock between her breasts and he teased her nipples with his cock, his balls falling onto her stomach. He slowly slid his cock then his tongue down her body until he was between her legs. Russell nibbled on her thong, kissed her thighs, then pulled off the thong altogether. I finally decided to join the action and came up behind Leanne so that her head was in my lap.

As Russell went down on her, I fondled her breasts and tweaked her nipples. Leanne was starting to move now, and I told her how hot she was, how much I loved watching her. Russell slipped a finger, then two inside her as his tongue swirled around her clit. His fingers moved fast in and out of her, and Leanne started to buck, her moans hushed as she pushed high in the air. I pulled her nipples just the way she likes just before coming, and she let out a scream and clamped her thighs tight around Russell's face. She twitched and rolled back and forth. Catching her breath, she started to calm and as she released Russell from her grip, I realized that she had my cock in her one hand and with the other, she was holding Russell's hand, their fingers interlocked together.

And like that super slow eyelid droop earlier, seeing her hand interlocked with Russell as she orgasmed with him would stay with me for a very long time. This time, it was Russell who went to the bathroom. Leanne and I curled up together on the bed. She was in her after-orgasm giggle. She kissed my arm as we held each other. We held each other, it seemed, tighter than we ever had before. It was a moment when we felt closer than I can remember. My beautiful wife that had blurred into a mother and housemate and dare I say, friend, was again my lover.

By the time Russell came back into the room, Leanne and I were still intertwined but Leanne had gotten me hard again—as if I had ever actually not been hard since walking back to the bar and finding her kissing Russell that first time.

Russell came over to us and started massaging Leanne's back and shoulders and ass while Leanne and I were kissing and caressing. "This is what I would do with my ex when she was making out with her lover, their breasts touching, their hands on each other's pussies." Leanne started to respond to his voice, story, and touch. I felt her legs part in that familiar gesture that says she is ready.

I got up and went to the base of the bed and pulled Leanne toward me and placed my dick right at the opening of her open, wet pussy. Russell was kissing her and fondling her breasts while she was stroking his cock and I slowly entered her. Russell's narrative switched and as I glided my cock into my wife he said, "You like kissing me while your husband fucks you, don't you?" She nodded, panting. He teased her, bringing his lips close to hers, "You like feeling my cock. You like it when your husband watches you." She nodded again and started to moan. "Yes!" she cried out. "Fuck me!" And she pulled Russell up to her so that his cock was right next to her mouth.

I slowed down and pulled almost all the way out. Time stood still. Leanne kissed the tip of Russell's cock. Her lips slid across the head of his cock like they were her fingers touching him for the first time. I moved a little inside her and then back out to the rim. Russell stood still next to her. She guided his cock into her mouth holding it there. Russell let out a sigh. Her eyes closed and her mouth and tongue caressed his cock. I pushed deep inside her, and Leanne started moving back and forth along his shaft. I met her rhythm and started moving faster in and out of her. When she slowed, I slowed.

Leanne pulled Russell out of her mouth and stroked him with her hand, kissing him along his cock then his balls, licking his shaved mound, while I would tease the outer edge of her pussy with my cock. At one point she was totally into pleasing his cock and her and my eyes met. It was the most erotic, loving, sexual, connected moment I ever felt with her or any another human.

When I felt her left hand on her clit, I knew we were close. She went full-in on his cock, and I went on my tiptoes and pushed fully into her, her fingers on her clit, Russell's hands on her nipples, my cock plunging deep inside her. I knew what she wanted. She wanted to feel me come inside her before she came. I pulled out and then back in slow. "I'm coming, baby, I'm coming," I said, as I pushed deep inside her. I tensed and pulsed into her with a huge, pent-up, load. As I spasmed, I felt her fingers moving fast against her clit. Her mouth released Russell's cock as she started to come, her moans loud, then silent, then a high-pitch scream. Russell finished his last strokes himself and came loudly on her soft chest. Leanne brought her hand to his butt and then helped him with his after-strokes while holding me tight with her legs wrapped around me. The three of us were in a post-orgasm melange intermingling twitches and coos and fondling until Leanne giggled.

Russell and I high-fived, somebody said something about room service and Leanne added, "and then round two?"

CHAPTER THIRTEEN

The Quarry

SO DARK. SO black. Colder than the air. Not a ray of light could get through. She stood at the edge and peered into the abyss. Her camera lay heavy across her chest begging her for direction. A cold breeze came from the quarry mak-ing her shiver even though the sun was high. A rare, Maine, sunny June day, but she felt the cold in every cell. Cold and alone and alive.

Across the quarry she saw a battered Subaru park and a young man emerge. From a distance, he looked like a Maine stereo-type. Flannel shirt, ruffled hair, untrimmed beard. She lifted her camera using its zoom to get a better look at the stranger. His back was to her, and she watched as he took off his shirt. His trim, straight torso was long and muscled. His soiled jeans hung low on

his hips without a belt; the pants held up by his distinct round butt. His movement was smooth and confident and with a hint of graceful femininity. She felt a twinge in one of her nipples and quickly lowered the camera.

Embarrassed at her voyeurism she turned and tried to photograph the quarry, to capture its depth. She struggled to get the shot. The glare, the darkness, the vast barren landscape. "It's hard to shoot isn't it?" Startled, she turned around and saw the man from the Subaru standing near her. He was now only wearing faded board shorts that hung even lower than his jeans had. The lines of his abdomen led to the top of his shorts and made her quiver. He had a towel over his shoulder. He spoke again, but she didn't hear him. She blushed. She recognized him.

134

"Oh, hey, didn't I meet you last night at the hotel?" His tone oddly low for such a young man. She struggled to place him, as he said, "You ate at Brunswick, right? I'm the chef, ah, let's see, you had the venison. Rare. A bottle of Haut Brion—nice, I respect a woman who knows how to pair." And she barely heard him because instead she was thinking, "Damn, he even speaks French with the right pronunciation."

"Keenan," and he put out his hand. "Oh, sure," she said. "Keenan, I recognize you now, just took me a second, out here, out of context. . ." she rambled nervously, "I'm Nora." And he took her hand in both of his. She felt him on her palm and the back of her hand. She felt his big, long-fingered, warm hands. Confident hands. Youthfully soft but calloused and marred like working hands should be.

"The venison was amazing, everything was. You're very talented, Keenan," she said, gaining her composure. "I wish I was talented enough to take a picture of the quarry. I was just mesmerized by the color of the water or rather the lack of color. Its stark beauty is shockingly—well—beautiful. Harsh and yet inviting."

Her voice was now drifting off into her museum tone. The tone she used back in Philadelphia where she was a director and fundraiser for the Philadelphia Museum of Art.

Keenan stood next to her and was silent, staring into the water. "I love it here. I bet it is hard to capture because the quarry is so raw. I love diving into the darkness," he said, and with what sounded to her like a 1,000-year-old grumble, he jumped high over the rocky edge and dove far, perfectly, into the ink. With barely a ripple he disappeared into the abyss for what seemed way too long to Nora. "How deep could it be?" she said out loud to nobody.

Keenan popped up to the surface and then, just as quickly, pulled himself up the jagged edge of the quarry and appeared right next to her. He dried off, and she was able to catch another glimpse of his taut, hairless, youthful torso.

135

"Isn't it cold? It sure looks freezing. And just how deep is it? I mean, why is it so black?" she said in a rush of words. She watched as he dried his legs, long and slender with calves that looked like a biker's. Calves formed the way her husband's legs were many years ago.

Keenan laughed, "Cold? You can't ask a Mainer about cold; we don't use the same scale as the rest of you. Roll up your pants and get your feet wet. I love a quarry baptism," he said and then that red-bearded angular face broke into a smile that made her feel like a little girl.

"Ok, but you have to find me a spot that I can, you know, dip into the water. The edge is too steep; I'm afraid I'd slip," she said as she bent over and rolled her khakis up, removing her flats.

Keenan motioned for her to join him a few feet away in a spot that didn't look any different to her than the one they had just left. She walked over and watched as his legs positioned themselves on the uneven rocks with one leg higher and a thigh gracefully turned out. He again motioned for her, and she was glad he didn't say anything because Nora would have found a way to beg off, but his Mainer silent motioning left her powerless. She took her sweater off. She didn't know why—she was just putting her toes in the water, but it just seemed like the sweater was in her way.

In a slow but assured way, he turned her, so her back was against him and he placed his hands under her arms. She felt the strong hands on the sides of her small breasts, and her nipples tightened again beneath her thin tee shirt. He lifted her, and she felt his beard against the back of her neck and a shiver cascaded from her neck right down between her legs.

Keenan held her perfectly still hovering above the water. "How could he do that and not be shaking?" she thought. And then he lowered her feet into the freezing, pitch black water, and held her there. She gasped. The sensation of the cold and water and the color and the twitching muscles of his forearms sent tremors through her. And a deep, deep voice as deep as the quarry itself said, "Alright? Again?" and he pulled her out to the edge of the water, his biceps fully flexed, and then he lowered her again into the water, and she felt her crotch get as wet as her toes. Her eyes closed. Lips parted.

She could barely look at him. He gave her his shirt to dry off and Nora was overcome by the shirt's smell of his sweat and earthy, chef scent—rosemary and meat and smoke. He then draped it over her shoulders, "Keep it. I have more in the truck. It's a Maine thing—flannel shirts."

The gorgeous, 20-something quiet, confident man. Half her age. More than half her husband's age. Her nipples were pressed hard against her bra and T-shirt. She put her sweater back on, thanked him, and checked her phone, pretending that she had to be somewhere, and drove straight back to the hotel. His moist, sweaty flannel shirt squeezed between her legs.

She turned off all the lights in the hotel room, even covering the glow of the clock and the AC unit. She wanted it pitch, quarry ink—black. She took off her khakis, T-shirt, and bra and laid down on her back. On one side of her, the T-shirt that Keenan had touched just an hour before, and on the other side of her, she carefully placed Keenan's flannel shirt.

She slipped a hand into the edge of her panties as she caressed and smelled his shirt. She ran circles around her chest avoiding her sensitive nipples and then back into her panties. She thought of his twitching biceps and slipped a finger into herself. His butt in his low jeans. His abdomen and those leading lines and as her breathing increased, she heard his gravelly voice say, "Again." She came biting the shirt, its essence on and in her—tasting him.

137

She laid in bed and giggled to herself as her heart rate returned to normal. She smelled his shirt one more time. "Again," she heard him say. Her hands drifted lower, and she caught herself starting to get aroused. "God, Keenan, what have you done to me?" she said aloud into the darkness of her room. She pushed his shirt aside, turned on a light, and put on a robe.

How she wished now she had a room with a bath in it. The old, newly restored Maine Manor was written up in the *Philadelphia Enquirer*, the restaurant got rave reviews, and she thought at the time that a shared bathroom down the hall was somehow quaint. A bath would be a good distraction, so she slipped her key into the old door and entered the Victorian bathroom and laid the robe across the antique dresser by the window.

The tub was a vintage claw foot that she knew from her museum work was an authentic piece from the 1800s. It was cold—like everything in Maine—but with the hot water filling up, the contrast was tantalizing, invigorating, and relaxing at the same time. Nora noticed that she was finally not thinking of

Keenan but of course as soon as she did, as her foot dipped into the hot water of the cold tub, images of him lowering her into the quarry ran through her and the rush of horniness throbbed her pussy—this time even stronger.

She stepped into the tub, looking down at her pussy as if to wonder what had happened to her. She ached in a way that she hadn't felt in a long time. Her vulva was swollen, clit standing out. That first orgasm wasn't relief but rather a prelude. She slid her fingers along the lines of her vulva. The crease felt even smoother than usual, and she squeezed, making her vulva even fuller and more sensitive. She wished Keenan was there, his rough, firm hand enlaced with hers, "Feel how wet I am, Keenan," she said out loud and moved so her pelvis was under the steady stream of the tub. She drove two fingers inside herself as the water rushed over her clit and she pushed her fingers imagining Keenan full inside her. Nora let out a moan, louder and louder, deeper and deeper. She cried out and holding onto the side of the tub—froze. A sound. The door opened. Shut and closed. She didn't even turn around.

138

He pulled her up, slow and steady, a towel in his arms. As he carried her, the tufts of his beard teased her nipples. And for the first time, he kissed her. His lips were softer than she had imagined. The mustache tickled her, and his full lips teased and caressed her as their tongues found each other. She moved her hand to his chest, the chest she had sneaked a glance at a few hours before. His smell was now real and pungent. His chest smooth to the touch; his muscles bulging to hold her.

He placed her on the dresser and kissed her chest as she ran her fingers through his short, unruly red hair. His fingers, those big, long, strong fingers holding her sides as his tongue explored her nipples. He slid his hands from her sides to her thighs and spread them open, her sex swollen and wet. He kissed and licked her throbbing, pulsing vulva pushing into his face, but then he pulled himself up, beard gliding along her torso, and came up to her mouth to kiss her again.

"I came twice already thinking about you," Nora whispered. He took her hand and placed it on his cock. She almost fell off the dresser. It was so smooth and thick. She was surprised by how soft the skin of his hard shaft felt. She wanted to see it. Taste it. But she didn't want to let go, his cock felt so good in her hand.

Keenan picked her up from the dresser. Hands under arms just the way he did at the quarry, but this time with her legs wrapped around him. He held her ass cheeks and lowered her onto his cock. She gulped as if to grab the air around her and force it to keep her in place. As she clutched the sides of the dresser he lifted her just so his cock was almost to the edge of her pussy, and then he lowered her all the way, and she felt his cock hit the back of her pussy. The sensation of her feet slipping into the cold quarry passed through her in a cold rush.

He lifted her and lowered her in short, rapid movements. She held on tight, taking in his scent, the muscles of his shoulders bulging with each thrust. His short, fast movements were mixed with slow, long thrusts that she felt push deep inside her. His hands squeezed her cheeks as if to lock his cock in her.

She felt the orgasm start deep inside her. The feeling so intense she couldn't make a sound. The thick black of the quarry flashed through her mind. The orgasm started deep in her and pulsed through her body and not until it reached her throat did she let out a guttural groan, scratching his sculpted back. Legs entangled around him; she shook, holding on, suspended mid-air in his arms. She twitched as aftershocks spasmed through her. She kissed his neck, his shoulder, tasting his sweat that she would dream about over and over.

139

He never flinched, holding her in his arms the whole time, never saying a word until she pulled back just enough to kiss him, and in that animal-man voice he throated, "Again?" and she playfully slapped him and nodded yes.

CHAPTER FOURTEEN

The Slither

I SLID THE key in and opened the door as quietly as I could. Hotel doors are so damn loud, but I treated this one like a resistance exercise, pulling it into place ever so deliberately. I had to juggle the door handle with full hands because I was carrying my pants and shoes, having taken them off in the hallway. I had undressed outside because the chance of change in my pocket jingling or a belt buckle clanking was not an option: I'd rather be caught in the hallway half naked than risk waking her up.

There was only one way to wake her. It's the reason she gave me her key the night before—curled up on the couch in our suite, her head resting between my wife's legs. "I like morning sex," she cooed and handed me the key. I took her hand and placed it on my still semi-hard cock, "My boys wake up early." I said, my voice barely a whisper. "Don't knock," she said now stroking me, "you and the boys just come right in." And she turned to kiss my wife on the thigh. A long, lip-teasing kiss.

There was a glow in her room—from a clock I supposed—

enough light that I could see her outline under the sheets of the king-size bed. Her long thin form bent, stark black hair splayed against the starched white pillow. Next to her the covers were pulled back. On the pillow by the hotel mint was a condom, a bottle of lube, and a vibrator. The setting signaled to me that she had prepared for my arrival and I wondered if the vibrator had already been used or was for us to use together. My penis twitched and pushed against my underwear. I slid off my remaining clothes and with her deep REM breathing urging me on, I slithered under the sheets.

At first, I was very still. I wanted her sleep consciousness to get used to my presence. She moved a little rolling onto her side, her butt facing me. I listened to her breathing, watched her lithe body rise and fall, the smell of lavender and clean pajamas teased me. I carefully stroked myself hard and moved a little closer, not touching her but close. Closer. And when she seemed to shudder a bit I placed my cock with the same precision I manipulated the door—lightly resting on the crease between her cheeks.

Her breathing returned to REM and I slowly, very carefully, slid up and then back between her cheeks. My staff grew and twitched with the slight movement. My heart beat so strong I was sure that the twitching, the throbbing, and my strong pulse would wake her. I wanted so much to touch her but held my hands still at my sides. Just my cock was making contact. And I continued to slide with the rhythm of her breathing—controlled, restrained movement. Every so slightly she began to move her ass with me. Her breathing and body movement changed, she was still sleeping, but now she responded to my movement.

I was nervous but very turned on. What if she woke and screamed? What if she woke and pushed me away? The unknown and risk of her reaction excited me even more. I ached to touch

142

her; my suppression was like being tied up by invisible ropes. Her cute ass, the sloping curve of her back and sides called out to every cell of my eager body. I wanted to touch her with my hands, feel her skin. I inhaled deep, I could smell her, I could sense her heat, but I couldn't make contact with her. A little sigh passed her lips, and her legs opened just enough that the top of my dick could feel how wet she was as I slid forward with her movement. I reached behind me and with the precision of a surgeon clasped the condom, opened the package, and pulled it out.

I again waited. I moved around her pussy with my cock until she shifted position. I deftly moved so my thigh was where my cock was so I could slide the condom on. In one contained movement, I exchanged my leg and cock again, positioned myself at a sharp angle and placed the head of my cock at her opening. I thought about the lube but decided she was wet enough.

143

I stayed right there; the head of my cock gently pressed just inside her pussy as I could hear her breathing quicken and her movement poised. I waited. A tantric wait. The only movement was me throbbing hard inside the rim of her pussy. Aching to go deeper—held in place by the possibility of discovery—the tension enveloped me and focussed all my kinetic energy to the head of my cock, twitching and vibrating just millimeters inside of her.

I could see her breasts, her nipples soft and begging to be touched. I imagined them on my lips, her nipple growing in my mouth. And then she said something, a name maybe, and I took the moment and slid in her. She gasped and pushed back against me. Her ass moved me a few inches across the bed. I laid my left hand on her side, finally touching her soft skin, as I slid in and out of her as she moaned with my movement. The tension in my body shifted from my shoulders and upper body to my pelvis. I moved with the release of my pent-up control. The sensation and feeling concentrated in my shaft; I could feel the walls of her vagina like a tongue in a first deep kiss. All my senses focused on my penis in a way I had never felt before. Touch and smell and sound and thoughts and fears disappeared into the background; my world funneled to our joined genitals. I moved my cock in her and through her like I was massaging her from within.

Her hands grabbed mine and moved our hands to her breast and now-hard nipple. "Yes, yes," she said. "Come inside me," and she moved my fingers to her neck and wrapped my hand around her throat, "Yes, yes," she groaned. I used my other hand to pull her hips toward me. My speed steadied, but my grip tightened. I felt an orgasm build, the tip of my cock on fire with all my reserve swelling it to beyond full. I pulled again and held still. I stiffened, and my still body froze, a Tantric storm moved my cock on its own. I let go. I came. With only the movement of my cock, holding her, digging my fingers into her flesh. A pent-up well of restraint shuddered into her. With my hand firmly around her throat, her rapid breathing pulsed through my fingers.

144

We laid intertwined like that for a few minutes while my heart pounded back to normal. She released me and laid on her back, a leg flung over me, the other spread across the bed leaving her wide open. I kissed her on the mouth, on the neck, her shoulders. My hands roamed her soft torso until I reached the inside of her thighs and she hummed to continue. I kissed her tummy and the top of her vulva. She pushed her thighs to give my mouth more of her.

She smelled sweet and salty, and I kissed and tongued her opening with a finger resting on her clit. I looked at her watching me in the dim room and saw her hands pinching her nipples. As I slid my tongue deeper into her, she pushed her clit against my finger. I moved my tongue all around her sweet opening. She let go of her nipples and pulled on my hair, her hips moving away and toward me. I moved my mouth to her clit and slid a finger slowly into her. Her small smooth pussy tingled to my touch. Once again my senses went quiet, and my mouth and tongue moved to the foreground of my body and mind.

She called to me in a deep harmonious way that sounded like a private hymn. My finger found her G-spot and her hips pushed away, I teased her spot and then slid another finger in and went deeper until I felt behind her G-spot. I pressed lightly and moved my finger in little circles. Her whole clit was in my mouth, and her husky tone switched and panted. I felt her clit with my tongue and kept my fingers to small movements inside her. When I slid my fingers back over her G-spot to her opening, she pulled my head hard into her. Her clit throbbed in my mouth and I felt her vagina fill and meet my fingers as I gently stroked her opening. She grasped my head, pushed it away then pulled my face to hers and in a loud "ohhhhh" released a stream. She held me above her and when I stroked her opening again she squirted onto my legs, paused then squirted again, emitting a purring-aw'ing sound. She pulsed and let another gush onto me. I held her butt cheeks in front of me and she let her weight fall onto me.

I kissed her legs, her thighs, her ankles, her feet, her toes, until I pulled slowly away.

I grabbed my pants and phone and texted my wife, "Come now. Door open," and then, "More condoms!" and after a pause, "and towels."

I flung open the hotel door, swung over the security latch so the door was ajar, and this time I didn't care about the noise. The door slammed hard. Loud. With unrestrained abandon.

145

Chapter Fifteen

IMAGINE, FOR A moment, your favorite restaurant. Pretend this restaurant is the institution of marriage. It happens to be the only place you can get your meals. Maybe the decor is attractive and contemporary and the service is impeccable. Or perhaps you have visualized your old favorite restaurant with the warm theme—it's familiar and comforting, and the staff is helpful and friendly. The food is delicious. Although the restaurant is not perfect, it is predictably good; that's why you've chosen to eat all your meals here, forever. Now imagine after a few years, the food served has less flavor, there is less variety in the meals, and the meals are sometimes not served at all. Nothing else has changed about the restaurant; in fact,

Erotic Pleasures and Long Marriages, Together Forever?!?

(a-THAT's-WHAT-SHE-SAID-COMMENTARY)

the staffing has improved, and the decor and menu were recently upgraded. Perhaps, one day, the meals cease to be served at all and, instead, the waitstaff advises you to bring in your nutritional shakes. They claim that everything else about the restaurant is still the same and, in some regards, the restaurant has significantly improved. You call over the manager, and he tries to convince you that you should be happy with the friendly service, the remodeled dining room, and the great atmosphere. The manager tells you to be satisfied with what you have and that a restaurant, if it is good enough, doesn't need to serve tasty meals or any meals at all. Nutritional shakes are good enough and good for you.

I imagine you would not be convinced. But somehow, many people are convinced that the giving and receiving of sexual pleasures, although not the only purpose of marriage or committed relationships, can be rightly omitted from marriage. Few couples know how to make the needed interventions in the kitchen if something is wrong with the food. And moreover, the culture tells us that only within marriage can we legitimately enjoy sexual pleasures. In other words, getting your meals elsewhere or eating at somebody else's restaurant is not an option; it is illicit. It's either accept the meals, or lack thereof, as served or quit the restaurant—these are the basic assumptions about sex in marriage.

Many couples, who very much love their partner and value their marriage or commitment, find themselves in a situation where their relationship is good, but the sexual desire for one another has waned; sex is uninteresting or is non-existent. Others may still have pleasurable sex with one another, but their sexual enthusiasm has diminished, and they long for the passion and intensity they once shared. Nothing may be wrong with the relationship per se, or with either individual psychologically or medically, but somehow the desire, intensity, and frequency of sex has waned over

148

time. Rarely do couples seek marital counseling or a certified sex therapist for this type of problem, a problem of desire; most just live with it.

In her landmark book *Mating in Captivity*, psychotherapist Esther Perel brilliantly explores how and why sex becomes dulled over time in average and typical marriages or long-term relationships, and explains why this is a problem of the institution of marriage or concept of marital monogamy, not of the individual. She found that the very qualities that characterize a typical modern marriage—closeness, familiarity, knowing all, and sharing—are the very opposite qualities, in many cases, that fuel erotic desire for a pair—uncertainty, distance, mystery, and novelty. "The Quarry" illustrates the longing and the human need for discovery and novelty. And dare I say it shows the strongest human sexual predilection: the biological preference for variety in sexual partners. This innate preference, of course, is nearly scrubbed from the female imagination through centuries of socialization. And Perel doesn't explicitly say promiscuity is innate and an essential ingredient in erotic desire, but you can probably read between the lines of her apt title.

Perel does say that the modern and romantic institution of marriage is asked to embody two contradictory forces—or flames, as she puts it—that often extinguish one another. A competent clinician, she shares solid advice for couples to create erotic space, cultivate seduction, share erotic fantasies, and make plans for pleasure as well as guarding against stifling closeness or over obligation. I say that those who practice consensual non-monogamy have done just that: they have reconciled the two forces finding a way to keep both flames burning—and they have challenged the idea that sexual non-monogamy and emotional fidelity are incompatible. They have also contested to the idea that sexual interests outside the marriage or long-term marriage diminish the value or importance of the primary couple's sexual relationship. Like a vacation that gives us new sights, sounds, and experiences and tends to live on and enliven our imaginations, a journey or vacation into new sexual territory as a couple adds dimension and interest to already familiar lands. In "MMF," the husband is pleased to see his wife in a new and exciting context and through this sexual experimentation they can discover and unpack the mystery of sexual desire. In "The Unicorn," both husband and wife enjoy the quirky, new woman. She does not diminish their marriage any more than a visit to an idealized ashram diminishes the love and comfort of one's own home.

Barry McCarthy, another expert in the field of sex therapy and relationships, describes how spouses become de-eroticized (read: de-sexualized) to one another. He describes that it even happens among couples who are capable of enjoying a healthy play of love and lust. He describes that two opposite forces seem to contribute to a progressive reduction in sexual enthusiasm in most couples—boredom and emotional disengagement, and increasing familiarity and comfort. I have observed that consensual non-monogamy, through an enactment of erotic scenarios, new and challenging, shakes up and transforms the sexual behavior of the couple and reawakens an emotional state that was naturally present at the beginning of the relationship.

Erotic Pleasures and Long Marriages, Together Forever?!?

In "Oz," Isabella and her husband are a typical, long-married couple. Isabella's husband is predictably enthusiastic about visiting a nude city. We can just imagine what our husband or wife would say about his immodest proposal. Forget the opening-up part, a factor not even known to Isabella and her husband at first, and just consider the risk Isabella takes by going topless—both are way out of their comfort zones. He prickles with anxiety. Her actions come as a complete surprise to her dumbfounded husband, and quickly remove the filters through which he has been habitually viewing her—wife and mother. Her husband sees and experiences her as a riveting and exciting sexual individual—a suddenly re-eroticized woman.

This type of shared excitement does not have to happen in such unconventional circumstances or such extreme forms for couples. In other words, the non-monogamous erotic scenarios probably won't be acted out by most couples, and don't need to be to get a similar effect. Re-eroticization, or sexual re-awakening, for a couple can occur by seeing our spouse in a new sexy environment, or when a spouse does something unexpected or shares an erotic fantasy. All of these activities can be considered sexually adventurous because they shake up the old sexual boundaries and habits. Remember, eroticism is not a particular sexual act. Eroticism is a process through which our "innate capacity for arousal is shaped, focused and expressed," according to the late Jack Morin, author of *The Erotic Mind*. I believe that eroticism needs to be an activity shared and cultivated especially for couples in long-term relationships.

Sexually non-monogamous couples are just regular people, no more interesting or unique than the average couple. They face the same sexual and erotic challenges as any long-married or partnered couple. But they have chosen to prioritize their sexual lives together and to break a core taboo—monogamy. In doing so, they create risky, transgressive, and new sexual scenarios regularly, and inject novelty, danger, and mystery back into their marital and sexual lives. They do this together, honestly and openly (not through cheating or secretly watching porn), and enter into a paradox of sorts: one in which sexual activity around or with others renews their sexual enthusiasm for one another.

CHAPTER SIXTEEN

The Architect

WHEN MY HUSBAND goes to the bar, or the bathroom, or for some reason leaves me alone in a lifestyle club, there's a chance, a pretty good chance, that when he returns, I'll be talking to, dancing with, kissing (or doing even more with) a couple or maybe a single man. Hey, it's the price he has to pay to be married to a hottie. Sorry for being so blunt and please don't think I'm a slut; these are encounters I rarely initiate. Now, of course, I can initiate, but if I do, it's never with someone that interests me sexually. It would be someone I thought looked lonely or had a funky hat; you get the point, right? And while we are making points, let's also be clear—I don't try to be a hottie and wasn't always. It's a new thing. It's as if at nearly 51 I was born again.

The reality is, at my age, the youngest kid having left home, my blinders came off, and Zander and I started swinging. I lost weight—a lot of weight—and I emerged what you might consider a cougar/MILF/

hottie. Today, I get checked out all the time. Before, only waiters checked me out.

Zander often tells me that it is one of his more dreaded and yet thrilling moments—that first view when he returns to see me kissing a man or a woman. There's something about him walking in and not knowing who I'll be with me that spikes a current of jealousy plus protection plus envy all equaling, God knows why, a major wood event for him.

But then there was the time in a lifestyle club when Zander returned from the bar not paying attention to me at all. Not slowly stalking in to catch me being naughty. He walked up to me like we were at the country club, and he had run into an old friend.

154

"I just met a guy who returned from Burma last week—can you believe it? The same tour we are taking. He loved it! See, it's going to be great! Nice guy, too. He said even the food was good." And on Zander talked about our upcoming trip to Burma, which, bless his heart, he has been planning and researching for half a year. I could have been blowing an entire cycling team plus the coach and Zander wouldn't have cared.

Zander has the enthusiasm and the energy of an undergrad but sometimes he misses the details. It never occurred to him that I'd want to talk to the guy, maybe get his name, or know whether he was even handsome. Even with a few bi experiences under his belt, Zander will never be actively bi. He couldn't tell you who was better looking—Brad Pitt or Dick Cheney—clueless. Note to self, Google "face blindness."

"Namaste! This your mate?" And a face appeared and kissed me on both cheeks—he introduced himself as Ian. A hand pressed against the small of my back as he kissed me. I tingled. Irish accent; a voice that sounded like it was from a distant radio show.

And his hand. I didn't even see his face or his body and I was blushing. Switch—on.

"The colonial life of Burma, still visible today in the way that Havana's history is visible between the rubble. . ." His voice was clear. Thick. Measured. I closed my eyes. The r's rolled. Authority. Talking of Burma was the canvas but his tone, the paint. A Latin rhythm filled the club. Ian held out his hand to mine and asked Zander, "May I have the pleasure?" Zander glanced at me, and my silence was his consent.

His steps were small, firm, and measured—like his voice. I moved my hips toward him, and he pushed me away with one hand and held me with the other. "Lead me," I whispered. And he pulled me firmly toward him, that hand on the small of my back, as he slowly spun me around him. He released me until only our fingertips were touching and then, in a sweeping movement, his hand high in the air, he wrapped an arm around my waist, dipped me, and flung me across the floor. I let go and nearly left the ground in his confident flow.

Another pull on my waist, and we were kissing. My eyes closed then sprung open and darted around the room. Too much too fast. He sensed my sudden caution but continued with a kiss that was gentle and boyish—careful. I gave in, opened my mouth to his, and tasted his Guinness-tinged breath, his hand moving higher on my back.

I was wet. On the dance floor. Wet in his arms. I leaned my head back, and he followed my lips, and we went deeper into a kiss that traveled from our lips to his beautiful hands. My legs twitched. He pulled back and bowed.

I left the dance floor blushing and looking for Zander. He wasn't there—I panicked with guilt. Guilt? Why? A dance, some kissing—nothing we haven't done, both of us, at the club many times. But this was different, and I was almost irritated with

155

Zander for not being there when I left the dance floor. Rather than stay and look for my husband, I went outside with the smokers, ironically, to get some fresh air.

Looking back into the club, I caught sight of my Irish-accented dance partner in a heated conversation with someone, and my irritation came back. When he moved to the side, I saw Ian was talking with Zander and handing him a business card. My stomach tightened. I just wanted to leave. Instead, I went back inside and joined the men, avoiding eye contact.

"Hey babe, listen to this—Ian here is an architect. His take on the Colonial architecture of Burma matches exactly what you were saying. Of course, our research came from Google Images," and both men laughed, with me joining in with an awkward giggle.

156

Ian kept talking but with his hand again on my lower back. He kissed me, and I reached for Zander's hand while falling deeper into Ian's embrace. My husband moved behind me so that I was facing and kissing Ian with Zander nuzzled against my back. Zander's hand cupped my ass cheeks; another hand was on my pussy—Zander's or Ian's? Ian explored my breasts, my neck, my shoulders. The excitement of first touch and discovery. His young, strong but tentative fingers tightened my skin. A rough callous of Ian's hand trailed and stung and tantalized me from just under my shoulder to the edge of my areola. I braced for the callous to meet my nipple and when it didn't, I turned so I made them collide. I moved my nipple around his beautiful finger like my tongue wanted to be on his dick. He held his finger stiff and erect, and my nipple became my tongue. I drew a quick breath and Ian kissed me, muffling my gasps as I moaned into him.

My hands ran through Ian's curly hair. Zander whispered in my ear, "Like him? Wanna bring him back to the room?" I quivered. Paused. "No, I'm good just the way we are." I breathed back.

"Ok, my love, I'm okay with it, if you are," Zander whispered again, and I felt a finger circling my clit. A finger I hoped was Ian's. I gasped and shook my head a little. A very little.

Ian gradually pulled away, and the three of us disengaged. Maybe Ian sensed my caution or maybe he was just happy with the flirting as it was. The rest of the night I spent talking with Ian. Affectionate, handsy, occasional kissing. Zander joined us off and on but then he found a couple from California. Just our speed, our age, good looking and funny. Zander introduced me to them—the woman was very flirty with me, a cute, butchy blonde. Zander knew my type. They invited us back to their room, but I balked—much to Zander's surprise, and actually to the surprise of everyone—and we awkwardly said our goodnights.

157

I was uncomfortable and for some reason irritated again with Zander. He barely noticed because when we got back to the room, I attacked him, pulling down his pants, and blowing him just inside the door then pushing him to the floor and riding him to a quick, nasty orgasm—for me. During and after the quickie I thought of Ian; his hand on my back, his lips, his voice.

The next day, over a long, late, lazy breakfast by the pool I casually mentioned to Zander, "I wonder what Ian is doing?" "Ian? Holy shit, look at the expression on your face, babe! Are you blushing? You really like him, don't you?" My face flushed redder than my sunburn. "Yeah, I guess I do."

Zander knows me better than I know myself sometimes. He suggested I text Ian. My blood rushed. After a lame objection, Zander urged me on. I texted him, "What's up?" You would have thought I was shoplifting shoes.

I had an exhilarating rush. I was picking up and coming on to a man for maybe the first time in my life. It was always Zander making the moves with couples. In fact, we were never sexual with just a single man—I never had the interest. And I never made the first-move flirt. Zander would always check out the pro-files and do the communication, or meet the couples in the bar, and I would give my yes, no, or maybe.

But now I was pursuing a single man who I thought was inter-ested in me, but he clearly wasn't chasing me. He wasn't texting me back. I kept the phone against my bare skin so I could feel the vibration alert me when he did respond, but I still couldn't help myself—I checked the phone obsessively like an anxious teen.

When I did finally hear from him, he was vague and friendly but didn't seem to pick up on my cues. Seducing Ian was much harder than I thought. Zander loved it. "Welcome to my world. The man's world! We take the initiative and wait for the signals, we try to interpret how much to push and no matter what, we assume rejection." I understood Zander's point, but I didn't care about the poor male conundrum. I was annoyed and horny and loving the chase even with the frustration.

Ever the optimist, Zander moved on and set up a date with the California couple we had met the night before. At first, I tried to convince Zander to cancel the date in the hope I would lasso Ian into a rendezvous. My last exchange with Ian I was more forceful, at least, forceful for me. Ian had texted that he would look to pick up a unicorn so we could have a foursome. I responded with my most pushy message yet, "Good luck with the unicorn hunt—I'm all in whether you find her or not." Send.

I was so worked up with my direct come-on to Ian and the frustration of having been ignored I could barely keep my hands off Zander, or myself—right there at the side of the pool. I jumped in to cool off—in every sense. But it didn't work. I moved to the side of the pool, and while pretending to do some leg kicks, I slid a finger around my clit, pressed hard and with ever-so-slight movement, and staring at a gorgeous young girl sunbathing nude in a lounge chair—her firm fleshy ass curved high in my line of

158

sight—I pressed and flicked my clit until I came in the cool, bright blue pool. Dozens of people around. Jesus, what was happening to me?

When I got out of the pool Zander was sleeping, and there was a text from Ian. "Met some people at volleyball. . .having drinks with them tonight, I'll let you know how it goes." I was crushed. How direct did I have to be? Maybe he truly wasn't interested in me. But then I thought, "There's no way he's not interested in me, the way he kissed me, talked to me all night, caressed me, danced with me, fingered me. Well, at least I think those were his fingers. . ."

"Drinks with the volleyballers sound nice," I wrote, "but why don't you meet me in our room for an aperitif? Come or don't—I will."

No response. Deafening silence. I checked my phone so often the battery ran out. Dinner with the California couple went fine, but still no word from Ian. Fortunately, the Californians passed on hooking up with us. Fine with me, I still had hope that we could find Ian and seduce him away from his volleyballers.

And sure enough, when we got to the club, there was Ian on the dance floor with a small group of people. My first, tacky thought was that they looked my age, meaning, at least 10 years older than Ian and, excuse me, they were not as hot as I am. Zander, my husband and partner in crime (and day-to-day hero), waltzed up to the bar and got himself a beer and a shot of tequila for me—chilled-double. I downed the shot like a freshman at her first frat party.

Emboldened by tequila, I snuck up behind Ian on the dance floor, put my arms around him, and as he turned around, I grabbed his shirt and pulled it off him. He didn't flinch. A boyish naughty smile grew across Ian's face, and he put a hand under my skirt and another around my neck. Oh, his touch—that hand. I swung an arm out and motioned to Zander who was standing a few feet away watching intensely to join us. I may have wanted Ian more than money, but I wanted Zander there, too.

The two men circled me, one on each side. I alternated kissing the two of them with (their) hands roaming all over me. Two fingers deep inside me, my knees bent in weakening arousal. Zander took my hand and guided it over Ian's pants to the throbbing mass pushing against his pocket. My skin tingled, goose bumps ran rampant. Zander's hand was guiding mine against Ian's pulsing cock.

I was soaking wet and buckling when Zander suggested we move to one of the platform beds on the side of the club. Ian paused and started to explain apologetically why he hadn't responded to my aperitif text. "I felt obligated to the group I was with, because in our culture. . ." I put a hand over Ian's mouth. "Shut up and fuck me. Now," I demanded. Zander gave me a light slap on my bottom. I love that goofball husband of mine. I forgot Ian for a second and just wanted to jump my man. Well, just for a second.

160

We reached the bed, and I went right for Ian's pants. I undid his buckle, pulled down his zipper, and caressed him firmly through his underwear. I could smell his cock. Musty. Spicy. I licked around the edges of his underwear, old-fashioned tighty-whities. I wanted that cock free and in my mouth, but I savored the moment. Ian mumbled, and I kept teasing him. My pussy felt like a bottle of lube had spilled in it.

I inched his underwear down with my teeth, his smell permeating my nose and wafting right to my peaking nipples. I licked and kissed every millimeter of his exposing crotch. And with the last pull, his Irish, freckled soldier popped up, and I dove on his tool with my mouth. All in. My mouth went to the base of his cock and hit metal—what the fuck? I pulled back and saw a thin silver cock ring around the base of his cock.

I had seen lots of men with rings but never experienced one myself. His whole package including the boys were inside the ring and protruding. I licked around the ring, his balls, and the head of his cock. He let out a distant growing moan, an Irish-brogue moan. I had found his spot. I flicked my tongue under the base his cock head, and he lifted his hips in the air so I could cup that round, strong, freckled ass. He tasted like a man. A clean, soap-fresh but slightly sweaty man. My hand glided over his cock as I licked his head. I could have stayed in that moment forever.

But I didn't stay there. I moved and took all of his cock in my mouth and it twitched. I love that twitch. And then I slowly moved down the shaft, and when it was almost all in my mouth, it grew again. Holy shit, that beautiful cock grew between my lips. Its girth hitting my molars. I promise on a stack of Bibles, or at least a stack of spa menus, I'll never forget the sensation of his cock growing in my mouth. I didn't move like I usually do, but instead, I paused to feel the throb against my cheeks. I loved it. That Irish talk-too-much, make-me-chase-him son-of-a-bitch was mine now.

Zander interrupted me, and I wanted to kill him. But as usual, he was right. Zander got on the bed and directed me to recline, so my back was against his chest. He pulled me gently by my shoulders so I was practically laying on him. Zander parted my legs wide and told Ian, "wrap that cock and do her," tilting me backward. Ian took a rubber and rolled it onto his dick in one stroke, leaned in and entered me. Zander held my tits from behind, his beautiful, sweet fingers knowing just how to tease my nipples, and then at the right moment—he pulled them.

Ian pounded me. Oh my fucking God. I had been fantasizing about this moment from the first time I saw him in the club. That

161

thick cock-ring-cock, his firm, pale chest in my hands. "Yes, fuck me! That's it. Fuck me hard!" I grabbed Ian's ass as he pounded away into me. I could feel his ass muscles flex in my hands as his hips moved his cock inside me—faster, harder. Zander was behind me sweetly whispering, "I love watching you—hearing you—feeling you." I wrapped my legs around Ian, and he slowed down, teasing me with his cock on the outer lips of my pussy— then in one long stroke—he went all the way inside me. "Oh, yeah!" I called out. His body started to stiffen, and I felt Zander's long fingers on my clit as Ian's cock stuffed my pussy. Ian was planking on his toes and plow driving into me. I felt an orgasm build way inside my pussy just as Ian let out a call like an ape defending his territory. He pushed deeper. He stopped with his cock hitting the back of my vagina and his whole body locked, rigid and without moving an inch he came. Loud, guttural noises. I felt him fill the rubber and his body shook in my arms.

Ian collapsed on top of me, his scent sweaty and athletic and sweet. I held him tight with Zander still under me kissing my neck. My pussy ached for an orgasm, but I held my Irish lover— the curly-haired, nervous architect that I seduced. "I'll come later in Zander's arms while recounting the scene of our passion," I said to myself. I just wanted to savor the panting, twitching Irishman. My conquest. My project. Who was the architect now?

CHAPTER SEVENTEEN

Unchained

I WAS ALREADY pretty worked up. Ok, so I had fucked my boyfriend and made out with my girlfriend. Like I said, I was pretty horny. I'd had a sweet clit orgasm and was ready for more. My boyfriend might as well be my husband. We've been together and know each other's every move and moan. David is my clit's best friend. I get stirred when I see David naked. I get wet when he gets hard. I come when he makes sweet love to me. My girlfriend takes me to places remote and special, like a weekend at a luxury spa. When I'm approaching orgasm I remember the first time touching Margo's soft soft soft skin, and that first kiss that made me nearly faint from the leap to the forbidden.

We were at the house of a friend we had met at Burning Man—an unofficial after-burner retreat weekend on a Sausalito houseboat. A funky confluence of elegant and rustic, the houseboat was a two-story wooden architecturally intricate design of multiple angles and levels with a deck that had a view of the Golden Gate Bridge, a hot tub, and two couches carved and polished from driftwood that looked like body curves in a forest of gnomes and elves. The houseboat design and style were an enigma and just like the home's owner, Jeremy.

And so it was after my David-and-Margo orgasm that Jeremy kissed me. Well—no, first he just sat next to me and slowly stroked my arms, and then my neck. He was soft but firm. Not pushy, he moved as if he had no agenda, as if that was all that was going to happen.

But there was something about the way he touched me, especially my neck, that made me relax and lean back into the couch. Relaxed and a little stirred up. He moved one hand down my chest, the other still holding my neck, and he traced my breasts—the underside of my breasts. I arched my back to reveal more of their softness, and my nipples preened, but he didn't go for them. His soft, but firm stroke held me in place; he took the lead.

His lips moved to the curve of my neck. My mouth opened, my eyes closed and then he kissed me. His kiss was gentle. When I pushed forward, he backed off a little and nibbled my bottom lip, and then in his own time he brought both lips back to mine. He tasted clean. He smelled clean. A masculine showered scent like organic, fresh soil. I inhaled and held it.

His hands moved back to my neck and with the same certainty and rhythm of his lips, he stroked me slowly and deliberately in counter-point to the electronic music coming from within hidden spots on the deck. My neck tingled, a buzz coursed to my lips. Then when I opened my eyes, Jeremy gazed at me like we were lovers.

I knew Margo had hooked up with Jeremy and his wife before, but I hadn't checked out Jeremy before that first kiss. I was falling under his sensual tango, and he looked ruggedly handsome. As if that mattered—I just wanted him to keep kissing me.

Oh, those hands on my neck. His lips teased mine, moving side to side and then straight on. When I kissed him back, he savored my lips as if they were a delicacy. I inhaled his now-more-pungent scent. Joe Cocker's raw voice played from a speaker behind me, Unchain My Heart." Jeremy moved the way Joe sang. Imperfect but abandoned, "Set me free." Joe sang, and Jeremy kissed.

When he pulled me up and off the couch I thought he was going to take me to a bed, but he didn't. He stood in front of me. Perfectly still. He was taller than I had thought and still fully clothed. Button-down, white dress shirt, and pinstripe suit pants—another enigma in casual anti-conformist Sausalito. My naked body, distant and foreign and naughty next to his formal, refined, dressed body.

His hands moved to the sides of my face, and he kissed me again. Just a little more firm. In small movements, he massaged my face and brought my lips to his. Oh yeah, I loved the way he moved my head to him.

He fully engaged his lips with mine, a little tongue and then he'd push me back just enough so I could see his eyes open and gaze at me. When I tried to kiss him back, he held my face in place and painted my lips with his sweeping thumb. Control. Oh, he tasted good. I couldn't stop my fingers from touching and flicking my tightening nipples. He looked straight at me, "I like that. Touch your breasts, your nipples." His voice steady and full.

He murmured how beautiful I was at the same time he kissed me, his hands caressing my face and neck. My fingers moved from my nipples to my pussy. I bumped his cock, touching it for the first time, billowing through his pants. He let out a low murmur, and his hands slid to my sides, to the curve just above my hips. He turned his hands over, and with the back of his fingers, he slid over my curves. I gasped. I never had my sides touched like that. A zone exposed, discovered. The image of clay turning on a potter's wheel flashed through my mind.

I dipped a finger into my pussy—wet, very wet. I rubbed my juices on the sides of my clit. His hands held me tighter. I pulled on my clit as his mouth pulled on my lips. He ran his tongue over my mouth and I imagined his lips on my vulva. I started to feel an orgasm build. Right there, naked and standing in his arms. He was still fully dressed, which added to his restraint and my desire.

Both of his hands found my naked ass. I moaned and leaned into him, a finger just inside my pussy, another tugging at my clit. When my hips pulsed, they pushed the back of my hand against his pants.

166

He bit me. Not hard, but enough to urge me on. My left arm draped over and tightened around his shoulder as I was about to come. My legs began to buckle.

My heels lifted, and I buried my face into his shoulder, his cotton dress shirt crisp and cool and clean. His steady voice chanted with Joe, "…under your spell. A man in a trance." And with almost mechanical movement and simplicity, he released his belt buckle and unzipped. "Unchain my heart. Let me go."

His pants slid to the ground. He pushed my hand away from my vagina, lifted and pulled my ass higher and apart. In a silent fluid maneuver, he lowered me to the top of his cock. I held his neck, sliding my hands under his shirt. I could feel the taut muscles of his shoulders. I felt his power over me. I wanted his cock inside me, but I was also afraid. His authority—thrilling yet dangerous.

His cock seemed to grow into me. Just the head was inside my soaking lips. I trembled in his arms. I dug my fingers into him. I bit his neck. "Fuck me!" I felt tears welling in a rush of pain and pleasure and wanting. The sweat on his shoulder tasted like an oak humidor.

His hands kneaded my ass and lowered me. Thick and stiff, I could feel his cock glide into my vagina. His hands pulled my ass in. He moved my bottom like it was my head going down on him. I pictured him masturbating. His strong fingers wrapped around his cock. He was stroking himself by squeezing and molding my ass cheeks.

I was his toy. It was his turn, and he was using my vagina for his pleasure. It was like I wasn't even there. His selfish desire a sharp contrast to my husband's kind—always putting me first— attention. Jeremy's eyes were closed. He was grumbling. I slid my tongue in his ear, "I'm your slut. Your whore!" I ate the words into his ear. "Your dirty fucking whore!"

He held my ass with one hand and spanked me with the other. I let out a cry. He thrust, somewhere deep inside me. I heard myself screaming. His head went back, the muscles of his neck bulging. His face contorted into a fierce scowl. "Come inside me," I begged. "Come inside your little slut."

He grunted. He growled. He lifted me all the way off his cock and then pulled me into his lap until his cock hit a spot even deeper in me that hurt good. I felt his hands nearly rip my ass cheeks, and he stopped. I felt his cock snap against my inner wall, and he came with a bellowing call that would stave off wild beasts. I shook. He shot again. Grabbing me like an extension of his cock. I flooded his lap with a rippling orgasm that throbbed me from his hands through my ass to the top of my pelvis. We panted. Holding tight. Small and lost in his arms—unchained.

CHAPTER EIGHTEEN

Barbie

GO AHEAD AND call me Barbie. I've heard it all of my life. Barbie. Got the picture? Blonde, blue eyes, white skin that doesn't tan (except with that nasty spray stuff), long legs, curves that accentuate my hips and, yes, boobs—so proportional and still perky that I've given up protesting, and now I just say, "Yes, they're fake." Even though, after nursing two kids, my breasts are still Barbie buoyant. And just to complete the picture for you, I'm married to an FBI intelligence analyst. True to Barbie profiling, my father was also an FBI man. Oh, and hubby looks like Tom Brady. All-American hunk; so handsome and beautiful and—wait, this isn't about him.

This story is about the full-swap party where I had sex with four different guys and two of their wives. But it's not about any of them. It's not about the tennis pro with the cock that looked like Michelangelo sculpted it. But yeah, wow, what a fabulous cock! It was thick and long both when it was soft and hard—which we all know doesn't always track. The big ones sometimes don't get bigger, but not the pro cock. And it was slightly flat along the bottom, so the beast fit perfectly in my mouth and even more so in my panting Pauline—as I call my nearly bald, with just enough hair to prove I'm a true blonde—vagina. Pauline loved that cock. But wait, this isn't about the tennis player or his spinner wife, with the pouty little... No, that's for another day.

This sexual adventure is about the man who I wanted from the moment I got to the villa but almost didn't hook-up with, and maybe technically didn't. The swarthy, beard-stubbled, bespectacled, older-than-anyone-else-at-the-villa, slightly removed, unsmiling, barely English speaking, full chest-haired, large with an extra layer of flesh, hook-nosed—Arab. The man my husband put on his watch list. As did I, but for different reasons.

170

Good Lord, he was the one. Even when I was fucking the tennis pro with the magic dick, I couldn't stop thinking about Farid, his impassive gaze peering through me. Whenever I caught a glimpse of him, he was out on the deck watching his wife as she got it on with everyone—and I mean everyone—at the party. And I didn't think he even noticed me—Barbie, all-American beauty that turns heads all day, every day. Is "aloof" an Egyptian word?

Truth is, I got a thing for brown men. Solid-built brown men. I don't know what it is; I don't even find them particularly handsome, but when I'm aroused, I want to be fucked by a Latin, Arabic, Indian, or any exotic brown man. Was it summer camp after eighth grade intently watching Raj play tennis? His lanky, tropical, taut Indian body would rock back and forth in graceful anticipation until the moment was right when he'd reach high into the air, his shirt exposing the dark border of his shorts, and he would lean far back and in a graceful storm of power, leap and sweep his racquet across his body sending the ball soaring like my burgeoning adolescent heart? Well, whenever it started, my body knew what it wanted—a man who knew how to handle me when the moment is right. And the moment was right.

The party had been going on for most of the night. There were breaks for drinks and snacks and dips in the pool. I was busy mostly with the tennis player and then his wife, and then the three of us. But throughout the night I never saw Farid with anyone except his wife—either alone or with whomever she was with.

While my husband was making the pouty spinner wife moan in whispy French, I schemed my approach to Farid. I couldn't read him. Was he only into activity with his wife or was his removed demeanor because he just wasn't attracted to me? There was only one way to find out; I had to make the first move. I put on a robe, a short cute robe but still a robe; odd that I had a moment of modesty even though I had been naked around everyone for hours, not to mention being very vocal for all to hear. And, I was nervous—not an emotion I usually feel at these parties. I felt my husband's eyes on me as I walked toward Farid sitting alone on a couch. My gait was slow; I wanted Hubby to know, to see, to hear what I was doing. What I was hoping to do.

Farid was polite; sophisticated but stoic. In broken, halted English he told me he was from Cairo. A surgeon and, yeah, I believed him. You should have seen his hands. Elegant but thick and sturdy with soft tufts of pitch black and gray hair on the tops of his fingers. I pretended to listen, but I just wanted to touch his espresso-colored cock—flaccid, short, and thick—resting on his smooth inner thigh. I asked him about his wife and while he was talking, I went to my knees and put that short fat little cock in my mouth. I urged him to keep talking. About his wife. About watching his wife. About anything. My tongue did a belly dance on his cock to the rhythm of the words rolling off his lips.

The little stubby Arab cock grew in my mouth. I love a grower. I could feel the head push and swell, his girth filling my cheeks. He stopped talking and ran his dark fingers through my blonde, freshly-fucked hair. His fingers seemed to grow like his cock and my scalp rippled with an electric tingle. His touch was firm, slightly rough but measured. I looked into his deep-set eyes, eyes made more mysterious by bushy salt-and-pepper eyebrows. A smile crossed his face that pushed the edges of his jaw into an angle that looked like one of my husband's fairway irons. His surgeon precise fingers were kneading my hair and scalp, his spicy cock in my mouth; I stroked his thighs, my transparent white hands on his cinnamon flesh.

172

I was intently working his cock, tugging his balls when he started to tense. I wanted him to come but I didn't. I wanted him to come in my mouth to feel that cock fill me up, but I also didn't want him to quit on me. I wanted to ride that thick, brown cock and look into his serene, confident eyes. I wanted to kiss him, tasting the lips that looked like they had a line of mascara outlining them. And as I stroked his Coptic scepter with my mouth, he said what sounded like an Arabic curse, and then he inhaled all the air around us, his chin pointed toward the ceiling, the veins in his neck pulsing like his cock. He came. And came. After a night of watching his beautiful wife get fucked by every man and woman in the villa, he had built up a huge, pungent load and I took it all into my mouth.

Tugging on my hair, his fingers pressed against my temples. That son of a bitch came a bucket load into my mouth and just kept pumping. My head, my face, my mouth all in his total control. I was so worked up a strong breeze could have made me come. Our eyes met, and he said something in a comforting, paternal, Arabic tone.

I nodded, urging him to continue talking. Still crouched on the floor between his legs, I started to play with my tits. At first a light touch on the side of my breasts and then sweeping around my hard nipples. He continued in his sexy, rolling, ancient Egyptian voice. And as I played with my breasts he got louder, and my fingers tweaked a little stronger, a little pinch and then I'd release, and then another little pinch. I moved closer, so his thighs were around me. My pale, delicate blonde white skin a striking contrast to his strong, full olive brown legs.

I slid my hand diagonally across my taut stomach, a light touch and in a slow glide, my hand went to Pauline. Hesitantly, I felt the top of my smooth mound. Farid's eyes now dropped to where my hand was. "Touch my face," I begged him and he slowly, with surgical precision, brought his warm, padded palm to my cheek. He held me like a sculptor admires smooth marble. I turned my face, and I could smell his hands. I tentatively brought my tongue to the fleshy base of his palm. My other hand was holding all of Pauline with the same grip Farid had on my face. I slowly moved the pads of my palm against my vulva. I slid my tongue across his hand until I reached his thumb, his fingers. My tongue followed my lips as I kissed and tasted and made love to his fingers. I looked up at him, his almond eyes fixated on me. Nothing in his gaze revealed a hint of his feeling, his arousal; his secretive, hidden repose was all the more frustratingly exciting to me.

I leaned back breaking free of his hand. "I wanted you from the moment I saw you," I uttered in a raspy, shaky voice. I ran my fingers along the sides of my clit with each stroke going a little deeper into the gap between my clit and lips. Farid droned in a strange but alluring monotone that sounded like a warrior's hymn. I dipped a finger under my clit just to my opening and pulled a little moisture up and around my lips gasping as I gave in to my private reveal.

I let out a little moan. I couldn't believe I was masturbating in front of this man. I flashed to my childhood bedroom discovering those first foreign, frightening sensations deep under the covers, biting the collar of my nightie, desperately trying to hide my pleasure, my embarrassment, my secret.

I leaned back further exposing Pauline to my lover. Farid's gaze was intense but detached, his Arabic words becoming more guttural like a far-off chant. Angry and poetic—his voice, his voice. I plunged two fingers deep into Pauline. My other hand went to town on her clit. I wanted to hold his gaze. To feel his control while I lost myself in his voice. Farid leaned forward as if he finally really saw me and he pulled me hard to his lips. His fleshy, stubbled, savory lips kissed me with fervent abandon. He pulled me back, his long fingers on my throat in a moment of near choking—he fixed his eyes on me, eyes wide with total obsession. In a frenzy of pleasure that he urged on with his mysterious words. Tasting him on my lips, I twitched urgently and came and moaned to the sounds of Farid's lilting, streaming Arabic. Weak, spent, satisfied, I blushed and fell forward—clutching his dark, primordial feet.

CHAPTER nineteen

I HAD SEXUAL intercourse for the first time, like many girls, in my late teens. Ronald Reagan was president. The ethos of the age could be characterized, in part, by his wife Nancy, in her war against illicit drugs: "Just say no." In 1986, over 50 percent of high school senior girls were sexually active. Although it was post-sexual revolution, young women knew to say no to sex publicly, but what took place outside the purview of adults or others, for girls, was more like "maybe."

What's in the Chase?

"Maybe I will if you love me" or "maybe I will, if you will, but you can't tell anybody." Girls who said "yes" without these declarative conditions, love and secrecy, and outside of a "steady relationship," were considered sluts, and they were shamed, even by those of us who were sexually active. If we talked about sex with our female friends, it

(a-THat's-what-she-said-commentary)

was about the relationship status or fear of pregnancy, not about pleasure, orgasms, or sex as an expression of our identity. Yet boasting about sex was a part of boys' behavior and developing identity. He was not shamed for pursuing sex for sex's sake, talking about sex openly, or having sex outside of a relationship—he was applauded by his male peers. A girl who actively pursued sex, or openly talked about their sexuality, was, in a word, inconceivable.

In "The Architect," Zander's wife chases a man and, despite her powerful attraction to him and her desire to pursue him, does so only when Zander encourages her. He knows that a sexual pursuit is both exciting and nerve-wracking. Men know this because they've had practice since adolescence. But Zander's wife, even in this unique and open sexual world of swinging, has to overcome her hesitation, and discover the inherent excitement in "the pursuit" or "chase." Where there is a risk, there is anxiety, but also the potential for greater reward and pleasure, no more so than in the erotic realm. This is somewhat obvious.

Less obvious is another excitement factor: power. In the 1980s it was inconceivable for young women to speak about her sexuality openly and freely. Today such discussions are commonplace—open and widely accepted. But sexual talk is different than sexual behavior. Surprisingly, even in the "open" subculture, certain types of sexual behavior and expressions of power remain gender-bound. In other words, in spite of the incredibly liberalized milieu, women's specific actions in this environment remain somewhat typecast: men pursue and women don't. The woman's behavior in "The Architect," an active and aggressive chase, is still less common in the real world of swinging. For some, this distinction may seem like splitting hairs, but I think the distinction is important.

When I was six, envious of my brother, I tried for months to pee standing up. I loved that boys could pee outside

What's in the Chase?

quickly and easily and that they could direct their stream on a tree, or make an arc or wave. I so wanted not to interrupt my play by having to use a proper toilet. And I wanted to pee in the flower bed or into our backyard canal. I eventually accepted my anatomy, the interruption of my outdoor play, and conceded to the use of a toilet. As a young woman I became aware of another male prerogative—not an anatomical one, but cultural: the ability to state what one wants directly and clearly without obsequiousness, apologies, or justifications, and the seeming directness and ease with which males went after what they wanted. It's not that a woman couldn't state clearly and exert her will directly, it was that males could do this without the burden of being called, directly or surreptitiously, a bitch, ball breaker, or, in the sexual arena, a slut. I became acutely aware and envious of the male prerogative to be assertive and exert direct power without apology.

Initially, I thought women in the open lifestyle were exempt from such gender politics. For goodness sake, they were having quite a lot of sex openly, frequently, and with obvious pleasure. But male and female sexual behavior, even in the lifestyle, still followed a larger cultural script where the exertion of assertive power in heterosexual sex was still mostly a male prerogative. Tradition holds that female passivity in the pursuit of sex is a result of her biology, shaped by evolution: primitive females were more selective (read: less promiscuous) to assure that their offspring had greater paternal resources for survival. Pop psychologists, my favorite of which is syndicated columnist the Advice Goddess, have cherry-picked all sorts of data to attempt to prove a working hypothesis such as "evolution shaped female's lower sex drive" or "females are more sexually choosy." I'd say that they have failed to consider that some girls in 1986 (not to mention primitive humans) were unsure of the details of human sexual reproduction. I would bet my last condom that early humans had no clue that sex was related to those cute little babies nine months hence, and they were just fucking because it felt good and aided in group cooperation, not because Miss Cutie Pie was looking for Mr. Right. In other words, I do not believe that there is a biological reason that females are less direct, assertive, or promiscuous in matters of sex. But I do believe there are cultural reasons why women don't do the chasing. And better yet, why (at least for this feminist writer) when a woman does chase, it is particularly exciting and exhilarating.

According to Jack Morin, author of *The Erotic Mind*, "overcoming obstacles" is a key mechanism in sexual excitement. Morin takes a look beyond the obvious obstacles in sex and seduction, to the developmental and psychological struggles all humans face, and how these become interwoven into what we find sexually attractive and most exciting. In "The Architect," the woman overcomes the first obstacle, which is Ian's distractedness and her uncertainty if he is attracted to her. Longing and anticipation are clear excitement enhancers here and for most people. The second, less obvious, obstacle is the struggle for power. Morin points out that there are two fundamental mechanisms to overcome powerlessness, to assert direct power, or to use submissive power to co-opt or join those in control. Women, though not powerless, have been culturally conscripted to

What's in the Chase?

use mostly passive or submissive power to get what they want—no place more so than in sex. In other words to say "yes," "no," or "maybe," not "I want this, and I am going to get it." When a woman becomes aware of what she wants sexually and then pursues directly, she is behaving unusually. Underneath this uncommon behavior is a larger psychological struggle—the struggle against a culture that deftly teaches women not to go after what they want in a direct, aggressive manner. And certainly not in sex. So, whether it is Barbie, whose blond hair and eyelid batting antics don't work on a preoccupied and detached man, or a feminist, relinquishing her control in a seduction, the search for power for women in the sexual arena is full of exciting potential.

Now, I know some readers are going to say that women have all the power sexually and apply a supply-and-demand model to sex and gender. In other words, women have all the control and power when it comes to sex because there is more demand for what they have than there is of supply. This idea is only true though if you believe that women's sexual drive is somehow less than men. It is not! It is just different and has been strongly shaped and influenced by culture.

Allow me to explain: female and male arousal patterns differ; men are aroused spontaneously, while females are more sensitive to the social and emotional context which may result in them appearing slow to warm to or disinterested in sex in some situations. But females have a similar core sex drive to men. In other words, they are just about as horny as men given the right circumstance and stimulation.

Their scientifically monitored arousal patterns, when shown erotic cues, will often belie what they might tell you about their sexual arousal—they are aroused but either will not or cannot, describe it. Read: they are horny, but they don't say so. Consider also that females have much greater flexibility and variety in what arouses them (genital measures of arousal have demonstrated this), and once they get going, they can go for the long haul and multiple runs. So, they are turned on by more types of stimulation than men but, again, they don't say so, and are less likely to indulge than men in what sexually stimulates them.

180

And we know or should know, that women can go on and on. There is little refractory period for women, and as a matter of fact, their clitoris becomes more sensitized with each subsequent orgasm. Think of women as the "diesel engines of sex" and men as the "formula one cars." Nowhere is this phenomenon more openly seen than in the world of consensual non-monogamy. However, most people, including sex researchers, have never witnessed human sexual behavior en masse where, as Terry Gould, journalist and author of *The Lifestyle*, aptly put it, the powerful moral and social constraints on sex, especially for women, are temporarily lifted.

You might assume that all women involved in the non-monogamy lifestyle, unlike girls of the 80s, are sexually assertive or aggressive, and fully comfortable and open about sex—embracing their sexuality as a part of their identity. The truth, however, is that some are, and some aren't. Sexual behavior, no matter how unusual, does not denote an identity or belief system. Consensual non-monogamy,

What's in the Chase?

however, does afford people, and especially women, the opportunity to explore new sexual behaviors in an environment where social judgments and sanctions are held in abeyance. In swinging, a sense of safety is also greater because of the formal and informal rules of etiquette, and because the activity is partnered (a protective factor). These factors allow women to explore their sexuality fully and without social shaming. A woman can act out her fantasies and desires; she can talk about what she likes. In other words, she can practice sex and the erotic arts. She can experiment, develop preferences, and ultimately, cultivate a voice of her own: a sexual voice. She doesn't have to wait to be asked if she wants sex or go about getting sex passively.

I believe that sexual non-monogamy, and swinging as an activity in particular, have the effect of equalizing power between men and women because they cleave sex from potential punishment, shame, and ridicule. Even so, exerting sexual power directly, for Zander's wife or Barbie, remains a big no-no. Old social beliefs die hard—long after the rules are blurred or eliminated. Aggressive women remain transgressive or rule breaking, and as such are more sexually exciting. The will of any woman courageous enough to discard "maybe" and determine what she wants sexually, and then pursue it directly and forcefully, is colliding with, and transgressing the will of the culture. This is the cultural will that has conscripted women to be only receptive to sex, not demand sex. This struggle for women is mostly invisible but is a power struggle for all women whether or not they are sexually open. The women willing to take the risk of asserting themselves directly in sexual matters are rewarded with greater erotic pleasure and welcomed into the sexual world men have enjoyed for a very, very long time.

CHAPTER TWENTY

Serial Love

DELILAH WAS THREE steps behind Franz as they approached the door and she stayed behind him as he entered and greeted Marshall, the host. Although the two men had been emailing each other for weeks, this was the first time they had met in person. Franz could tell from the way Marshall looked at Delilah and then kissed her on both cheeks, that he was a good match for her. Franz stepped back to see his Delilah through the eyes of Marshall. She was elegant and soft even with her dramatically short blonde hair and distinctive angular features.

Marshall was swarthy and happy in his element, smiling and playful as he took Delilah and Franz around the party introducing them to the couples who were not already engaged. Franz was not, as you might expect, checking out the women and looking for potential partners for himself. Franz had only one concern—his wife. This was their first "sex party," as Marshall had described it in his emails, and Franz knew Delilah was hesitant, although when they were in the car, she confessed to being turned on—an apprehensive turned-on. They had been with other couples, a few single males, and they had visited some clubs, but a sex party was different. The host made it clear that the affair was full-swap—meaning if you were coming to the party, expect to be having sex with other people, not just your partner. Not a requirement, as such, but an expectation. This scene was not for a first date, and it was not a meet and greet.

Delilah never initiated these encounters, but Franz knew that if he did the research well, and the people were compatible, Delilah would have a good time. A good time for Delilah meant Franz might also get some sexy fun, but most importantly Delilah would have a newly enlivened feeling of sexuality that would add to their sex lives, and that was a win for both of them. Occasionally, when Delilah was in a heightened state, a long night at home making love with Franz when they could take their time and play after her first orgasm, Delilah would say, with eyes closed and in between gasps, "I want a hard cock in me while I blow you. I want to have another cock getting ready for me. I want to be fucked all night long." And once after sex, Franz asked her if that fantasy was something she ever wanted to fulfill, and she laughed it off. Franz also fantasized about her with multiple men but wasn't sure it was something he wanted to move past fantasy. The invite to the sex party was a possible fantasy realization set up.

Franz made a cautious assessment of the couples and their compatibility with his beloved Delilah; compatibility was essential if they were going to stay at the party. Franz liked what he saw. There was a varied age range and a few foreign languages bantered about. There was a selection of men he thought Delilah would find acceptable, and acceptable was ok. Delilah is not a

184

prude or she wouldn't have been there. She just wasn't driven to this world the way Franz was. He got aroused from the whole process—communicating with the host, looking at the profiles of some of the couples that had RSVPd from the same site where Marshall had found Franz, imagining the scene. Delilah knew this and was fine with it. Her moment came after the action.

Franz went to the outside bar to get glasses of champagne. Two couples were on lounge chairs—both women on their knees giving blowjobs. Franz noted a tiny, curvy redhead for a possible interlude for himself later. When he walked back into the living room, Marshall was affectionately kissing Delilah. They were standing, Marshall naked, Delilah dressed, her hand firmly on his waist. Franz stayed by the door and watched. He loved Delilah. He loved watching Delilah. He could view her activity all night and never touch another woman.

When they began exploring this lifestyle, he thought he might be a voyeur or a cuckold because he got so aroused from watching Delilah. But he learned a cuckold got off on being humiliated by his wife when she preferred another man and a voyeur is mostly interested in strangers. Franz liked watching his wife because he loved her and he loved seeing her as a woman in every way. And Marshall was just her speed; he started with kissing and caressing. Delilah looked beautiful to Franz in this early taxi on the long runway to take off.

The host's wife, Annalise, joined Franz and put her hand on his bottom slowly fondling him as they silently watched their spouses kissing each other. Franz turned to kiss Annalise, and she returned with a soulfully understated kiss that captured Franz's erotic core; his hands slid to her soft curvy sides. As they kissed, Annalise slowly unbuttoned Franz's shirt and ran her hands over his trim chest. Franz returned the attention to Annalise's naked, peaked nipples as his pants fell to the carpet.

Annalise led Franz to a chair and motioned, smiling, for him to sit. She positioned Franz so he was facing Delilah and Marshall, still kissing in the center of the room. As Annalise caressed Franz, Marshall was undressing Delilah as he moved his mouth down her body. Franz was captivated seeing Delilah shiver when Marshall touched her vulva with his lips.

Annalise matched her husband's motion and kissed then completely engulfed Franz's cock in her mouth. She was intense and moved her head up and down in a way very different from Delilah. Franz watched Annalise devour his member and then glanced up to see his Delilah's legs wide open with Marshall's large head between her legs. Delilah was moving her hips in rhythm and threw her head back as she approached orgasm. Franz caught her gaze as he, too, was close. Oh, that look on her face, close to orgasm by Marshall's mouth, not the usual way for her to come, brought Franz to the edge. Franz watched his wife as she thrust her hips to Marshall's mouth and then her body went stiff, and she appeared to orgasm, but Franz wasn't sure—the body he knew so well, the orgasms he knew so well, they seemed different from across the room.

Franz pulled Annalise up as he felt himself coming close and told her, "get a condom and mount me reverse."

Annalise put a condom on Franz as Delilah did the same for Marshall. Franz moved toward his wife and motioned for Annalise to meet him on the couch-fold-out bed across from his wife and Marshall. Franz directed the scene so the two men faced each other and then the two wives climbed on in reverse cowgirl. It took some arranging and the men had to overlap their legs which was a first for Franz being so close to a man's body, but Marshall seemed nonplussed. The excitement of the moment put Franz at ease, and as soon as the women mounted their men, Franz forgot about the awkwardness of the man to man contact. The women

186

were now fucking each other's husbands facing each other, licking each other's nipples and kissing. Franz knew his wife loved to kiss women. She was new to being bi, and her biggest turn on was a female that was a good kisser.

The two women rode the men and fondled and kissed each other until, in a smooth acrobatic move, Marshall removed Delilah, put her on her back and entered her missionary style. Delilah gasped; Marshall thrust hard and fast with Delilah holding his waist, her back arched to meet his thrusts.

Although Franz had been close to coming a few times, he held back with his focus centered more on the pleasure of the two women. Franz rarely had an orgasm when he was with another woman saving that for his wife, and he knew that was not unusual in swinging couples—especially for the men.

187

Annalise climbed off Franz and slid next to her husband and Delilah. Annalise licked and kissed and played with Delilah's nipples while Delilah had a hand on Annalise's ass. Annalise moved a hand to Delilah's clit and flicked it while Marshall pumped her to a deep guttural orgasm. Delilah's cries filled the air of the party—captivating, arousing, and filling Franz with pride at his wife's satisfaction.

Champagne cooled Franz's tongue and his desire—for the moment. The little redhead was dancing with Annalise, and Franz saw his chance. Delilah was in the bathroom. He would have preferred his wife to be there because he had a better chance to make his move on the woman he most was attracted to at the party. She was small but perfectly proportioned with a butt as perky as her boobs. Annalise introduced her to Franz, Sabine from Montreal. Sabine's French accent enhanced her desirability and drove Franz to a new level of nervous attraction. Annalise diplomatically danced away to leave Franz alone with Sabine and his growing desire.

Sabine was an awkward dancer, and though Franz struggled to keep in sync with her, he did manage to slip a hand on her glorious bottom–firm and high but smooth and freckled. He slowed her clumsy dancing enough to get both hands on her ass. Sabine responded casually; she was bubbly and smiling and seemed entirely comfortable with Franz when Marshall interrupted to introduce them to a new couple who had just arrived.

The new couple was a sophisticated slightly older pair, the man rugged and large, intense and a little anxious. Franz knew Delilah would be attracted to him. He couldn't tell you why, but he knew her type and the new guy fit her criteria of appealing men. The woman was pretty with beautiful eyes and a quick, easy smile that contrasted her serious husband. As Franz sized them up and tried not to lose Sabine's interest, he heard a familiar sound.

188

Delilah was on the couch on the balcony, her beautiful face looking to the sky with a woman's head between her legs. She was leaning on a man whose hands were caressing her breasts. Franz was so completely caught up with the sight of his wife's pleasure that he didn't notice Sabine slip away from him.

Franz pretended not to be too infatuated with Delilah and poured another glass of champagne. When he turned back to his wife the man was between her legs, his cock entering her. The woman laid next to them, and Delilah's hand was on her pussy. The man moved slowly then would rotate his hips eliciting a little gasp from Delilah. She pulled the man to her lips and kissed him with a hand behind his neck. Franz leaned against the wall and watched his wife with his full erection in his hand. He was immersed in the ecstatic moans of his wife. To Franz, it was like he was making love to Delilah and seeing her in full passion, his experience more full because he wasn't the actor in the play but the audience.

Franz barely noticed the new couple next to him watching the ménage-à-trios with Delilah. The wife reached for Franz's cock, and the husband put his hand over his wife's wrist, so they were both stroking him. Franz turned to kiss the wife, gazed into her eyes, and his hand found the man's growing penis. Franz had stroked a few men in the passions of swinging, but he had never experienced a cock grow in his hand (except his own). The man's cock was both familiar yet very different. His hand experienced all of the sensation instead of feeling his cock and hand when he masturbated. They played standing up, Delilah's moans and then post-sex coos in the background.

189

Franz and the couple moved to the bed where Sabine the redhead was kissing a woman in full body embrace. Franz put on a condom and pulled the new wife toward him by her thighs and quickly entered her. Her husband stood next to them watching and stroking himself as Franz pulled and pushed the woman on and off his cock. The wife pinched her nipples, and Franz pulled her, so he was deep in her—she rolled her beautiful eyes, and Franz pulled out slowly. "Wonderful," she panted. Franz felt the man's body next to his and looked over to see Delilah sucking his cock.

Delilah relished that cock. Licking the shaft, then running her tongue up and down, a pucker to its head, then pulling the long cock far into her mouth. Franz felt the wife grabbing his ass and took over the movement. Delilah stood up and bent over, so she was next to Franz and the wife. The husband entered Delilah from behind. Franz tried to reach his hand under her while staying in the wife but found Delilah's hand already on her pussy, furiously fingering herself. Delilah was calling out, "Yes, fuck me. Yes!" Franz pulled out of the man's wife as Delilah fingered herself faster and faster, the husband grunting behind Delilah. Franz pulled off his condom and stroked once, then gripped his cock tight; he could hold back no longer and he came on the wife's stomach, Delilah jerking herself into a full-on trembling orgasm. The wife fixed her gaze on Delilah but slowly rubbed the cum on her stomach like she was applying body lotion. The four collapsed on each other. Franz felt Delilah's heart pounding on his side and the husband's cock pressed against his leg.

Aware of the irony, with limbs still intertwined, Franz introduced Delilah to the new couple they had just had sex with. The foursome stayed on the bed, stroking, kissing, and giggling about their adventurous sex lives until another couple on the bed got into a full-on fuck session, and the two couples decided to shower together. On the balcony the dried off, shared a cigarette, and somebody, somebody from heaven, Franz thought, brought shot glasses of brandy and chunks of bittersweet dark chocolate.

"Men need to rest. Woman don't. It is biology, my friend," Marshall said lounging next to the spent Franz. "Even with Viagra, we need rest but 'V' sure helps," and Marshall handed Franz a blue pill. Franz took it and swallowed it with brandy. Delilah was back in the main room sitting in the lap of a very long-legged man Franz hadn't noticed before. She was laughing and playing with his ponytail. Franz couldn't believe she was still going, but he loved it—he loved her even more for her openness, her joy, her frank embodiment of her sexuality.

Franz sat with Marshall, and they watched as Delilah mounted the seated man. Delilah caught Franz gazing and she mouthed, "Love you, honey" as she moved up and down, raising high and pausing then lowering herself staring at Franz and Marshall, biting her lower lip. Franz recognized the look on her face. The biting on the lip was when she was attracted to someone or something—think ice cream when she was a little embarrassed at indulging.-the lip bite. But then the way she moved on the man, her fourth that night, was almost mechanical like when they had sex in the middle of the week, tired from a long day, and she just wanted a quickie, not a marathon. The seated man was her quickie.

Franz met Delilah in the shower again. He washed her back, following each swipe of the cloth with a kiss. Her back, her bottom, her thighs. They barely spoke, the music from the party muted through the open bathroom door; their communication was with their hands and lips. When their eyes met, Franz, looked at her with the pride of a parent at high school award night, her returned gaze was shy, eyelids lowered in modesty, but then she'd pinch his butt, stick out her tongue. Franz loved the mystery of his Delilah. Sexy womanly, joyfully girlish, powerful and sweet, all in a potpourri of expressions along the complex spectrum of Delilah, his love.

After the shower they circulated the party, flirting with their new–old lovers. Franz found his redhead lying on her back getting pounded by a man he determined to be older and heavier than Franz, which gave him hope for a chance with her. The man was holding Sabine by her ankles lifting her ass off the bed. With each thrust, she called out, "Oh, oui! Oh, oui!" Franz stopped and stared and for a moment closed his eyes to savor Sabine's calls. Delilah appeared by his side, "Well. that was interesting. Two men just offered to D-P me. I guess that means two cocks in my vagina at the same time, right? Or is that vaginal and anal?" Franz was taken aback by her use of the words so matter of factly as well as her apparent interest in doing whatever D-P was. Before he had a chance to ask who the men were and how she felt about it—two men appeared.

One was an older, thin, and strikingly good-looking Latin with a full complement of chest and body hair. By his side was the husband of the redhead. Sabine's husband put his arm around Delilah, "I am the right size for anal, one of the few advantages of my lack of size," he said, laughing at himself. Delilah bent over, inspected him, and then took his cock into her mouth, "Um, lovely," she muttered, "let's give it a try. Franz, are you okay with this? I'd like you to be with me." Franz nodded and so did his cock.

The four of them walked to the bed where the redhead and her lover were just getting up. The larger Latin man laid on his back, almost fully erect, and he put on a condom. Delilah followed his lead and laid down on top of him, kissing him, and stroking his slim hairy chest. She lifted herself and easily slid onto his cock. She turned to Franz now laying next to the Latin man and leaned over to kiss him, a long full, loving kiss—all the time moving her hips on top of the Latin guy. Behind her, the redhead's husband was stroking himself and positioning himself to enter her. Franz handed him a bottle of lube and a rubber from a bowl next to the bed that had been graciously provided by the host. The smaller man lubed himself and Delilah and slowly entered her.

Delilah held still, gripping Franz's hand and not uttering a sound. She held on to Franz and the Latin man and the redhead's husband began to move in shallow in-out movements. Delilah tightened her grip on Franz's hand, looking the Latin man in the eyes. Then, as if coordinated by a director, the small man pushed inside as far as he could and stopped, and the Latin man took over the movement. "Oh, yeah, fuck that is good. Oh, my God, I can feel my G-spot. Yes, that's it, Oh, God, yeah!" Delilah let go of Franz and wrapped her arms around the handsome Latin man's neck. "Don't stop, just like that." But the Latin slowed down and

192

changed his rhythm, pushing his pelvis higher. "Oh, oh, oh," Delilah panted. She suddenly stopped, "I think I have to pee." The Latin pulled her back onto him, and the small man behind her followed him pushing to her depth. "Go with it," the Latin man said with cool confidence, "That is not pee you're feeling. Let it go. Let it go," he said in soft accented English, and he held her tight and the two men moved in rhythm like a suave tango dance.

Franz watched his wife go into a trance, her head rolled back, eyes closed, silent, and then with a long moan her thighs tightened and butt rose. Franz saw Delilah's shaking then he felt the sheets now soaking wet. The men stopped in unison and Delilah rotated her hips in slow movements against the two men; her butt cheeks relaxed and a gush of fluid flowed as she lifted up. Delilah looked at her husband, a huge grin on his face, and she collapsed in a fit of laughter—her first squirting laughter.

CHAPTER TWENTY-ONE

The Men's Room

WE WENT TO watch. It was a Wednesday evening, no big parties scheduled. No dates. We had already had a carnival of action over the weekend. No expectations. We went out for dinner and then to the club. Dance, have a cocktail or two. Maybe play a little, but probably just with each other.

Every year we plan our summer vacation, and for the last six, we chose to return to Barcelona. You know the refrain—exquisite architecture, friendly, safe, casually elegant, late-night prodigious dining, clubbing, beaches, and even affordable if you have dollars. And then there is the pace and mystery of the most foreign of concepts, the siesta. Add the siesta's long, outdoor lunch—always with wine—to the list above and you have that often uttered phrase, "the Barcelona lifestyle." And in the last few years, that phrase expanded when we discovered, "Psst!"

Psst! was one of Barcelona's best lifestyle venues. The club had three areas; the downstairs was a straightforward nightclub/bar, dance floor, darkly lit. The place was not too busy. It was pretty much the flirt bar where you could check some people out—maybe run into a friendly couple. We didn't stay long.

Upstairs was a large open area with another bar, a few circular bed/couches, and mostly men hanging around. This was typically not our scene. The unattached men milling around and the utter randomness always seemed off-putting to Melissa and me. Because it was upscale and in suave Barcelona, the men were dressed and dressed well. Melissa noticed and liked the way the Spanish/Catalan/Barcelona male took obvious care in their appearance without being too obvious—not as fastidious as the French, or as forward as the Italians, and certainly not American sloppy. Even I took extra time getting ready and have taken to the occasional scarf. And although it was a highly sexual scene, there was a sense, like their dress, of reserve—not the underlying aggressive feel we get in clubs in other countries and in rooms like this.

196

On one of the beds, a couple was having sex, the man on top, the woman's high heels bouncing on his shoulders. The woman was very vocal, but we couldn't see the couple well because around the bed were people, mostly men, watching, some with their cocks out. We strolled through the room to the door leading into the couple's nightclub.

The bouncer nodded to us and opened the door. I looked him in the eye and made a comment about it being a slow night. I wanted to be sure if I came out of the couple's club to use the bathroom the bouncer would let me back in without Melissa.

The scene was as expected. Maybe 30 couples. A good mix of ages and types. We found an area where we could watch much of the room so if there was any action we had a view. We watched, we danced, we played a little ourselves. We ran into a Russian couple, Yakov and Anna, who we had seen and chatted with a few times during other nights at Psst! By far, Anna was the most beautiful woman there. Model, take-home-to-mom beautiful. Strikingly pretty and sexy in every way. Face, hair, slim, tight body—and Anna was very young—probably in her early 20s, a good 25 years younger than Melissa and I.

Like a lot of younger people in the lifestyle we had noticed they seemed not to be as wild as we were. They mostly watched although once I saw her kissing another woman. We talked with them a bit and at one point Melissa and the husband Yakov were kissing, making out like long-distance lovers reunited. It was super hot for me because Melissa draws a boundary at guys under 40. I knew this was crossing a line for her, and I like when she crosses a line.

I also knew not to push it with Anna. She was clearly beyond me. We talked and watched and I was just happy to be so close to her. She had on a top that, when I got the right angle, I could see her incredibly cute, tiny, perky naked breasts. There were probably gang bangs going on in the other room, but I was more turned on by watching Melissa kiss a handsome 20-something and getting a peek at supermodel boobs.

The Russian flirt faded, and more couples showed up at the club. And then I recognized the shoes. It was the woman from the other room who had her heels in the air as her husband fucked her with a circle of men around them. I pointed her out to Melissa, and we watched as they danced by us. She was not at all what I had thought.

She had grayed, carefully styled hair and was, at least, 50— and dare I say handsome. She looked like a partner in a CPA firm. Melissa whispered to me, "Damn, good for her." We were practically staring at the couple. They seem totally relaxed, dancing like they were waltzing at a wedding.

It was a perfect, quietly sexy mid-week night. Flirting, watching, hearing. Another drink and a few more dances. We were standing by the bar when Melissa gave me the it's-time-to-go look and took me by the hand.

As we entered the single men area, now a bit more crowded, Melissa led me straight to a bed in the center of the room and to my total surprise gently pushed me down. Not a word. She just bent over me and unzipped my pants, pulled them down, and went down on me. She watched me intently as she did her magic with her tongue.

Some people came around us. A man went behind Melissa and slowly ran his hands along her back. Her eyes closed for a moment and I could tell she liked his touch. His hands went to her skirt, skimming over her bottom, and down her naked legs. Another man standing next to us, a dark, trim Spaniard wearing an expensive dress shirt with cuff links, took out his cock, and Melissa took him and stroked him. She moved her head from my erection and looked up at the Spaniard and then the cock in her hand.

198

He was only semi-erect, and I could tell he was as big as I had ever seen. His penis looked like an expensive dildo. Perfectly proportional, smooth with a dark brown even tone. His cock grew in her hand, and she could barely get her fingers around it. With a full fist at the base, Melissa turned so she could wrap both hands around him like a baseball bat. He was so big there was still room for maybe another hand.

Melissa let out a long "ahhh," and I looked up to see the man behind her had lifted her skirt and was playing with her pussy. I didn't like that I couldn't see what he was doing and didn't want the stranger to enter her, so I told Melissa to switch positions with me. Melissa laid down with her head in my lap so I could sit up and watch. The man who had been behind her went to his knees and started to kiss her thighs. He spread her legs gliding his hands over her and kissing all around her vulva.

The Spaniard came close to Melissa's head, and as she fondled him, she kissed and licked his cock stretched out across her face. People had gathered around, and some were playing with each other as they watched. The man between her legs moved to Melissa's clit and delicately brought it into his mouth. She moaned and did the same with the Spaniard's cock—taking the big head between her lips. The man between her legs then moved his tongue to just the opening of her pussy, and I could see his tongue toying with her opening. Melissa squirmed and took more of the Spaniard's cock in her mouth with a fist still around the base.

The man going down on her moved his tongue back to her clit and put two fingers into her. Melissa moved to him and they rocked together. Other men on either side of her were holding Melissa's ankles, keeping her legs open. She kept the Spaniard in her mouth, and another cock appeared in her other hand. Melissa twisted, her hips moving in the air. I could see the muscles in her legs tighten, and she attempted to close her thighs, but the other men kept their grip and her legs wide open. The man's fingers were moving fast and angled high in her, and Melissa's butt left the bed. Hands went under ass and held her as she took on more of the massive cock in her mouth, and Melissa had an orgasm so strong her hips slammed into the face of the man between her legs.

I motioned to the men holding her ankles to let go, and she twitched and twisted with a wave of spasms. I leaned over Melissa, and we kissed gently and deeply. Melissa pushed away from the man going down on her and his helpers. And that's when I noticed the Russian couple watching us, and I asked them to come closer. Melissa kissed Yakov and then Anna and then back to me. Melissa ran her hands over Yakov's chest and unbuttoned his shirt. I took out a condom and gave it to Yakov. He looked at his wife, and she nodded saying something in throaty Russian.

Yakov moved between Melissa's legs and unzipped his pants, his shirt open and his hairless, muscled chest hovered above her. Melissa caressed his taut chest and shoulders as he entered her. She wrapped her legs around him, and he moved slowly in and out of her, intently watching his wife and Melissa kiss. The Spaniard appeared, and his cock came between the women. Melissa moved her mouth away from Anna's and guided her hands onto the massive shaft while she went back to sucking his cock at the same time.

200

The gorgeous Anna moved in slow motion toward me. She looked at me with longing—yearning. Her long eyelashes descended in a pirouette of desire as her lips neared mine. I brought a hand to her beautiful face gliding from her neck to her cheek and then my thumb lightly across her lips. Her tongue met my thumb, and then we kissed. A kiss I thought would never happen. Anna's lips were delicate but firm. She tasted of sweet champagne. I moved my hand to slide into her shirt and her tiny tit filled my fingers. Her nipple got hard and long, so I moved my tongue to her cleavage and took her whole breast into my mouth.

Yakov was watching us and moving faster into Melissa. Strange hands from the other side of us had pulled up Melissa's blouse and were toying with her breasts and nipples. Yakov started to get louder, and Melissa grabbed his pale white, strong ass, and he thrust into her faster and then pulled out of her and stroked himself, coming into the condom. Anna moved to her husband, and they kissed as she gently took his condom off and led him to the bathroom.

Melissa still had the Spaniard next to her, holding his member like an old friend. She watched me and guided my hand to his cock. The Spaniard let out a moan, and I stroked him with Melissa. I moved to Melissa's other side, so she could stroke him and me at the same time. The man who had gone down on her was massaging Melissa's naked, glistening body with one hand, the other stroking himself. Melissa looked at the swarthy Spaniard, told him she wanted his beautiful cock inside her, and then sat up and got on all fours.

The Spaniard put on a condom and got behind Melissa as I sat in front of her. Melissa went down on me as the Spaniard positioned himself behind her, putting his dark hands on Melissa's smooth ass arched between us men. Before his cock even got close to her, she let out a deep moan. Yakov and Anna returned, and Anna went to the Spaniard and deftly used his penis to tease Melissa. Anna held his cock and slid it between Melissa's cheeks following it with small kisses. I had a perfect view of Melissa's beautiful back and the dark Spaniard next to the blanched white Russian. Anna took off her top and was standing topless, her breasts looking even smaller naked. Her firm stomach and the outlines of her core muscles exposed with the graceful movement of her hands. The lines leading to her vagina were clearly defined ending at the top of her jeans.

Her beauty stalled the action as Melissa, and all the men, watched Anna. When she came to where Yakov and I were at the top of the bed, she turned her back to me as Yakov unzipped her jeans. I cupped her ass cheeks through her jeans and felt as awkward and nervous and excited the first time I dry humped a girl. Her ass in her jeans felt so good in my hands that I hoped Yakov would be slow to remove them. And then they came off, her pink satin thong triggering a gasp from somewhere in a room of gasps.

Anna slid under Melissa, so they were able to kiss while the Spaniard eased his way into Melissa. Melissa hovered over Anna her breasts lightly touching Anna's thin frame. And then Melissa went from "ohhh" to "awww." The Spaniard was halfway in her, and she looked up from Anna to me, "Oh my God, he's so big," she said almost pleading. The Spaniard, dress shirt still on, his thick torso towering above the women, his cock half inside Melissa. She wiggled toward him, taking him as much as she could. She held her breath and then exhaled, "Holy shit, he totally fills me up." Anna reached up and held Melissa around the waist, their breasts pressed together. The Spaniard stood still, and Melissa began to move. Anna moved her legs, and I could see her rubbing her vulva against Melissa's thigh.

The Spaniard started to move his hips and Melissa called out, "Oh, yes, fuck me with that big cock!" The Spaniard grabbed Melissa's hips and pulled her toward him as he thrust his torso forward. Melissa screamed, "Yes! Yes! Yes! Fuck me with that giant dick!" Anna held her tight and started to moan in low sweet coos. The Spaniard slowed down for a minute, and Melissa begged him to keep fucking her, but the Spaniard pulled out and told Melissa he wanted to be on top. She moved so Anna was next to her and went on her back.

202

The Spaniard entered her again slowly, and she motioned to Anna to kneel on the bed in front of her and position herself so Melissa could lick her pussy. Melissa dove into Anna's bald lips while cupping her cute little-girl ass. The Spaniard buried deep in Melissa, and she let out a groan and pulled Anna's pussy closer. The Spaniard moved in half strokes pulling out and then pausing, and thrusting half way and then pausing, and then thrusting all the way into her.

Anna was facing me, and we kissed as the Spaniard built up his rhythm. Melissa was screaming into Anna's pussy, and the Spaniard started to mumble some Catalan chant, and then he let out a growl like a mad matador. He pumped his orgasm into

Melissa as she twisted. But Melissa was unable to utter a sound, her mouth planted on Anna.

Anna pulled away from our kiss and grabbed Melissa's face pushing her into her pussy and used her fingers on her clit while Melissa tongued her. The Spaniard kept pumping into Melissa and Anna started to come. She rose up, her lithe body a ballerina rising from a stage. Her breasts were pointing across the room. Melissa's mouth followed her and the whole room stopped to watch Anna. She fell back onto Melissa, her thighs hugging her face. Anna fingered herself to a quivering orgasm, her thighs clamping Melissa's cheeks, her exquisite face jerking forward. With each wave her chest heaving, her breasts flattened to just hard, long, pink nipples piercing the air above her and into my waiting hands.

203

Yes, it was a Wednesday when were just there to watch, except it wasn't us doing the watching.

CHAPTER TWENTY-TWO

THE IDEA OF group sex probably cannot be separated from the cornucopia of both artistic and pornographic images dotting our imaginations. When we are not sexually aroused, both the idea and images of group sex seem lurid and unappealing. But, aroused, more commonly than any other thought or image, sex with more than one person present is the most common theme of all erotic fantasies according to sex researcher Jack Morin. This is true for men and women of all sexual orientations. In other words, when our bodies are sexually aroused, lots of other excited and desirable bodies pop up like daisies in the springtime, and fuel our real or imagined sexual experience.

the future or Past of Sex?

In a sense, all swinging is a form of group sex—two cou-

(a-that's-what-she-said-commentary)

ples, or one couple and a third. The group sex, however, portrayed in "Serial Love" and "The Men's Room" is, in swinging parlance, considered fast lane, advanced, or hardcore. When Jim and I first encountered swinging, we didn't realize that sex clubs or sex events even existed. As a couple, we had stumbled into the idea of non-monogamy quite by accident. I had confessed my sexual involvement with Juan, a friends-with-benefits arrangement, on an early date with Jim, attempting, unsuccessfully, to convince him that I could only be sexually active with one person at a time. Instead of being angry or put off, he was curious. Eventually, he confessed that he became aroused at the thought of me being with Juan or any man, and he wanted more details. Though these confessions were a turn on for both of us, I was only remotely aware of the fantasies and images that floated or flashed through my mind while sexually aroused. Only after broaching the subject of non-monogamy with Jim did I take a closer look at my sexual fantasies. I noticed that more often than not, they involved multiple people having sex with me or watching me having sex. I had slowly pulled back a veil that shielded me from my own socially forbidden fantasies with the help and curiosity of a new lover but within safe and private confines. Nothing, however, neither pornography, artistic portrayals, descriptions, my own craziest sexual fantasies—nor my years of psychiatric work witnessing the most unusual and sometimes disturbing human behaviors—would quite prepare me for the fast-lane sex that we later witnessed.

It's my old default—intellectualization. When confronted with something shocking, strange, or even repulsive, I don't run away, I don't jump into the action. I put on my glasses— now over 40, my bifocals— and take a closer look. And did I get an eye full! By the time we started the workshops, Jim and I had read all we could about non-monogamy and sexual behavior and had interviewed a lot of people. We had heard of sex events and clubs but had only witnessed and participated in pretty soft action ourselves. I was curious about, but not particularly motivated to go to, the harder sex venues and could not quite fathom what took place there or why.

We both understood that human beings were the most sexual of all mammals—in fact, naturally hypersexual and promiscuous (though sexism even seeps into so-called scientific explanations of female sexual behavior—I'll get to that later). We all think about sex a lot, and sublimate the drive into all sorts of creative and, sometimes, problematic endeavors. Few researchers would counter this observation. But if you have any doubts that sex doesn't permeate the human culture, turn on a TV or radio, look at the Google results for sex: sex and more sex, billions of links. Or open a Bible or look at the more fundamental religious practices—sex and lots of special attempts to control, especially female, sexuality over the ages. As we researched and tried to understand better group sex and what we were witnessing in the lifestyle, we were first confronted with a dearth of information. Most of the psychological frameworks for understanding group sex were either absent, useless, or very negatively biased. The only psychological explanation that attempted with some accuracy to describe the turn on of group sex was asserted by Jack Morin. He explained that group sex, when imagined, confirms our own irresistibility. This made sense—and there was even a Cheap Trick song, "I Want You to Want Me," humming the confirmation. However, as we heard more from the sexually adventurous, we found that even this astute psychological framework could not fully account for the many fantasies of an average non-swinger, nor the sexual practices of the hardcore swingers. These were people who were, by all accounts and purposes, utterly conventional, except in their unique group sex practices.

It wasn't until a workshop where a sweet, bookish college professor, perfectly average in her real-life sexual history, quietly confessed that she often fantasized with enthusiastic pleasure about being gang banged, did we begin to understand both the turn on and paradoxes of group sex. She said, "I don't understand it myself, being raped is appalling to me and nothing I would ever want to do in real-life, but it's where my mind goes at the moment just before I cum." Rape was, in fact, a multiple person fantasy and a real turn on for her. We learned later that it was also a turn on for many ordinary women. The irresistibility factor certainly could not explain this group sex or multiple partner turn on. So, if not irresistibility, then what?

We discovered that the allure and pursuit of group sex point to a shared history, hidden in our minds and, for women, expressed in her anatomy. But to understand the allure—fantasized or real—I had to get past my cautious instincts and tendency to just hypothesize about it. I needed to observe it firsthand—in person, lights on, in the open—not in furtive pornos, back rooms, or where the participants were being paid or coerced. We were lucky in that we could observe it in places where the population of women was equal to or exceeded the male population, and where the women were calling the shots, and the sex for sex's sake—venues like those in the stories. The social constraints dictating appropriate sexual behavior were temporarily lifted here, and people were allowed to indulge in their sexual desires in these places safely. What we witnessed was more complicated than what we expected.

There is nothing quite like seeing women in the throes of orgasmic ecstasy. Though I had seen print copies of *Playboy* once or twice, I had never really looked at pornography until recently. I had no idea that there was an entire genre of visual pornography, or erotica, that focused entirely on women having orgasms, with much visual attention focused on her face and her expressions of pleasure. This genre is riveting. I thought that perhaps it was riveting because it was novel (our brains like novelty). But after seeing and hearing orgasmic women, with their vocalizations and incredible endurance, in open settings, I realized it was riveting not just because it was novel. It was riveting because humans respond to this emotional expression, an expression of intense pleasure, just as they respond innately to the expression of intense pain or sadness—they respond with captivated attention, and sometimes action.

We found that the real-life group sex events were not a flailing mess of humping bodies (contradicting some of the lurid stereotypes). They were more of a casual social scene where about only a third of any given group were actively engaged in a sexual act at any time, and a third were eating, drinking, chatting, or resting. The most interesting and impressive third were the observers. This third was observing the "diesel engines of sex"— the women—as they warmed up slowly, and then in some cases, took on one male sexual partner after another, or a single, very fit, male partner for an extended period. Other women surrounded this woman, stroking, petting and caressing her—sometimes also penetrating her. The women would have increased, and sometimes waxing and waning, expressions of authentic pleasure, calling out, moaning, giggling, arching, and squirming—and the observers, both men and women, took obvious pleasure in watching her pleasure. The observers did not necessarily become actively involved in a sexual act even though we could presume that they were sexually aroused. They were just enjoying the pleasure in someone else's pleasure. The irresistibility here was not a narcissistic phenomenon where sexual arousal is enhanced because of an erotic fascination with oneself (I am so horny because I am so wanted). As a matter of fact, the women in the ecstatic sexual states were largely unaware of what was going on around them. But for the observing participants in these events, the emotional expression of pleasure itself was, in fact, irresistible!

There was more, though. The multi-orgasmic women, often at the center of these sex events, were still shocking and a mystery to me. I immediately thought, "This couldn't possibly be real," but it was, again and again. The events were planned, but the women's experiences were authentic. Because I am a pathologist of sorts, a psychiatric one (a friend used to joke with me that I'd write a book one day titled *Let Me Tell You What's Wrong with You: Your Psychiatric Diagnosis*) my assumptions naturally went in two directions. One was that these women were the outliers, perhaps with a much higher sex drive because of a hormonal or mood imbalance. Or second, that there was just something wrong with them— maybe they had been abused, and this was a way to work out their trauma and regulate their emotions. But because sexual pathology and emotional disorders have been thoroughly researched, and we got to know the participants well (they were not in fact troubled in any way, and their behavior was thoroughly enjoyable to them), I had to put aside my tendency to pathologize. I knew and the research bore it out—sexual trauma or mood problems may result in compulsive or impulsive sexual behavior but, more typically, it results in avoidant behavior. And with either, compulsive or avoidant, the sex is distressing. I knew that my reaction and tendency to pathologize had been shaped more by the social strictures and taboos around sex than by what was happening for these women at the group sex events.

I have to be honest, too, I was a little envious of these women—they were multi-orgasmic. I experienced both joy and pleasure in watching them, and though I did set aside so many social taboos around sex in the last few years and enjoyed my body in so many new ways, I was skeptical that I could be multi-orgasmic too. So naturally, I started taking a closer look at both the conventional notions about female orgasm and the latest science. I thought I knew a lot, but what I found shocked me—not just the pure facts, but the implications of the facts when taken into the context of these somewhat unusual and little-known group sex events.

Let me explain. The female clitoris has an external, hooded gland (the clit) with twice the nerve endings of a penis head—most women are familiar with their clit. Less known is the internal anatomy of the entire clitoris body. It is a large structure consisting of inner wishbone shaped corpus cavernosum with soft parts called the "bulbs of the vestibule." The clitoris is bigger overall than an average penis, though most of the structure is hidden because it is internal. The wishbone corpus wraps around the vaginal canal and fills with blood, like the penis, when aroused. The female clitoris, in its entirety, actually exceeds the blood-carrying capacity of a typical penis. The blood is what engorges the penis and the clitoris and sensitizes it. In the penis, it makes it erect. In the clitoris, the blood causes the clit and the tissues surrounding the internal clitoris to bulge or protrude. Interestingly, the clitoris has virtually no refractory period, unlike the male. That is because the blood in the clitoris is not entirely emptied upon orgasm, like the blood in the penis is upon orgasm. And the clitoris, having retained blood, becomes more sensitive (sometimes uncomfortably sensitive on the external gland) and engorged further and further with each subsequent orgasm.

The women at these events were having multiple orgasms. And it was evident, given the female clitoral anatomy, that any women could have multiple orgasms—potentially—one after another continuously with increasing intensity, stopping only because of physical exhaustion. Men, we knew, couldn't. But why, then, were women popularly and universally informed that their orgasms were unreliable and the so-called fact of their unreliability was backed up with exhaustive research meant to make women "feel normal" when they could not achieve an orgasm during sex? Now, I don't want to be melodramatic here, but having lived in

the future or Past of Sex?

Salem, Massachusetts, I do need to remind you that not too long ago witches were identified by their clitoris and then burnt at stake. I'd say that the Western cultural associations have always been formed by men to see that women's pleasure is not revered.

Though I don't think that there is any conspiracy here to deny women their rightful orgasms today (or to be burnt at the stake)—just look at the recent incredible vibrator technology. But I do think that the "science of unreliability" didn't take into account that the female sexual engine was a "diesel engine"— slow to start with penetrative sex, but long-running. Sex researchers have focused on the fact that the orgasm plays no part in human female ovulation and, thus, reproduction, unlike other animals. Also, the external clitoral glans is located, on average, pretty far away from the vaginal opening. So the motivating promise of reliable pleasure couldn't even explain, from an evolutionary standpoint, the persistence of the human clitoris. I do think that the researchers, while pondering the mysteries of the continued existence of the female clitoris and orgasm, neglected to consider any other type of sex other than monogamous, heterosexual, penetrative sex lasting, say, about 15 or 20 minutes. The 15 or 20 minutes, of course, takes into account a little post-feminist foreplay and the average time it takes the "formula one car" to ejaculate. Fifteen or 20 minutes was not long enough, as far as we could see, for a typical female to orgasm with penetrative sex alone, much less for multiple orgasms to happen. One thing was for sure—these researchers never saw what was going on at a group sex event. And, we think they also did not consider how sex happened among early humans or what purpose sex served other than procreative.

In the last 20 years or so, a few brave anthropologists have attempted to debunk the notion that sexual monogamy in humans is innate. And, like the big brother who informs sissy there is no Santa Claus, these anthropologists are none too popular with some of their peers and the public. One sissy, an oft-quoted evolutionary biologist, has garnered celebrity based on her theory that there is endocrine evidence for monogamy or pair bonding, including and by presumption, sexual monogamy, deftly, but I think inaccurately, wedding the two. At orgasm, women experience an increase in oxytocin, the "cuddle" or bonding hormone. She states that this is "endocrine evidence" for pair bonding and, thus, monogamy. A host of pop psychologists have further extrapolated on this idea in an attempt to explain why females are more picky or selective sexually—more naturally monogamous. They assert that the bonding hormone, a product of orgasm, helps to ensure that the product of sex—babies—would be well taken care of or protected by the stronger or more dominant male.

I'm not going to defend big brother anthropologist or wholly dis sissy, the evolutionary biologist. All one has to look at is the real evidence, aptly summarized by psychiatrist Cacilda Jethá and her psychologist husband Christopher Ryan in *Sex at Dawn*. Or check out anthropologist Meredith Small's research. It shows that primitive humans before the development of agriculture (not that long ago on an evolutionary scale) lived in small, non-monogamous groups where high promiscuity, especially female promiscuity,

the future or Past of Sex?

and social cooperation operated synergistically to ensure fecundity and survival. And, by the way, primitive humans had no idea how babies were made. So even if Jane felt that she had found "Mr. Right" based on the pleasurable oxytocin rush after good sex with Tarzan, she would have had no idea what she was in for nine months later. So probably the oxytocin rush Jane experienced was a hormone facilitator of group bonding, not pair bonding.

So what does psychology, social convention, anatomy, anthropology, and evolutionary biology have to do with group sex? We are not exactly sure, but we think a lot. During our inquiry, our questions multiplied: why would perfectly average people, with no experience with multiple-partner-sex report that, when aroused, thoughts or images about multiple partners pop into their imagination and fuel their arousal? Why would the practice of group sex persist over time under the threat of significant social sanction? Why are women more likely to achieve orgasm during long periods of penetration and stimulation, much longer than one male could provide? Why do swingers universally report intense feelings of closeness with their spouses and their other group play partners?

If we were to guess, we think that non-monogamists are accidental tourists in an ancient sexual territory. This sexual territory is a place where "normal sex" actually took place in small groups, frequently and promiscuously with no regard for exclusivity. And that sexual pleasure, especially the gradual, slow and lasting pleasure of the female, and her riveting emotion expression, her orgasms, served to call together and bond the group. The ancient sexual territory resides in our brains. And when we are turned on, we tune in.

CHAPTER TWENTY-THREE

I'm Fat

I DON'T CARE what Jorge says; I'm fat. I feel fat. I look fat. Ugh! Not that I've looked in a mirror below the neck, at least not since Isabella was born and certainly not since Ryan racked my body with his 9.3 lb grand entrance.

So when Jorge said he wanted to book a long weekend at Caliente, the nudist and swinger resort, I told him I'd rather give birth again. I mean, really? Nude? In harsh daylight around a sunny Florida pool? You got to hand it to him; he asked me a week later while he was giving my cunny a lingus. He told me he wanted to go down on me at the pool with an eager man watching me. A stranger with a raging hard-on, a hard-on that would end up in my hand, with me stroking it. Not bad, right? Jorge is good. Not to mention I look my best laying down, you know what I mean?

So, when I was calling out "yes, yes" to his artful tongue, he took it as "yes." Yes to the trip. He booked the

room and I promptly bought a one-piece bathing suit. A long
weekend in the warm, breezy Florida-in-winter sunshine was terrific; I just wished I didn't have to be naked.

I'll be as objective as possible. I'm pretty with a young-looking
face and my hairdresser, Ramon, has my blonde, thinning-but-
still-wavy hair looking awesome. At 46, I still look like I belong
with the younger moms—well, most of them anyway. That's the
good news. But I'm 10, ok, 15 pounds overweight; I haven't seen a
size four since college. My butt is cute but only in select pants—
a dike-y pair of cargos that make my butt look higher than it
really is and don't kid yourself—I have those cargos in every color
including camouflage which is not just dike-y, but full-on
butt.

I hate my breasts and, seriously, they hate me, too. They
are huge but not in a fun way. In the right bra they get looks
from the dads at Ryan's T-ball league, but without major structural
reorganization, they hang and sway at the mercy of gravity. When
I nursed, I was on constant suffocation alert. Shall I go on? I have
a little mid-section paunch that, let's face it, is never going away.
The gap between my thighs hasn't allowed light to pass since the
days when I could eat a french fry and still sleep at night.

That's it. Attractive, young face, sexy Ramon-inspired hair
(although I worried the Florida sun and humidity would turn me
into a frizz ball before I left the Tampa airport), a cute butt— if
I'm lying on my stomach—and breasts that could feed a baby-and-
me class. Oh, and, of course, my Latin husband is better looking
with each crease in his swarthy face. The paunch he now sports
somehow makes him look like a sexy chef who knows just how
to handle a woman in a way that younger fumbling fingers could
never do.

I have been to Caliente, and I know they aren't all 20-some-
thing, childless, workout goddesses. In fact, those youngins are

the last to take their clothes off. There are plenty of deflated breasts that make my ample ones look, at least when I'm laying down, attractive to somebody. So, I know the world is not made of perfect bodies and I had TWO NURSING CHILDREN damn it! But this is how I feel. Sexy? No.

Swinging I'm fine with. I may look like a Rubens painting, but I must have a lot of testosterone because even with a sex life most of my friends don't believe possible, I still manage to turn the kid's nap time into a little me time, if you know what I'm saying. So a hot threesome with a pair of hard cocks will keep me masturbating long after the kids have outgrown their naps. God help me when the kids go to school all day—I'll need to rearrange the laundry to make room for a case of batteries.

219

As any woman who has gotten their children to nap long after they need to knows, moms know strategy. And I hatched a plan. Avoid the pool. I'm fine in the evening at the bar and nightclub and by the hot tubs in the moonlight. I just had to avoid the naked daytime. Jorge loves the pool because, of course, it's his chance to check out young bodies, so I needed to find a way to let him have his pool time and my indoor vaca.

What can I do all day at a nudist resort beside staying in the room? Hello, spa! I booked every treatment, massage, yoga class, mani-pedi, makeover they had. Hey, it cost a fortune, but as we all know men lose all sense of budget when it comes to sex, and I told myself that I would go on a shoe fast until Christmas. Strategy.

It didn't hurt that the masseuse I booked looked like Jorge's nephew if he lived in the gym.

Strategy, check. One piece, check. Sexy nightclub outfit in camouflaging black and a bustier that would have made Newton reconsider gravity, check. But as cocky as I sound, I was plenty anxious. If one, I mean just one, mini-skirted, perky-titted thing gives me the head-to-toe look, I swear Jorge will be buying stock in Kleenex and hand lotion.

We arrived Saturday morning; the hot air hit me in the jetway as we de-planed and I felt my shoulders lower. By the time we got the rental car—a convertible (Jorge knows how to seduce me), I didn't even care what it did to my hair. The clear blue sky, bright sun, wind in my face—I was quickly thawing both physically and emotionally.

Driving into Caliente is, surprisingly, mostly beautiful. I mean, my image of swinger places was more seedy than luxury, which is what I thought about the lifestyle people before we jumped into this world. We checked in. I was wearing cargo pants and a shirt that made my cleavage sweat. A tattooed girl came behind the desk, her tight shorts showing off a terrific ass didn't help my insecurity. We headed to our room where Jorge got naked right away and was ready for the pool. What's with boys? They sure love having their willies out. I put on a fluffy robe and informed Jorge I was heading to the spa and that I'd meet him at the pool later, and then I mumbled—out of his earshot, "when the sun sets."

Jorge just smiled, totally oblivious. He just wanted to take his little friend and dangle by the pool. Just for effect, he brought a book that I guarantee will be nothing more than a coaster. I started with the yoga class, in my one piece, thank you very much. Then I glided from one indulgence to the other. I texted Jorge to meet me inside for lunch then continued my luxury tour ending with the massage.

The massage room was candlelit, so I got naked and laid on the table, on my stomach. I positioned a towel over as much of me as possible. I was excited and nervous to be naked and touched by the masseuse. I heard a person come in and with a low, new age-y whisper say, "I'm Blair. If you have anything special you want me to work on, or areas for me to avoid, just let me know. Otherwise, I'll be quiet, and you can just close your eyes, relax, it's ok if you doze off."

I looked up and smiled and told him to do whatever feels right to him. He was young and handsome with a thin hipster beard, but my view was mostly of his legs visible from his short, short shorts. Smooth, tanned muscular but soft-looking legs. I didn't want to close my eyes but the moment the warm oil drizzled over my back, and his long fingers roamed over my skin, I let out a sigh and let go of checking him out further. Thoughts of him judging my fleshy body dissipated as his plying hands wandered.

Oh, Blair. He knew what he was doing. There was never a moment his warm, firm hands left my body, keeping tactile contact as he plied my muscles with expertise. He kneaded my shoulders for so long I thought he'd never go lower. In long strokes, he loosened my stiff back, and when he focused on my butt, I might have slipped out an "I love you." When my legs came into play, he wasn't shy about my inner thighs and spread my legs just enough so his godly hands lightly tickled my lady bits.

At some point, I found myself turned over, and he cajoled, pulled, coaxed my fingers in a way that made me want to swear off new shoes forever. He treated my breasts like I was the only woman in the world and although my eyes were closed—and I was in a state of drifting sensuality—I could have sworn he kissed my nipples.

And then I woke up. Blair was gone, the room dark and quiet. Every inch of me was oiled and calm. A sheet covered most of me. I laid there for a long time hoping Blair would return. I was too blissed to move. I was imagining Blair's legs and feeling the oil between my legs and with my eyes still closed I must have drifted off to sleep again because the next thing I remembered my Jorge was gently nudging me awake.

Jorge was super sweet, and he helped me dress in my robe and held my hand all the way back to our hotel room. We took long showers and made slow comfortable love. We went to the club late, and the word was the action was out by the hot tubs. The Caliente hot tub is more like a warm, but shallow, large meandering pool. Jorge spotted a redheaded MILF he saw by the pool earlier in the day and positioned us nearby. I got naked and quickly slipped into the water. Perfect! The only part of me you could see was my face and, of course, my tits that floated high like a nubile teenager.

222

The redhead was about our age and cute and fun and, true to their reputation, vocal. She was with a man who clearly adored her, and the attention he paid her was both sexy and comforting. Jorge ever-so-slowly moved us toward them. The redhead sat on her man's lap and slowly rode him. I moved a hand near hers, and she readily took it then leaned over to kiss me. Her thick, out-of-control red hair swarmed our faces, and as she kissed me, she let out little moans. Jorge knew how to pick 'em, and he deserved in on the action.

I took the redhead's hand and guided it to Jorge's soldier. The look on his face was worth the price of admission. The MILF moved from kissing me to kissing Jorge, she then gave him a tug and told him she wanted him in her mouth while she was riding her man. Jorge pulled himself to the side of the hot tub and gave her little-big-Jorge just like she asked. Now she was really moaning, and I loved watching the action. Technically I was temporarily left out, but I have to say I usually am not the one watching, and seeing the smoky redhead, her eyes closed, moaning and sucking my Latin God, was enough to get me off with a little starter orgasm by my hand under the water.

Some other people were coming close to us, and I could hear some slurping and kissing. A very sexy, totally tattooed youngish, fit girl that I swear I saw that morning behind the reception desk joined right in. She went for the MILF's left breast, and I took the opportunity to caress T-girl's amazingly high, hard, round bottom. Tattoo Girl reached for my breast and then turned to kiss me. She tasted of weed like the nasty girl she was. Oh, this girl did it for me. She was butch in her aggressiveness, and her taut body was muscular. My hands ran down her thighs, and she felt like a soft man. Thoughts of Blair, the masseuse, ran through my mind, his sexy legs a male form of Tattoo Girl's thighs.

I could hear the familiar sounds of Jorge ramping up to an orgasm, and I turned to give full attention to tattoo girl. "Sit up here," I said and patted the edge of the pool, "I want to go down on you." Tattoo Girl bit my upper lip and grabbed my crotch with a firm handshake, "Deal, but first I want to bury my face in your fantastic tits," she said in a surprisingly feminine voice. She took my breasts in her hands and kissed the inner curves of my cleavage flicking my nipples with her thumbs. She dove deeper into the gap between my breasts pushing my breasts against her cheeks. I could feel her moans vibrate through my skin and felt her pussy rub against my thigh. She made love to my breasts, feeling them with her hands and moving her face from side to side, kissing and moaning.

There is something about the reception desk employee who I had seen before in clothes and now naked and fucking me with a crazy passion that made the experience even more naughty. Her youth and tattoos and her firm boyish body. The way she was moving her pussy faster and faster against my thigh. I felt like a fucking goddess. I heard Jorge rumble to nearly a howl as he came and that pushed me to take charge. "Now get up there," I barked, to the receptionist. "I want you to come in my mouth."

Tattoo Girl hopped up on the side of the pool where I stood thigh-deep, and I went right for her clit. I took it all in my mouth, she put her hands around my face and twisted her hips to my sucking. I held her thighs and could feel the muscles twitch. Oh, she tasted good down there. I pulled back and kissed her inner thighs. I ran my tongue along the thorned rose tattoo and inhaled deep the scent of her open lips. I looked up and saw her nipples pointing straight ahead, the tattoos on her arms, her choppy butchy hair, her gaze focused right on me. I owned her. Me: the mom who worried about being seen naked was fucking this gorgeous, bad-girl, sex creature—a long, long way from mom-land. She was a wild child who wanted me, damn it!

I went back to her clit and as I wiggled two fingers into her vagina. I heard Jorge behind me and felt a cock push up against my butt. Oh yeah, just what I needed, I wanted a cock in me right then. Tattoo Girl was pressing me into her pussy, moaning and calling to me, she held me so tight it almost hurt. I fucked her with two fingers then three. I felt a cock at the opening of my pussy. "Fuck me, baby!" I called out the best I could while still buried between T-girl's thighs. "I wanted to fuck you all day. I couldn't stop thinking of you." And he moved his cock a little inside me. But the voice wasn't Jorge's. And the cock wasn't either. I pulled back from her pussy to see Jorge facing me next to Tattoo Girl. Confused, I looked behind me and saw masseuse Blair's beautiful face. He leaned over me and kissed me deeply. His firm lips tasting like massage oil and he pushed his long cock into me, it drove slow and deep to spaces untouched and I almost came right then.

Blair kept telling me how sexy I was, how he was hard all through the massage. I pulled my fingers together and slid my whole hand into Tattoo Girl. She screamed, "Oh yeah, you're fucking me—fist fuck me!" And she pushed and pulled and bucked against me as I drove my hand in and out of her. Blair egged me on, "Fuck her like a man!" and he pumped his long cock into me. I felt his muscular legs smack against me. Tattoo Girl was yelling that she was coming. Blair spanked me hard, "I love this ass. I'm going to come, baby. You are making me come. Can you feel how hard you make me?"

Tattoo Girl squeezed her thighs together, my hand deep inside her. A hand went to my clit, and I shuddered on the brink. I pulled away from Tattoo Girl's shaking body, turned around, and leaned back against her. I looked over to Jorge, watching with a satisfied and proud smile, stroking himself hard again. Blair gazed at me with, dare I say it, with love and gently leaned in to kiss me like a nervous first date peck.

Blair entered me from the front, and I saw his sexy face tense as he moved those straight trim hips. Tattoo Girl held my breasts, pinching and releasing my nipples. I felt a finger on the edge of my asshole. I pushed against it, and the finger slid in. Blair held his cock deep in me and made small, determined thrusts. "Fuck, you are sexy. You had me so turned on today I had to jerk off." And my orgasm, poised for launch, tweaking the nerve endings around my vulva, began its ascent through me.

I saw Tattoo Girl and Jorge playing with each other but watching Blair and me. "I fantasized about fucking you while I came all over myself." Blair huffed between thrusts.

I felt my asshole pucker. Then a wave went from the walls of my pussy, spasms clutched Blair's cock creating a heat wave that grew to a fire around my clit and a shock went through me in electric slow motion right to my throat. I pulled Blair into me hard and held that cute little ass. I wrapped my legs around him, and I shook. And I shook. "Beautiful. Beautiful. Beautiful. Beautiful." he whispered, and I shook again.

A month later, snow falling outside our bedroom window, I was in a black see-through negligee doing a lap dance for Jorge. I teased him with my breasts and when I turned to let him touch my exposed bottom I heard Jorge, heard Blair say, "Beautiful. Beautiful. Beautiful. Beautiful."

CHAPTER TWENTY-FOUR

Youth

I'M NEARLY 60 years old. Well, ok, I'm 60. One. And I'm in a relationship with a 33-year-old woman. A relationship of sorts. Actually, my wife and I are in a relationship with a couple in their 30s. Sounds crazy, right? It's not. It's real. It's a fun, fulfilling relationship. Still don't believe me? I'll explain.

Let's get this out of the way. I'm not rich, don't have a huge dick, nor am I so handsome my age doesn't matter. Now that we have that out of your mind, take those three things and dial them back. I'm fairly successful, have an above-average dick, and I'm told that I am okay looking. But I am in no way exceptional. If I walked into a crowded room, maybe one or two heads would turn.

Regarding looks—I don't look 61, yes I've been told that, but so what? Maybe I look mid-50s, even early 50s at most. The fact is Ashley is a young-looking 33 and she's crazy about me. Ok, I got ahead of myself. My looks, however, are not non-descript—how's that

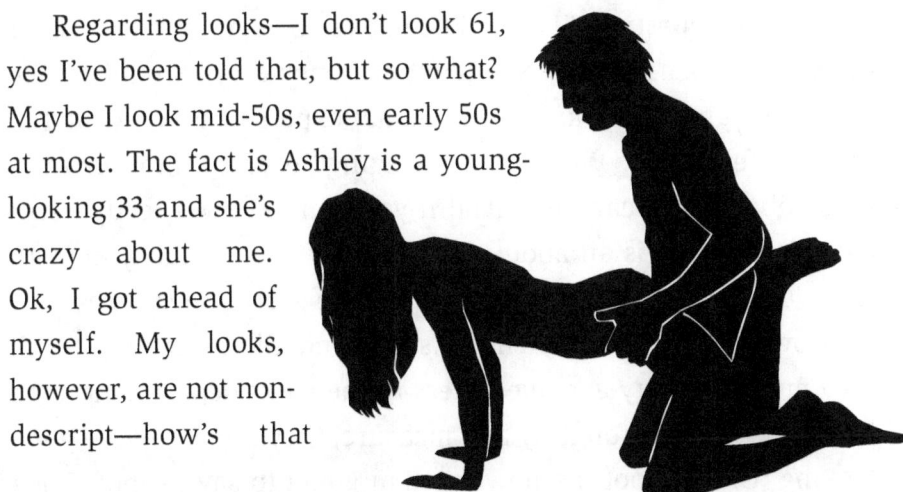

for a double negative? I'm pretty much all Italian and look like it. My face has angles. In fact, I look tough. By appearance, people think I'm a badass. Truth is, I'm a pussycat. Probably because people think I'm tough I've never really had to be. But I am, hopefully like most people six decades into life, confident in who I am. I made it through a war and some tough times; I take trouble in stride.

So I have unusual looks—not traditionally handsome, boyish, or with symmetrical features. And I'm a little fleshy. I work out once a week—that's it. I'm not flabby, but you wouldn't look at me, especially naked, and say I'm in great shape. Enough about me. I mean, I think we needed to get the, "what the hell does this guy look like?" out of the way. So, that's done. Now my wife, Genevieve—she is a beautiful woman, and when she wants to, she can look hot. She has great legs and looks killer in a miniskirt. She's resisted the 50-something fashion of short hair and has kept her wavy mane blonde—well, most of the time. Genevieve looks pretty damn good. Three kids nursed but her breasts still have life in them, and her ass is a nice handful. She may not look 57, but she sure doesn't look like she's in her 30s either.

As to the question, "Would I be in a relationship with a 33 year old without Genevieve?" No. Without Genevieve, I would not be lucky enough to have any of the sexual experiences we've had in the past few years. We started swinging 30 years into our marriage, about five years ago. And if you don't know already—successful swinging is all about the female. If you are lucky enough to have an engaged partner, you will have great experiences.

Now to our young friends Ashley and Gio. You may think they must be pretty average or less in the looks department to be interested in us. Wrong! By any measure, they are both very good looking. Okay, shoot me now, but I'm going to say it—hot. They

228

are hot. Ashley is a dirty blonde. Very dirty, haha. Sorry, I deserve that eye roll. Anyway, she has an awesome body—slim but firm. Big-nippled, upright large boobs that are so full and high that sometimes they look smaller, until my big hands are barely able to cover them. Ashley has a flat tummy with those lines that lead to her shaved, nearly-flat pussy. Tiny, hard ass and strong legs that control my movement when her legs are wrapped around me. And she's pretty. Not a great beauty but a sweet, soft face with a killer smile that goes from charming to "I'm gonna rock your world" instantly.

Gio is no slouch. He must work out a few days a week because that 30-something body is rock solid. He's a bit shorter than me but a much better-looking guy with a freckled good-boy look that I have seen heads turn toward. And he's got a thick cock that, God bless him, is always ready to go. And they are both professionals with graduate degrees and serious careers. So I guess my point is they could have the pick of the swinger world in any age group.

So, do you want to know how we became swingers after 36 years of marriage? How we met Gio and Ashley? Probably, but I'm going to tell you about what it's like to be with them, and let's see if you still want to know that other stuff.

After we make love, Ashley likes to sit next to me with her legs over mine. She takes my fingers and uses them to stroke her arms, legs, and breasts. Her slender, soft hand caresses and guides my big, Italian man-mitts in a self-massage that has the revealing-boundary cross of masturbating together. My fingers, held in hers, lightly stroking that tight smooth skin, those delicious breasts. That's fucking hot (there I said it again—hot—so sue me I don't care—hot). And before the hand dance across her body, our sex is great. Kissing her strong lips is fricking amazing, but when she takes my hands in hers and traces her body with my fingers, that's my take-home, play-it-over-and-over personal movie.

Last night we started dancing in the living room. I held her by her waist and with a flick of my hand pushed her away, holding her hand then pulling me back to her. A hand on her back and I led her body close to me then I pushed back. When she was in my arms, we kissed. I didn't let it go on too long before I changed our position so I could see her body move, her hips, the small trim hips move in a figure eight. I then pulled her into me. She gave a little gasp showing me it was the give and take—the tease—that she liked.

230

I eventually moved her to the couch and positioned her so she could watch Gio and Genevieve, who were already in full-on acrobatic intercourse on a mattress on the floor. I leaned over her, held her arms back and kissed her. I teased her lips with little gentle bites. We were naked, and my dick was suspended over her. When she tried to reach for it, I held her back, nipping at her lips. When she panted that she wanted me inside her, I instead moved between her legs and went down on her.

Her thin pussy lips tasted like sweet sweat; her clit rose from her flat vulva pushing into my mouth. I ran my tongue in between her lips and over her clit as Ashley squirmed and moaned for me to keep going. I turned my face sideways, so I was playing her long clit like a harmonica, licking and sucking it in my mouth like a lollipop.

I moved next to her squatting on the couch; she took my cock first in her hand then her mouth. I fingered Ashley around her clit and then a finger inside her. I could feel her bumpy G-spot and tickled it with my fingertip. She took all my cock in her mouth and pushed her pelvis into my hand.

Genevieve was practically screaming behind us on the floor with Gio's thick cock pile driving her. Ashley was swelling my cock as she started to moan, and she let go of my cock as I moved back between her legs. My middle finger still inside her I took her whole clit in my mouth, and she began bucking until she let out a deep grunting sound and came, her clit throbbing in my mouth and her soaking pussy drenching my finger. Her thighs, thin and strong, clamped my face and shook until I was almost suffocating.

With barely a moment to recover, Ashley joined me on the floor and took me by the hand, so we were on the mattress next to Genevieve and Gio. And then Ashley sat on me. She moved ever so slow and strong on my lap. I cupped her undulating breasts and pulled on her nipples. Genevieve and Gio got on either side of us. Gio kissed his wife while Genevieve took one of Ashley's nipples into her mouth. I moved my hands, so one hand was on Genevieve's ass and one on Ashley's. I moved a hand to Genevieve's soaking pussy, and Gio brought his cock to Ashley so she could take it in her mouth. Genevieve then joined Ashley alternating between kissing her and sucking Gio's cock. Watching the two women kiss each other and move their lips on either side of Gio's cock right in front of me brought me to the edge. With a rasta-rhythmed squirm, Ashley rode my cock until I came as far into her as I could, filling the rubber with a flood of cum.

The two women let go of Gio's cock and moved to my face and kissed me as I continued to spasm inside Ashley. I finally went limp—the girls and Gio gave me a group hug. Ashley rolled off me and into Genevieve's arms. I got up to get a drink and took a moment to recover. When I looked back Ashley was on the floor; Genevieve was on top of her rubbing her breasts and pussy on her thighs. Gio was perched above Genevieve, his cock poised to enter her from behind. I took a slug of OJ and a shot of tequila and finding our little sex bag popped a Viagra.

231

I went back to the action and traded kisses with Genevieve and Ashley as my wife was approaching another Gio-activated orgasm. Ashley and I moved to Genevieve's breasts, and when I slid a hand to Genevieve's clit, I found Ashley's hand already there. We teased her clit while Gio slid his dick in and out of her. Genevieve was screaming now and Ashley gave me the cutest smile, and we fist bumped each other.

The Viagra was kicking in; Ashley noted my erection and laid on her back next to the panting Genevieve, who spread Ashley's legs wide so I could enter her. But I resisted the entry and stroked her firm young body from head to toe then did the same with my lips and tongue. Her large breasts were pointing straight up, and I took each one into my mouth, so her nipples were tickling the roof of my mouth. I moved down her and traced the lines of her pelvis with my fingers then my lips then my tongue. When she begged me to fuck her, I positioned myself between her legs and teased her vulva with my now-hard cock. I used my cock like a dildo and rubbed her inner thighs, her lips, and her clit. I loved the way she begged for me enter her, and I resisted as long as I could.

Holding my cock like a rolling pin I teased her opening, putting my cock in just a bit then pulling it out. I could hear Genevieve sucking Gio, and his moans, and him telling her that he loved the way she teased his balls. I then entered Ashley all the way and her legs wrapped around my back pulling me into her. I thrust in slow, steady strokes and Ashley lifted up to kiss me. I felt her nipples brush against me and her lips lock tight onto my mouth. I pulled back against her thighs, and she tried to pull me into her, but I kept my cock at the front of her pussy. She begged me to fuck her harder. She bit my lip and then my neck. I plunged my cock full into her pushing her into the mattress and Ashley cried out. I felt a flood of wetness surround my cock, and she twisted and crooned and pulled me with her thighs. "I'm cumming," she called out, and I slammed into her—holding deep inside her while she ground against me, biting my neck.

Ashley held me tight and twitched below me as if her finger was caught in an electric socket. I held her, and we kissed and kissed and kissed. My hands ran along her sides, her taut smooth, skin etching into my memory. I rolled over and cuddled up close to Ashley. I looked across the room and saw Genevieve sitting next to Gio kissing him with her hand on his cock.

Ashley swung her legs over me, the signal we are entering my favorite post-sex phase. She took my hand and gently positioned my fingers over her shoulders then she lightly guided my fingers over her body. Her glistening, satiny skin sent rushes of shocks between us. Ashley took my fingers and hovered over her breasts, around them, under them, just barely touching her nipples. She guided me on a tour of her beautiful young body. My 61-year-old, seen-the-world, big Italian hands commingled with Ashley's fingers in a delicate, romantic slow ageless waltz.

233

As to why I have a lover 30 years younger than me? I asked Ashley—she moved my hand to the side of her breast, we touched her together, we watched as her nipples puckered.

CHAPTER TWENTY-FIVE

Famous

WHEN WE WALK into a room it's easy to know who the men will be attracted to. It's different for us females sometimes we don't even know who will turn our heads—well, sometimes. But when we saw Anthony, well, I'm sure we both knew Anthony was going to make our night interesting. Even if he wasn't famous, he had presence. When he walked into the room the energy changed, the room turned toward him. The fact was, I recognized him, not enough to know his name or in what context, but I sure noticed him. There was not one particular feature that stood out although he was traditionally handsome with a strong jawline. But good looking doesn't always turn me on; in fact, if a man is too handsome, I'm a bit put off. Trouble alarms go off.

When I say Anthony had strong features, I mean particular and distinct. A symmetrical face but almost a little odd looking. You know, like when you can't look away? But you could see why the camera liked him. You got the feeling he was formidable. Did you ever look up a celebrity and discover they went to Yale Drama and you thought, "Of course he did!" That was Anthony. And he had a moodiness in his demeanor that I wouldn't say was a turn on, but was somehow alluring.

I wasn't surprised to see him at the party; it was after all what we called a "limo party." A carefully selected group, each of us picked up in a limo and brought to a townhouse in Georgetown where it was understood that discretion was impera-tive. Washington is a strange mix of discretion and, "oh well, fuck it!"

236

We were used to being around high-powered people— politicians, diplomats, deal makers—but not typically movie stars. It was exhilarating. High-powered people, we have found, have high sex drives. They can be kinky or weird but are almost always fun and exciting. But even in this environment, Anthony stood out. The men wanted to meet him; the women wanted to fuck him. Pretty obvious. So in the classic model of game theory, I ignored the target. I assumed the hotties would go after the celebrity, and that would leave the normal over-achievers for me to pick from.

There was one girl who caught Anthony's attention and, for that matter, stares from the rest of the partygoers as well. She was so comfortable in her beauty that you couldn't hate her. I'm sure she was stunning as a baby and was used to the admiration. Her olive skin, full wavy hair, and long tapered hands reminded me of a Persian princess. She looked young, but you knew she wasn't. She had the clothes and style that telegraphed a European sensi-bility. A refined sexiness in her tailored linen pants that weren't tight but draped enough to show her curves, and a chiffon shirt unbuttoned low so you could see her small breasts barely cradled in a delicate, lacy bra. She knew what she was doing, and she was going to have the pick of the room; Anthony was the prize. The two celebs were out of our league, certainly off limits to my husband and me.

We circulated and avoided the two stars of the room but to my surprise Anthony found me. "I read your article in the *Atlantic* about the shared economy and sorry, I don't buy it. Don't you think it's just another cog in the capitalist wheel? I mean, it's not more egalitarian, it's just more efficient, right?"

"Um, well, how did you recognize me? I'm not exactly a public figure?" I said with a thinly veiled acknowledgment of his fame, but of course, I was happy he recognized me and impressed with his commentary and contention.

237

"Oh, it's not so bad being famous," he said, moving the conversational chess pieces two moves ahead of me. "Being recognized is good for the ego but not in the way you think. You see, people recognize me and think they know me. They make judgments about me which forces me to know my true self. It's a good discipline. It's a relief in a way. Embrace it," he said, with the same piercing eyes and intense look that makes his performances so engaging.

"Ok, I said, so be it. So, yes, the shared economy is just a turn in the economic evolution like swinging is an evolution of the sexual economy." I retorted, kind of proud that I turned the conversation to sex.

"I see," he said, and he paused and fixed that intense gaze on me. It was uncomfortable. I wanted to fill the silence, but I held on.

The empty moment was so long, so intense. I just gave up—I turned and walked away. "I don't need to play games with a pompous celebrity," I thought. "I'm here for some fun." I found my husband who was laughing it up with a group of lobbyists, so I joined him. At least the lobbyists are authentic in their bullshit.

And then the little group went silent, and I turned around to see Anthony behind me. "May I kiss you?" he asked, his unsmiling focus fixed on me.

"Maybe," I said, surprised but enjoying the attention, still figuring he was a Hollywood playboy used to getting his way. "I'll tell you what, you may kiss me if you can get the Persian princess to kiss me first," and I motioned toward the beauty across the room.

"Screw you," Anthony said, and I felt the eyes of the room on us. "I'm not your pimp."

238

"Now you are," I said, figuring I had nothing to lose at this point, and I might as well push it as far as I could. "I'll let you watch if you are a good little pimp," I said, upping my bitch to his movie star brat.

"Okay," he said, "come with me." And he took off across the room. I grabbed my husband and followed Anthony as he parted the sea of onlookers. He interrupted the princess in the middle of a flirt with a gaggle of admirers. He leaned in and whispered something in her ear. She checked me out and with a return whisper Anthony took her hand and guided her to a bedroom upstairs. His confidence and power over the most beautiful woman in the room was infuriating, but I have to admit, there was a rush straight to my kitty. We followed.

In the bedroom, the princess approached me with a sly, playful, slight smile that betrayed her serious yet seductive look. She unbuttoned the first button of my blouse and kissed me first on the exposed spot just above my breasts then moved to my neck. With me putty in her hands, she kissed me with those beautiful Persian lips that flushed me like a shot of Courvoisier searing my throat.

Anthony leaned in to whisper into her ear, and I pushed him away—pushed him hard. He stumbled backward and onto the couch by the bed. Princess responded by pulling me closer. Oh, her lips, her eyes. Half open, dreamy, almond eyes. Her scent faint and expensive with hints of patchouli after a light champagne rain. I ran my fingers across her face, tracing her lips as we kissed, a finger slid into her mouth. Princess made love to my finger, her tongue slowly teasing it while those sweet, full lips played tiny notes along the base of my finger. I pulled back to watch her and our eyes met. I blushed, I was so taken with her I had to look away. Then I saw Anthony and my husband, now sitting next to each other on the couch, intently watching us. Silent and focused. I looked down and saw Anthony's hand on the bulge of his pants.

239

I kept my gaze on Anthony as my hands went to Princess's side, her bright white, delicate, sheer blouse heaven against her dark skin. Still standing, we slowly unbuttoned each other's shirt exchanging kisses and touches with each small reveal. Princess made small, soft sounds—the murmurs of anticipation. I wanted to taste her nipples but took my time admiring her tiny breasts barely covered by her lacy half bra. Her scent built with her heated breathing, and I inhaled deeply with a hand on her tiny chest.

As my lips moved toward her nipples, she pulled me back to a kiss. This time a strong full-on, head-sideways kiss. I felt a hand reach under my skirt and a finger circling my clit. I was so wet, my heart pounding in my chest. I couldn't believe this beauty was making love with me. I was momentarily embarrassed by my own arousal. I reciprocated with a hand to her pants, a button undone, a zipper, down one tooth at a time. Her cooing gave way to deep "ohhhs" and her finger slid inside me—I could feel my wetness on my thighs. We continued to kiss, her finger in me and mine touching her mound through her slight satiny thong. I could smell her musky kitty, and the scent drove me to an orgasm standing, kissing, holding her small puffy kitty lips in my hand. As I bucked against her hand, Princess kissed my neck and shoulders.

I took Princess's pants off, her panties, her bra, exposing her naked lithe body before me. I guided her to the bed. Anthony and my husband were still in the same position on the couch but now, their pants off, cocks out. I took the rest of my clothes off and laid Princess down. I kissed and licked her toes watching her tongue rim her own lips framed between the tiny hard nipples of her flat chest.

My hands ran along her long model legs and inside her thighs. I slowly pulled myself up and moved my nipples along the length of her legs and then alternated nipples hovering and slightly touching her clit peeking between her lips. Princess watched me, biting her lower lip, her hips moving in rhythm with my nipples.

240

I moved my breasts slowly back and forth tracing the lines leading from her hips to her mound. Her abdomen was defined, and my nipples slid along the creases of her V-lines that led from her abs to her mound. Princess leaned her head back and let out a moan. I had found her spot. The beautiful lines leading to her pouting, rotating kitty. I licked slow and firm along the V, and when I got to her clit, I licked deep between her clit and her kitty lips.

Princess called out, and I pulled her clit into my mouth. She wrapped her long legs around me. Her musky, clean scent filling me, "Oh yes, ah oui!" she called out. I pulled away and lay on top of her. My thigh pressed against her wet kitty, and we kissed, rolling into each other's arms. "Take me," she called, "make love to me." I felt the dawning of another orgasm start along the curves of my bottom. I pulled up and positioned my legs, so our kitties were pressing against each other. "Oh my God," she called, "your pussy feels so good on mine."

I sat up and held one of her legs high and against my chest. I scissored and rubbed and teased our pussies together. I looked over, and Anthony's hand was on my husband's cock. The sight of my husband being fondled by the intense Anthony changed my rhythm into a full-on fucking motion. I thrust into Princess's pussy, and she emoted deep whimpering sounds, her fingers pinching her own nipples. I hit her kitty harder and harder with my clit. My husband was now fondling Anthony, a first for him, a boundary broken. The two men were stroking each other while I fucked the Princess. I fucked her. Kitty to kitty. I fucked her like I know Anthony wanted to fuck me.

CHAPTER TWENTY-SIX

AS YOU PROBABLY can guess, I am sexually open. My openness, however, was not natural or comfortable, and it was distinct from my sexual practices. My decision to engage in non-monogamous, recreational sex came after some hemming and hawing, and though the activity was far from traditional, my general attitudes about sexuality remained more conventional at first. Sex was secretive and naughty, and this, was, well, just over the top. Gradually my attitudes toward sex widened, my judgments softened, and I came to delight in the raw and varied expressions of human playfulness embodied in open and shared sex. I no longer viewed pleasure, including sexual pleasure, as taboo.

To Be Naked or Not?

Public nudity, however, was different. It was not a "maybe," nor was it a happy accident when Jim suggested

(a-THAT'S-WHAT-SHE-SAID-COMMENTARY)

that we go to a nudist community in the South of France, where I would be obliged to take off my clothes and walk around in the unforgiving light of day. It was, instead, a swift and decisive "no." And then I met the French and a few stout

Germans. But first, I want to share my initiation into public nudity.

I'm a redhead. This fact would have little significance if I had grown up in the northern regions of Scotland or in Norway where the aurora borealis turns and glows for some odd and sparse population. But I had grown up in Florida, a few blocks from the beach. A recurring conflict between my mother and me, was, of course, my desire to go to the beach and sun myself, and her efforts to save me from death by melanoma, or at least from a scorching sunburn every time I spent more than an hour in the Florida sun. In my 30s, motivated by the threat of cancer and early wrinkles, I developed a religious commitment to zinc oxide and routinely carried and used the "for babies—delicate skin" version of pasty white sunblock. The travel-size version of sunscreen allowed in carry-on would have covered a thigh and breast, so I left my bottle at home confident that a naked city would have a French version of pasty cream pour les enfants, and it did. I eagerly bought the largest tube.

244

On our first day in the naked city, in spite of the naked goings on all about us, my clothes stayed put. By late afternoon we thought the best place for our first foray into defrocking would be not at the super-marche or cafe, but rather the beach. It was less intimidating and seemed more natural, a small step from topless, somewhat familiar to us, to the full Monty. We made our way down the boardwalk to the beach's edge, where the initiated only had to remove sandals. I tentatively slid off my bottom—I was sure everybody was looking at me but of course not a soul was, not even an older man. I was just another naked body in a sea of

To Be Naked or Not?

nudity, apparently invisible. I grabbed my newly purchased sunscreen and slathered with vigor my face, my legs, and arms. I was nervous and glancing about while rubbing. It wasn't until I squeezed the last glob into my palm and began slathering my breasts, did I notice a pair of kids (yes, nudism is wholesome and a widespread practice in some parts of Europe) staring at me. I looked up, and absolutely every passerby was gawking at me.

"Oh, no!" Jim yelled, "look at yourself." I first saw my arms, then my legs, and then my torso—blue! Bright, hospital-corridor, flat matte blue paint. I looked at the now empty sunscreen tube in my hand, and the description written in French, and realized it was for babies and intentionally blue so mommies could see if they missed a spot. I would have turned bright red from embarrassment if I wasn't already blue!

"Don't just stand there—rub it in!" I yelled, now not caring who saw as Jim vigorously rubbed every, and I mean every, inch of my body until the blue dye faded—with all of the beach to see.

Nudism and sexual adventure are not one and the same; in fact, they have very little to do with one another. Nudism embodied a philosophical mindset and developed out of a separate set of social conditions in Europe, where the public nude body was regarded in non-sexual terms, and nudity was thought to be beneficial to physical and mental health. The two recently crossed paths—only because the nudism venues were more tolerant and open to the sexually adventurous. In the large nudist venues (called naturiste in Europe) with activities catering to the lifestyle (clubs, hotels, and such), there is an easy, almost invisible social contract in place. This contract respectfully parses the two, so that there is no mistaking an adult setting or activity for a family setting or event. And most sexual adventurers are not nudists, and most nudists are not sexual adventures— just in case you were wondering. But nudism, much more than sexual non-monogamy, by spotlighting the naked human body, helped me to confront and understand the social conditioning that distorted my perceptions of, and feelings about, my body. It also helped me discover the unfettered delight and pleasures of having a healthy body. Let me explain.

It feels good to be naked. If it were up to toddlers— those uncivilized little animals who also eat with their hands—humans would never wear clothing, at least in a warm, or climate-controlled setting, and forks and spoons would be confined to the floor or rubbish heap. But we are not toddlers, and we eventually concede to wearing clothing, not out of some natural desire to dress, but basically by conditioning. Experts in child development note, of course, that toddlers resist being clothed. This is well understood by parents.

But experts assert that the resistance stems from the toddler's own desire to exert their developing will in dressing themselves and that their will exceeds their ability to do so efficiently, resulting in parent-child conflict. This, I believe, is true to some extent, because babies are unable to object to being diapered and clothed. They are thus conditioned to being dressed, growing to like clothing and, sometimes, the process of dressing. But having raised my own children

To Be Naked or Not?

in a warm climate, and having allowed my toddlers to run about naked in the house and yard, I can assure the experts that my children would have remained unselfconsciously naked for a long time. Naked, perhaps, until they figured out (probably at age eight or nine when children actually finally develop some form of social self-awareness or self-consciousness) that the neighbors were not naked and that they strongly disapproved of their freakish, hippy practices—or until their mother was turned in to child welfare authorities. My children would have done so because it just feels better to be naked. Clothing squeezes, pinches, binds, and itches—and is hot. And if everyone had been naked in my neighborhood—the children's whole world at the time—my children would have gladly remained naked indefinitely.

I enjoy dressing up and adorning myself with clothing and jewelry as much as any other fashion-conscious woman. However, clothing is a social construction, often a necessary one, enforced to a greater or lesser extent by one's culture. Nudity is only a spectacle when everyone around is clothed. And a clothed (or blue) body is a spectacle only when everyone around is nude. And nudity, forgive my redundancy, is merely natural—it feels better. Just ask any toddler.

When nudity is the norm like it is in the naturiste communities in Europe, the exposed body is not a spectacle. Furthermore, the nude body, in general, possesses no special sexual fetish or magic. Because of the sheer quantity of nude bodies, the nude body is demystified and is, in general, desexualized. The subtle and not-so-subtle differences between bodies fade. This is not to say that as individuals we are not sexually attracted to certain body types, clothed or unclothed. We are. But the image or idea of an idealized body, say a Victoria's Secret model, disappears in the mind's eye because it just does not exist. What exists is a sea of skinny, fat, taut, tall, short, droopy, young, old, light, or dark. A body is just a body. Like a pair a khaki pants—boyfriend, skinny, button down, fly, crop, flair—is just a pair of khaki pants, no matter what the Gap wants us to believe.

From a distance, without focusing in on the minutest of details, they all kinda look the same.

However, when the body remains mystified, meaning we see only very few nude bodies live and in person—in contrast to the hundreds or thousands of nude or seminude bodies we see in media portrayed images—our idea of the body is distorted. These pictures have been picked, poked, posed, and brushed. Because we are inundated and exposed to only altered images, we naturally internalize these and then proceed to compare the idealized and distorted images to our real body.

For the first time at the naturiste communities in Europe, I saw, in quantity, what real bodies looked like—and it shattered this imaginary ideal I carried in my head. I became average, ordinary, and okay. And boy, was it a relief. My body was just an ordinary nude body—a little sunburnt and a little blue.

The woman in "I'm Fat" struggles with, like many perfectly healthy, average women, her self-image and her self-esteem in respect to her body. She, like most women, has an inner critic comparing her own body to a socially

To Be Naked or Not?

constructed idealized image of a female body—a body that essentially does not exist. Her body "could never live up" to this image. And she, like most people, believe that this is the only body that should be exposed publicly—anything else is gross or yucky.

So, you might say, what difference does this make? "I don't want to go grocery shopping naked. I don't need to be naked. I just am interested in sexual adventure." Well, it does make a difference. The body is at the center of sexual and sensual pleasure. If the mind is burdened by unfavorable comparisons that fill us with negative thoughts about our bodies, it's hard to enjoy the visceral experiences of the body. In other words, we don't feel with our eyes, we feel with our bodies. When confronted with a sea of real bodies in a relaxed environment, the degrading inner critic that exists in every woman's head is first given focus and then is given pause. In the pause, the inner critic is presented with ample evidence that a body is just a body, and that no ideal body exists—or, if it does, it is a rare, and not often sighted, bird.

Nudism quieted my inner critic. Nudism will never be accepted into U.S. culture. If it were, however, it would serve as a much-needed cultural anecdote to the contrasting and unrealistic obsession with the perfection and imperfection of the human body. Nudism normalizes the variations of the body by fully and publicly revealing it and helps to neutralize the psychological and cultural distortions about the body. Like pleasure and sex, nudity, I discovered was not just for the young, firm, and fit. For me, this discovery was more important than any discovery about my sexuality, because the pleasures of sex were just one function of the human body. On the other hand, our minds, especially those of women, are continuously evaluating our bodies. When the basis of the evaluation is distorted, we feel bad about our bodies no matter how well they work. Like the men and women in these unique communities in Europe, I am freer thanks to nudism—naked, blue or not.

CHAPTER TWENTY-SEVEN

Happy Ending
(Oz Revisited)

JOSH ONCE SAID that everything was different after our first experience swinging in the South of France. My husband was right. On that trip, we bit the apple of couple knowledge that we can't unlearn. And now it's four years later and we have followed what we now know is a typical pattern of swingers—each year we get more involved.

The first year we went for two days and stayed five. By the time we had landed in Virginia, we had booked a week for the next summer. The last day of our second year at the Ciudad Naturiste our son texted that he wanted to spend another week in summer camp—we decided to do the same and paid for another week at our camp: sex camp. The third summer we stayed a month and this year we are moving into the condo we bought. We are hooked.

It sounds cliché, but our best friends are now from the lifestyle. It's as if once we discovered that we could have sex with other people and that swinging made our marriage stronger, we felt connected to others who have made the same discovery. We share nudity, sex, and intimate details with our lifestyle friends. Three things—big things—that we don't ever experience with "vanilla" friends. I have a few, well maybe a couple, of close long-time girlfriends with whom, over the years, details of our sex life have been shared back and forth but there is still a wall between us that doesn't exist with swinger friends.

Our oldest and still-closest lifestyle friends are a couple from Paris—Quentin and Frederique. Through them, we have met many other people who frequent our funky village, the Ciudad Naturiste. We met them our first day of the first year at the village the day we had an adventure at the giant bubble bath party, the Savon—where I had my first experience with a woman. Oh, and another man. And while I think about it, with both of them, and Josh. . . And well, you see my point.

After our Savon encounter, we were starving and exhausted and spent the night in our dorm-like room eating pizza and distracting ourselves with Netflix. The next day we took a long walk on the beach—naked. We rented a lounge chair on the beach, and I did something even more decadent than group sex—I read a book—a silly romance novel about a housewife who has a crush on her kid's soccer coach. At that point, the normally risqué story seemed quaint but was the perfect beach guilty pleasure.

We drank rosé, said hi to Monique—our new friend who had told us about the libertine life, and we giggled about our crazy experiences from the day before. I got so horny laying naked in the sun, and thinking about what we had experienced, and oh, it didn't hurt seeing endless naked bodies, that I would have made love to Josh right there on the lounge chair. Later we would find out just a 10-minute stroll down the beach it transitions from

252

families to "adult," where "sex on the beach" is more than the name of a naughty cocktail.

As the sun lowered, we made our way back toward Thebes, the building where we were staying. We stopped at L'attelier, a sidewalk cafe of sorts with tables on either side of the walkway leading to Thebes. The chairs and tables were facing the path, so people watching was required. And what great watching! People of all ages and body types and nationalities strolled past us. As evening approached, some nakedness gave way to sarongs and even some clothes. People were drinking a milky-looking liqueur, and Josh ordered one—pastis, which we learned was a substitute for absinthe when it was made illegal in France a century ago. The cool Mediterranean breeze, naked people, sipping an exotic aperitif, and all surrounded by sounds of silky French—well, I just felt like my Josh had stumbled onto planet pleasure. Looking back, we couldn't have imagined how much our lives had changed.

253

Funny thing, marriage. Long-term marriages—like Josh and me. Having a child changed me—changed us—in good ways, but also in not-so-good ways. Let's just say there's nothing fun, attractive, or sexy about negotiating with your husband over who is picking up Brandon from the speech therapist's office. Our daily routine in Northern Virginia is a dance of survival. Josh is a great dad and pretty good husband and, let's face it, I can be inflexible at times and I'm no picnic either, I'm sure.

Previously, when it came to our sex life, I just lost interest after Brandon was born. Sex seemed like another task I was doing to please somebody else. I would just as soon get my nails done (not that I ever had time) and indulge in some chocolate. Sex wasn't painful. There was no physical reason I lost interest, I still enjoyed it when we made love, but I was always tired, and sex sometimes felt like work. I hate to admit it, but there were times when Josh would want to make love, I'd claim to be too tired. But when he was in the shower, I would use my vibrator, jeans barely unbuttoned—I'd be done in a minute.

When two close friends got divorced, and both were because someone cheated, the news hit me hard. One night when Josh gave me a patronizing peck on the cheek with not a hint of intimacy and then rolled over without even trying to make love, I went into the bathroom and cried. Josh had stopped trying.

I realized I had become complacent about our marriage and our sex life. A voice inside me said, "You are losing him and each other." I thought of the pop-psychology and annoyingly anti-feminist book, *The Proper Care and Feeding of Husbands.* Although the thought of being a traditional wife was repellant, I had to confess, at least to myself, I wasn't caring for Josh. And Josh was just going through the motions of being a husband. Our relationship had become tasks and chores. Instead of caring for each other, we were acting more like roommates and co-parents than lovers.

The next day I decided to take control of the situation and arranged a babysitter for a date night and then went to the mall and to Victoria's Secret. I felt silly, like a '50s housewife, not the feminist woman that I felt I had become—but I persevered. I got completely naked in the changing room and tried on a short, pink babydoll that had a see-through bra, satin bottoms, and a tantalizing bow. I tied and then undid the bow, and I watched in the mirror as the outfit fell off of me—I repeated and this time did a little wiggle of my hips and brought my chin to my shoulder. I giggled at my own silliness—I was doing a striptease for myself. I re-did the bow, and the satiny lace did something to my nipples that had them peaking like it was the first time I had felt them. I looked around. Nobody was watching, of course, and I slid my hand under the cup and over my breasts and massaged the satin over the tops of my thighs. I was stirred in a way I hadn't felt in years.

Hanging on a hook from a previous customer was a bra and panty set that I would never have chosen. The bra was a soft, unstructured cotton that reminded me of an adult training bra that barely covered my boobs. I let out a sigh when I leaned over and my stiff nipples poked out. I put the thong on and my-oh-my, the panties completely exposed my butt, the slight cord tickling and provoking me between my cheeks. My lips were barely covered, a fleshy gap was exposed that made me blush and shiver. I was wet. I bought the babydoll, lingerie set, and some expensive massage oil.

On the way home I got waxed—everywhere. I canceled the reservation at our favorite restaurant and booked a room at the Ritz. Just before Josh got home, I took a shower, feeling my smooth hairless body, and aimed the shower head right at my clit. I somehow stopped just before I came. I wanted to be on the verge for Josh.

I put on the panties and bra, a dab of perfume here and there, and then slid on a loose shift that I pulled from the back of my closet. I was humming, no, *singing*, while getting ready. I even wore stiletto heels, and that's a line I thought I would never cross again.

The sound of the garage door opening triggered my heart to beat faster. It had been a long time since my heart raced when I heard Josh pulling in. And I liked it. I went into Josh's closet and picked the Valentino shirt that had I bought for him years ago that still had the pins in it. I even brought out his skinny jeans that I had told him looked silly on him.

When Josh saw me in my print shift and heels and the clothes laid out on the bed, I was ready for a storm of questions. He didn't notice. Not a single question. I told him we had a babysitter and reservations at the Ritz. "Ok," he said, checking his phone. Boy was I right—we sure needed a date night.

It worked. The next morning I woke to Josh bringing me breakfast in bed and under a plate of heavenly quiche was an itinerary for our first trip to France. I've been waxing ever since.

When we arrive home from our summer adventures, we don't have sex with anybody local. It's too risky with our jobs and family life. If we go on a trip, yes, we might meet a couple for some play time. But the memories and stories from our time in the naked ciudad keep our sex lives alive and steamy. I even told Josh the story of the Victoria's Secret's dressing room while we were making love once, and added that I had to pull over on my way home and masturbated in the minivan on the side of the road. Hey, a little artistic license never hurt.

256

So back to our first trip to the ciudad and the day after our encounter at the Savon party. We were sipping our pastis and watching the kooky world go by when a gorgeous couple passed and then turned back to us. I recognized the bronzed man as I had seen him naked when we first walked out of our apartment. I had seen a lot of naked men by that point, but his body and, well, his package stood out—so to speak. "Nos voisins!" he said with a raspy, throaty French. I didn't know what "voisins" meant but pretended to while he leaned down to kiss me on one cheek and then the other. He smelled like coconut oil and sweat and—don't ask me why this turned me on—but he smelled faintly of a cigar, and that must have triggered a bad-boy gene that went right from my cheek to zones unknown.

"Voisins," I later learned, meant neighbors. They had the condo below us and it was much nicer than ours. The floor was bamboo and the furniture clean Scandinavian design against wall-high mirrors and gray lacquered cabinets. The exceptional feature was a big terrace with a couple of beach loungers and a table with chairs and a grill. The neighbor, Quentin, introduced us to his fiancé, Frederique. "Call me Freddy," she said as she kissed me on both cheeks and when she touched my side it was a simple (perhaps innocent) gesture that spurned goosebumps.

Freddy was cool. She was polite but not quick to smile. She wore a mostly see-through lace, but almost floor-length, negligee that gave an inkling of her physique. She was not impossibly thin like so many of the French, including her husband. Without the visible muscles of a woman who worked out, I got the impression she was in good shape and strong. Her beauty was subtle. She wore no makeup but her lips looked painted, and her eyes were blue and bright behind glasses that seemed like she was wearing them to hide her looks. Aloof. Confident. I was intrigued and a little intimated. Josh on the other hand later told me he was immediately attracted to but also afraid of her.

257

Quentin then introduced us to another couple, a tall blonde with a body that looked like a swimsuit model, but whereas Freddy exuded confidence, the blonde beauty was the opposite. She looked furtively as we did the cheek kisses and awkwardly kept her hands to her sides. The man with her looked so much like Quentin that I was immediately confused. He, too, was handsome with a day-old stubble, impossibly thin and fine, pointed, French features. Another man entered the apartment, and I caught I glimpse of him—older with ruffled, messy hair, and a naughty grin.

Quentin poured chilled white wine that tasted so good—dry and herby—that I had to supplement it with water so I wouldn't drink too fast. There were olives, a soft, gooey and pungent cheese that barely stayed on the narrow slice of dried baguette toast, and potato chips that were so wafer-thin and delicate, I wondered if they could be even be considered potato chips. The music was an ambient, smooth rhythm that seemed to pulse with the distant Mediterranean.

We spoke about the wine (they bought a case at a vineyard they visit each time they drive from Paris to the coast), the best boulangerie in the village (the one in the campground and well worth the longer, albeit naked, walk every morning), and where they tell their family they are when they are really in the ciudad (Euro Disney, of course).

Josh was speaking with the shy blonde, and I was completely entranced by Quentin when I noticed Freddy, with a whip in her hand, teasing the older man whom she called Simon. The man took the whip, a purple leather flogger with a handle and strips of loose leather (I later learned the straps are called falls because, I, um, now have a small collection). He ran the straps through his thick, sturdy but smooth hands and said something in raspy, smoky French, and Freddy turned around, clasped the table in front of her, backed up, widened her long legs, and pushed her butt into the air.

258

Simon lifted her lingerie and exposed her full round butt. He brought the whip close to her skin but didn't touch her. Instead, he ran the straps through his hand then slapped his own skin with it. The muscles of his solid forearm popped up and jerked. Each time he slapped his hand, Freddy moved her butt and made a gasp. Quentin moved his gaze from me to his fiancé and Simon, but he never stopped speaking, "We bought this apartment three years ago..." His casualness, while talking to me and absently watching his partner being teased by another man, was shocking in that it wasn't shocking. The blonde and the Quentin look-a-like shifted their stances to watch Freddy but they still kept drinking and talking. Josh, on the other hand, was all eyes on Freddy and the whip. Our eyes met, and we both smiled a couple's knowing smile and then quickly went back to watching the action.

As Simon air-whipped Freddy he motioned for me to approach. I came to him with a torrent of thoughts running through me. "Was he going to whip me and did I want him to? Did he want me to whip Freddy?" He turned from me and then gave Freddy a hard slap with the tip of the straps. Freddy tensed and bucked but didn't utter a sound. "The end of the falls makes the skin burn—Freddy likes that," he said to me in flawless, softly German-accented English. I later learned his accent was from speaking Belgian Flemish. Simon handed me the whip, and his large muscular fingers rested on my slight hand as I grasped the handle. He moved my hand in his and quickly snapped the whip against Freddy's exposed bottom, and this time it was me that gasped. Oddly my thought was, "Uh oh, I think I like this. . ."

Freddy flinched and moved her butt down and then up and I could see the puffy bulge of her vagina through her panties. I was shaking from the strength of the German-sounding man and the sight of Freddy's vulva and red butt. "Touch me," Freddy said, "feel my skin." I lowered the whip letting the strips of leather cascade over her back and bottom, and I gently felt Freddy's pink cheek. It was hot and soft, and she wiggled to my touch and slid her butt higher, so my fingers followed her cheeks until I nearly touched her vulva. She wiggled so I could feel the hill over her lower cheeks and the valley leading to her lips. Her skin was smooth, shaved, and warm. A raft of perfumed scent gave me a shiver. Freddy rotated again and moved in small circles guiding my fingers to a spot just below her opening. My knees gave a little, and Simon spoke in his native tongue—guttural and commanding. He brought our hands together again and smacked her, cracking the whip like a locker room towel snap. Some of the straps hit my fingers that were still on her bottom. I was the whipper and the whippee.

I looked up and saw Quentin take a sip of wine and lower his chin, gazing at me as if he was looking over imaginary reading glasses. Quentin's look was so direct and raw that I slid my hand away from Simon and the whip and came to Quentin. His fixation on me focused on my lips, and his hands went to my neck. His long thin tapered fingers wrapped around to the bottom of my face. He pulled me toward him but bypassed my mouth whispering something in French and then, "Watch Simon—we call him Magique Fingers." And Quentin spun me around and pulled me tight to his side like the lead in a tango.

I looked around for Josh, having been so lost in the intensity of the action I had forgotten about my husband—a slight moment of guilt arose but dissipated when I found him in a similar position staring at Freddy and Magique. Josh was next to the blonde, a hand somewhere behind her and her hand slowly tracing the bulge tenting his sarong. The other Frenchman, the Quentin look-a-like, was on his phone and plating something in the kitchen seemingly unaware or uninterested in what was happening on the terrace.

Freddy was still holding the side of the table, her bottom exposed in the evening air. Her panties had fallen to just above her calves, stretched wide like a lingerie restraint. Simon had the whip in one hand and a finger in Freddy's vagina. She was moaning now and moving her hips to his movement. Magique took the straps of the whip and from underneath her, tickled her clit while still having a finger inside her. Freddy called out and pushed the table so hard she almost fell over.

Quentin left me and went to his fiancé. Freddy grasped Quentin's waist as if he was the table. Stoic and calm, Quentin's hands held his partner's waist as she bucked and squirmed and moaned and cried. Quentin was dressed in a cotton shirt and linen pants without any of his body exposed, he held her but did not participate. Quentin propped up Freddy for her pleasure, not even touching her breasts or himself. He was casual and confident and selfless in the way he attended his lover as she was being pleasured by another man.

Magique dropped the whip and fingered her with two fingers like a sculptor's hands on clay. Freddy shifted and squirmed, holding her husband tight, and then she went stiff, raised her head, hair flying and pushed her husband away. Magique's fingers followed her movement staying inside her and Freddy brought her fingers to either side of her clit and she squirted across the terrace. The stream shot far and then Magique twisted his fingers and she screamed and shot again. Freddy shook, grabbed her husband as Magique triumphantly pulled away from her. I nearly fainted.

Freddy kissed Quentin and Magique and left to go into the apartment. I turned to see Josh, holding the blonde's hand and looking like he had just witnessed a miracle. I was so aroused and stimulated and light-headed, I felt as if under a spell. Quentin's spell. He approached me, and I felt scared, vulnerable—he could have done anything to or with me—I was powerless. Quentin kissed me, his tongue stalking, licking, teasing my lips. A hand was on my lower back just above my butt—oh, how I wanted him to grab me. "We are going for dinner, tapas. Join us." He whispered. "People dress here at night, you know."

His words pulled me back to the present. It took me a minute to realize he was telling me our beach towel sarongs were not appropriate if we wanted to go to dinner with them. I pulled away from Quentin, thanking him and then went back for one more kiss. I found Josh once again talking with the others as if Freddy's squirting was a course between entrée and dessert. "Honey, I'm going to go back to the room and change—you stay here. I'll bring clothes for you." Josh looked at me like I was telling him I wanted to drive our son without a car seat. His look reminded me that we just witnessed a woman casually squirting on an open-air terrace while I made out with a man and he fondled a model beautiful blonde. "I know honey, we have a lot to talk about, but right now I'm going to get dressed. Hydrate—I'll be right back. I love you." I kissed him, handed him a glass of water and nearly ran upstairs, relieved to be alone for a minute to at least try to ground myself.

I put on my Victoria's Secret panties and the only dress I had. As I slid on the clothes, I thought about quickly masturbating just so I could take the pressure off and maybe keep myself from acting like a teenager with the Frenchies. Just as I touched myself, I heard a call from outside our balcony and stopped, grabbed some clothes for Josh, and headed back downstairs.

262

When I walked into Frederique and Quentin's apartment, I got halfway through, and stopped dead in my tracks. Along a low wall on the side of the terrace, I saw Josh, my sweet-husband-dad encircled by the two women. On one side the blonde was kissing him, her breasts exposed a reddish nipple between Josh's fingers. On the other side was Freddy, dressed again in her floor-length lingerie, stroking Josh's exposed erection. I was shocked. It just hadn't occurred to me anything would happen without me there with my husband. The scene struck me as somehow a betrayal even though we had crossed a dozen boundaries in our short time in the Village and only minutes before I was kissing Quentin, silently begging him to do more to me. But I nevertheless felt betrayed, even jealous, that I could leave my husband for 10 minutes and come back to him fully engaged with the two women. The action was both disturbing and arousing. To this day, I often replay that moment when I walked in on him with the two women on the terrace.

When the blonde's hand met Freddy's and they stroked Josh together he let out a low moan I had never heard from him. As I watched—transfixed and still—I felt a hand on my bottom. I let the hand roam without looking to see who it was until I felt, no smelled, the refined woodsy scent of Magique Fingers. "Watch them," his voice said as the hand on my bottom pulled aside my panties. Quentin passed in front of me, kissing me with full abandon before approaching the women and Josh.

Quentin took the whip from the table and ran the falls over the blonde, who by now was sucking Josh's member. The other Frenchman came next to Frederique and pushed her head down level with the blonde's, and in a slow choreographed dance, unbuckled, then lowered his pants, unwrapped a condom, rolled it on, and entered Freddy. Quentin had somehow done the same so that both men were behind and inside the women while the females were bent over kissing each other with Josh's penis between them.

263

There were so many sounds of moaning and flesh slapping that I got lost in my own pleasure and let go joining the chorus in a voice that came from deep within me. I called and screamed, perhaps for the first time, or certainly the loudest. A crescendo of sounds melded from our joint pleasure into a harmony of passion. I felt like the first violinist in a philharmonic, with Magique's fingers the bow on my fretless neck.

An hour later we had ordered and eaten every tapas on the menu and had drunk carafes of wine that didn't get me the least bit drunk. And maybe my favorite part of the night: finding out that Frederique was the former mayor and now city manager of a town south of Paris; the blonde a professor of sociology and widely published; and Quentin and the other Frenchman were in finance. Yes, they were all professionals except Simon—Magique Fingers. He's an artist.

After dinner, the two couples and Simon went to a club, but Josh and I opted to go home. The evening had been so charged;

Josh didn't want to dilute the experience with even more crazi-ness. "Let's go home, cuddle up, and savor what we just saw and did," Josh whispered to me, and I readily agreed. We lay in bed, intertwined and silent for a while. "Yesterday the scene at the bubble party was a free-for-all sex party. But what we experi-enced tonight was so different, and I can't quite put my finger on it," Josh said quietly as if contemplating the difference between jazz and blues.

I listened to him think aloud, but I was silent in a state of bliss-ful shock myself. "Basically, we were at a neighborhood cocktail party, but instead of some people off to the side watching the game, here they are having sex." Josh continued as I swung a thigh over his legs. "I mean the sex was no different from the wine or chips or casual conversation." I love my Josh— my thinker with boyish curiosity. Josh recalled every detail of the scene on the terrace, and I realized that I had been so lost in the moment that I barely recalled anything. Well, except for Simon's twitching forearms and Quentin's salty kiss.

I was less interested in the social aspect of the party, but more fascinated by what it had done to me. Josh asked how I was doing and I whispered, "Numb. Tingly. Alive. Young. Sexy. Grinning. Dreamy," and I rolled on to Josh so that I was completely laying on top of him. I kissed him slowly and deeply, "In love," I said.

We made sweet love that night, me on top with my legs pressed together and Josh's thighs wrapped around me. I woke up sometime later, Josh breathing deeply beside me. I was aware of a vivid dream and the image of Freddy's bottom red from the whip. My groin ached. My vulva seemed to be twice its usual size. I squeezed my thighs together and tried to close my eyes, but my agitation only grew. I nudged Josh but he was snoring. I undid my legs and touched myself; I was so wet it surprised me. For some reason, I wanted to resist masturbating—my dream state

264

of arousal so intense it was as if I was afraid I couldn't control myself.

There was moonlight coming from the balcony, so I opened the sliding glass doors and let the cool night air breathe across my naked body. A giggle and then a muffled voice came from below. I walked to the edge of the balcony, looked down to our friend's terrace below, and saw part of two lounge chairs pushed together. Quentin was standing and slowly thrusting his hips into a woman with only her legs exposed to my view. The other chair was a tangle of bodies, but I was focused on Quentin: his long sinewy limbs, his tiny hips moving in careful rhythm. Now I didn't resist and touched my nipples which puckered to the breeze and my pinching.

265

Quentin looked up, and our eyes met. His expression didn't change as if he expected me to be watching him. He pulled his hips back, and I saw his long erection spring out of the woman below him. I lifted a foot to the balcony's railing opening my vagina to him, to my fingers, to the sea. Quentin brought his hand to his erection, and I saw the head of blonde hair disappear below his shaft. I glided a finger inside myself as I touched my clit. I shifted my view from Quentin's staff to his piercing eyes. I heard a woman moan and a strange ripple went across my shoulders. I couldn't hold my orgasm any longer and said, maybe called, to Quentin, "Come with me." I heard a noise behind me. "I'm watching you," Josh said in a whisper. "Come now—I want to see you come." I pulled back—caught in the act. Heart throbbing. I bit my fingers and then gave in—gliding two, three fingers inside of me like the thick digits of Magique Fingers and I called out—the animal in me uncaged. Quentin stroked himself and shot across a naked body, and I bucked and screamed. The next thing I remember, I was laying on the balcony floor—Josh holding me tight.

I can hardly believe that's me as I write the account of our first time in France. These wild sex adventures don't happen every day for us—even at the ciudad—but a few encounters a year can be like a relationship resurrection. We might meet a couple on the beach, have a drink with them and maybe dinner—perhaps sex as well. Sitting next to us at a seafood restaurant one night we met a British couple well into their 70s; they had been coming to the ciudad for over 20 years. "I suppose it's our second home now," the man said in drawn, proper English. "We aren't swingers really, oh except for the odd foursome," he said as if to say he wasn't a golfer except for the occasional 18 holes.

266

We have found the inclusion of sex into a social interaction seems to be more common with some Europeans—French, Dutch, German, Scandinavian, and, for some reason, Israelis. Oh and Brazilians and. . . Well, we have met a lot of socially progressive people and our night with Quentin and Frederique and friends was our intro to a world we still find wonderfully confounding and exciting. As the stigma of sex lessens for us, we have found boundaries fall through many social situations. Last year we saw a man go to one knee and propose to his wife in the middle of the Savon bubble party. We met a young couple from Barcelona who went to a sex club after their wedding—she in her traditional white wedding dress.

Last week we crossed another line. Quentin and Frederique decided to officially marry at the ciudad—naked. Quentin wore only a bow tie and Frederique, a beautiful white lace veil and matching garter on her right thigh. The guests and even the officiant were all naked although a few women were more formal and wore pasties. The officiant was especially handsome: my Josh, dressed in only a Washington Nationals baseball cap. I was, I have to say, beaming as Frederique's maid of honor, wearing only long, white, bead embroidered gloves.

Josh read a poem and spoke of the love between the couple who had become our closest—in every way—friends.

"Do you both, before these naked witnesses, pledge to do all in your power to make this a happy and enduring union?"

The couple together said, "We do."

They exchanged rings. Thankfully, Josh had talked Frederique out of using a cock ring for Quentin.

Josh paused, "By the power vested in me through love and friendship, I pronounce you husband and wife."

We cheered, and Josh turned to Quentin.

"You may now kiss the bride, the bridesmaids, and my wife, the maid of honor."

CHAPTER TWENTY-EIGHT

LAST WEEK WE went out to dinner with our good friends Ruben and Lea. And yes, we are friends in every way. Jim and I arrived at the restaurant first, got a nice table in a corner, and ordered drinks. They arrived, and after hellos and another drink, we switched seats, so I was next to Ruben, and Jim was with Lea. Eventually the affection we all share turned into hand-holding and Lea's head on Jim's shoulder. As the server arrived with our food Jim and Lea had started kissing. The waitress did a movie, no cartoon worthy, WTF double take. It wasn't the first time that happened when we were out with friends and, no doubt, will not be the last.

friends Lovers or Hippies?

When we entered the non-monogamous lifestyle, Jim and I did not expect this kind of soft, loving affection to occur. In fact, it is what we feared. We were seeking

a-FINAL-SHE-SAID-COMMENTARY

sexual adventure, not friendship. As reality show participants say, "We're not here to make friends." We feared the closeness and the affection with lovers that is normally reserved for married couples. But somewhere, sometime, and somehow—and without conscious intention—we transitioned into a closeness that has brought wondrous joy to our lives.

Americans, especially, love to label, segment, specialize, and categorize themselves. If you practice yoga, chances are you are into Hatha or Kundalini or Hot or Bikram or Acro or X yoga. The dating site OkCupid has 13 sexual orientations (including "other") and 22 genders. Go figure? Non-monogamy is no different. There are soft swap, full swap, kink, S&M, same room only, open, poly, no single men, just curious—the list is as varied as there are people.

Sexual practices and interests can change over time for individuals, but especially for the non-monogamous since, by definition, they are engaging in an adventurous activity together where they are more apt to be exposed to new things and learn more about themselves and others. Jim and I have developed and changed, and at times stepped back from the lifestyle, in the course of opening our lives to sexual adventure.

On our first visit to an S&M club, Jim saw a female acquaintance in a submissive bondage scene, and he became so upset that I found him outside unable to talk for fear of breaking down in tears. I, on the other hand, had put on my clinical hat and was dispassionately observing the woman and her partner although I admit being slightly aroused by the scene. So, we learned that this practice isn't a preference for us—at this time.

When we try something new, there is always excitement, nervousness, and fear, but most importantly there is discovery. So although bondage, domination, sadism, and

Friends Lovers or Hippies?

masochism (BDSM) practice isn't our thing, we have found emotional closeness with others, like with Ruben and Lea, to be an unexpected positive addition to our lives.

I wouldn't say we were poly—Jim and I love each other and are as committed a couple as any. I don't think either of us is ready to feel happiness when our partner falls in love with another person as polyamorous people do nor am I interested in parsing and discussing practical realities like cleaning and paying the bills with more than one person. However, we have allowed ourselves to become surprising close and affectionate with some of our lovers.

Cuddling up with a man, sometimes next to or very near Jim, is yet another boundary I thought would never be crossed. And in these intimate moments when trust and caring, and even love—that ridiculously broad term—are shared without the fear of hurting my partner or our relationship, well, I feel enormously lucky and enriched.

Perhaps the intimate boundary crossing was unintentional on my part, but I think Jim knew this kind of closeness was possible. I call it the post-hippy effect. Jim had lived in counter-culture communities in California, Oregon, and India, where nudity was common and sexual boundaries were blurred. Jim may have later "straightened-up" to raise a family, but while the hippy could wear a suit, he couldn't ignore what he knew and what he experienced. So when Jim's kids were off to college and the suburban home was empty, that free spirit came out in our relationship.

Jim and I had been to Rainbow Gatherings, albeit in different decades. The annual, week-long, hippy get-togethers in national parks have been occurring since the 1960s. The events are pop-up societies of cooperative living—building camps, making meals together, communing with music and nature. There is nudity and public displays of affection and sex. But what the events really represent are people living by their intuition—and human intuition and instinct is characterized by the desire to live together and be together in small groups—sharing, loving, working, and learning together. They even call themselves a family—the Rainbow Family— and they address each other as "brother" and "sister." Folks seek an extended family in all sorts of settings, including, of course, traditional church, but the Rainbow People, unlike the religious, are guided more internally than by top-down structure. I got merely a taste of the alternate life, unlike Jim who actually lived as a hippy.

272

The social re-ordering that took place in the 60s and 70s is evident in the new generation of women who have truer agency and independence in the way they are approaching love, relationships, and sex. Recently we met a woman, the daughter of French hippies, Camile, who asked, "Why wouldn't you have the love of as many people as you could?"

Camile's blunt rhetorical question shifted my attention to the larger picture of the change at hand in female sexual behavior, role expectations and, ultimately, the changing belief systems around gender, sex, and marriage.

I am professionally and personally intrigued by today's post-feminist, sexually open, and fearless female. I don't fully understand and cannot emulate what many younger, freer women are experiencing today in a world where they are more and more financially and sexually equal to men.

friends Lovers or Hippies?

But I am having a lot of fun conducting the research in the meantime!

Young women are coming of age at a time when they will choose their sexual and romantic partners with even fewer of the established boundaries that were present in previous generations. But the absence of these boundaries means women will also have to navigate their own set of rights and wrongs. Imagine, it was less than a generation ago when it was scandalous to be divorced or to live together before marriage. Now marriage is an option, not an obligation.

In addition to the shift whereas women have more economic power, social norms have changed so that women, especially, have more freedom sexually and in relationship choices. But this boundary-breaking by women—the shameless expression of her sexuality, I think, will do even more to shape what relationships will look like in the future. Females are now making choices about long-term partners after having many and varied sexual experiences and having more information about relationships. This experience, even if she chooses a conventional relationship style, will not be forgotten.

When my daughter was going through puberty, she asked me why her period takes up so much time and energy. I explained to her that reproduction is the primary purpose of human animals. Reproduction is survival. Believe it or not, humans could survive without pizza and Netflix but we, as a species, must reproduce. And as reproduction is the purpose, sex is the drive to reproduce. Reproduction is the function; sexuality is the complex operation.

Of course, her reaction was, "Whatever, Mom. . ." and she went back to her pizza and Netflix. But I rambled on. I wanted her to understand why suddenly boys and men of every age were looking at her differently and why she was noticing those annoying boys in a new way. Sex is so dangerous, taboo, regulated, and so glorified because it is our most primal drive. I want my daughter to understand both the function and the complex operation. She has to; this knowledge is power.

At times I can't believe we've written a book about sexual adventure. It was only 10 years ago that I had ever heard of the word "polyamory." I had been in a strictly monogamous relationship from age 19 to 45—my entire adult life.

274

When Jim and I set out on this adventure, I assumed that the sexually adventurous were just naughty people doing naughty things in secret. But as we researched, observed, and became subjects ourselves, the full world of consensual non-monogamy was revealed to us. It unexpectedly, but fundamentally, changed our ideas about sex, marriage, and even family.

Of all things non-monogamous, polyamory was especially perplexing to me. My initial response to polyamory was, "Why in the world would someone want to negotiate all those relationships?" While married, I had had an unusually close-knit family. My ex-husband and I had moved back home after graduate school. Frequent family and holiday celebrations required elaborate negotiations, and a family-owned business blurred the boundaries of private and commerce. When my daughter was born, the hospital staff had to ask my garrulous aunt, uncle, and a couple of stepparents to move to the waiting room, noting with an eye roll, that I had a very big family.

My experience of married family life was, I think, a bit unusual—I'll call it "old school." On the surface, no one would call the consensually non-monogamous (CNM) old school—blasphemous, maybe! But when the deeper needs and desires of people practicing CNM are considered, they are not much different from the traditionally monogamous couple or traditional family unit. The needs and desires are basic: the needs for emotional connection, belongingness, safety, and security, and the desire for freedom and pleasure.

The changes in relationship structure from when people were married for life to now—when marriage itself is optional—has not changed the fact that people have the same needs for love and attachment. Not everyone can have a large close-knit family—one that provides a sense of belongingness. Not everyone can have it forever.

Polyamory is not perplexing to me any longer. I see and understand their desires—it was what I wanted when I married so young. I wanted love and belonging. The polyamorous are just going about it in a different way and with greater freedom than I did. And the sexually adventurous are doing what the name implies—looking for adventure. But what they often find is a sense of connection and friendship, and even love.

This is what Jim and I found. Good luck in your adventures. Let us know what you discover.

CHAPTER TWENTY-NINE

What the Fuck?!?

Common Questions and Uncommon Answers

Q: What is swinging, do normal people do it, and how is it different from other forms of consensual non-monogamy?

A: Swingers are married or romantically committed partners who consensually and openly have sex for fun with other couples. Sex is considered a playful, recreational activity, done with others, but with the purpose of enhancing the erotic bond of the married or partnered couple.

Swinging has informal rules, like a game, but it is also considered a form of spontaneous play—for adults. Some call it the "lifestyle," and sociologists and investigative journalists have documented the swinging practices, people, and their locations. Swinging is quite a bit different from other consensual non-monogamous arrangements in that the couple is typically not looking for romance, emotional support, commitment, or fidelity with their serial sexual partners. Some people confuse open marriages or relationships with swinging. They are not the same thing. In open relationships, partners have sexual and sometimes romantic relationships with others independent of the couple. Some people may have heard of polyamory. Polyamory involves a complex relationship structure and style involving multiple mates. Swingers or lifestylers are distinct from these, in that the swinging is a temporary activity, not an alternative relationship form or structure.

Swingers, except for their nontraditional sexual activity, maintain emotional, financial and romantic fidelity to one another, and generally, when they have sex with others, it is together, either in the same room or close by. And swingers are normal—some sociologists even assert they are quite conventional—in that their sexual activities and adventures are done with the purpose of enhancing the sexual pleasure and erotic bond of the married couple, thus, better ensuring the longevity and stability of the otherwise traditional marriage. Swingers take joy in the sexual pleasure their partner receives from others and feel that their activity enhances other aspects of their marriage or commitment to one another.

278

The majority of long-time swingers are long-term married couples, 20 years or more. However, millennials who may be in a committed relationship, but are not married, are participating at higher rates. Swinger couples date online, go to clubs, gatherings, and themed resorts. Unlike the lecherous portrayals in popular media or perhaps in our imaginations, swingers look like, act like, and hold many of the same values as any other group of folks. They are not much different from the people you might meet at a Rotary Club meeting in a midwestern city, except for the racy outfits and slightly fitter bodies.

Q: I'm afraid my spouse will fall in love with someone we meet on our sexual adventures—how can I be sure that won't happen?

A: It probably won't happen. If you decide to open up, hopefully, you are in an untroubled relationship where you are still very much in love. Consider opening up like the skydiving or the triathlon of sex. If you have serious health problems and are looking for a sport, you should probably start with physical therapy, and then move on to speed walking. So if you have relationship problems, we firmly discourage opening up. It will be hazardous to your marriage or relationship.

When a relationship embodies qualities of compatibility, clear consent, openness, honesty, closeness, and flexibility, and there is a firm and explicit commitment to one another, some of the difficulties encountered in opening up can be navigated more easily. Then sexual non-monogamy can be taken for what it really is—sexual adventure, a fun recreational activity that couples do together for each other's pleasure.

All forms of consensual non-monogamy have informal rules and guidelines that most couples learn about together, and that help to ensure that any intense feelings between non-partnered couples are not nurtured if not specifically consented to. It helps to know that falling in love is not only a phenomenon of sexual attraction but also a process that takes time and means. The process of falling in love occurs when two people who are attracted to one another share deeply held feelings and information. Most couples that swing, for instance, lay down ground rules that prevent this falling-in-love process from happening.

So, for instance, a rule may be that a spouse does not have face-to-face or electronic contact with the other couple without you there or without your knowledge. It is standard practice in the swinging world for only the same genders to have contact with one another outside of the "date." It also helps to know that some forms of consensual non-monogamy are not like traditional dating, where you are looking for someone that is both sexually attractive and embodies the qualities that make them a suitable long-term partner. The purpose of dating in swinging, for instance, is to find other couples who are physically and sexually attractive, but not necessarily compatible and suitable for a long-term relationship.

That being said, some long-time swingers or lifestylers, do report that they form ongoing friendships with others.

Couples also know that sexual contact does sometimes generate the feeling of closeness and intimacy. The intense energy and feelings are more akin to crushes than to love. Smart couples, if this is not part of their agreement, discuss this fact and explicitly make a commitment to guard against cultivating deeper feelings with others. But this doesn't mean that the couple doesn't talk about or denies feelings—just the opposite, they acknowledge feelings, and in the process of talking about them, the pressure or energy of the crush is relieved.

280

Q: **But can't it happen anyway?**

A: Sure, it could happen. It is a known risk. And sometimes you may discover that your or your partner's communication skills are not up to par, or perhaps you or your partner need to cultivate more sensitivity for one another's feelings. But remember most relationships fall apart because of longstanding lack of emotional connection and communication as well as deception, lying, and cheating.

Q: **What about STIs?**

A: Some sexually non-monogamous persons may have a slightly higher risk of contracting a sexually transmitted infection. Some STIs don't have obvious symptoms, so regular medical monitoring for STIs is essential. Condom use should be default and is imperative. Expect to use condoms and, if it has been a while, learn how to use them properly. There are condoms readily available in club settings. We suggest that you speak to your primary care doctor about the risk of sexually transmitted infections and the suggestions for monitoring and reducing risk given your high promiscuity choices. A gynecologist for women may be your best source of information.

Q: What's the difference between consensual or ethical non-monogamy, open, swinging, and "the lifestyle?"

A: The terms are often used interchangeably, but they may mean different things to different people. So, for instance, people who call themselves lifestylers are seeking recreational sexual activity with others and may also be looking for friendship and companionship with other free-spirited couples. Consensual or ethical non-monogamy is more of a general concept that defines the boundaries, practices, and informal rules that people who have sex outside a traditional couple relationship or dyad. We define swinging as the actual activity when married or partnered couples have sex with other couples for recreation and fun.

281

Q: Can we just watch?

A: This is a common question, and the answer is yes. Going to a lifestyle club or event as a couple and watching, or fooling around with one another in the presence of others, is a fun way to enliven your sex life. You may have people flirt or ask to join, but you can politely decline. Most people are very respectful, and if you encounter a problem with a pushy person, you can always notify staff. Reputable clubs cater to couples, and they want their business. Pushy, aggressive, or disrespectful behavior is generally highly frowned upon. There are some events that explicitly say, "This is a full-swap event," which is the term used when all participants are expected to be sexually active with others at the event. If you are not sure, ask the organizer of the function for clarification.

Q: **Are people going to be hitting on my wife?**

A: If you attend a lifestyle event or club, it is a sexually charged atmosphere, so there is going to be a lot of looking and flirting. Generally, though, people don't touch before asking. And the men are, on the whole, particularly respectful. Compared to a singles club full of booze-fueled 20-somethings, the men are generally polite and deferential to the women present. Many venues are couples only—single men are not allowed and, if they are, there are usually rules of decorum that are enforced by staff, or the single men are separated from the couples. Also, there is no reason for sexual pushiness, because, well, there is no shortage of sex—sex is a sure thing even if it is just with your spouse. But if someone becomes aggressive, notify staff, and they will probably be removed from the venue.

282

Q: **Do I have to take one for the team?**

A: Sometimes the math seems impossible in lifestyle dating, and there are some situations for couples that are non-starters. For instance, if the prospective date has hygiene problems or has posted a picture from 20 years and 40 fewer pounds ago, a couple may want to have a signal for calling it quits or moving into a just-for-drinks mode. Couples sometimes know one another so well that explicit verbal communication is not needed—they just know intuitively what is going to work for their spouse or partner.

A smart couple should talk up front and then along the way about what they like and don't like, including how to start or end a particular encounter—for any reason. Although the likelihood of a perfect foursquare match at every encounter is rare, experienced couples find that their sexual attractions and tastes expand over time. Experienced couples also know that sex is not a long-term commitment. If their partner is having a lot of fun, they may choose to hang in there with a less than ideal fourth.

Q: **What do I do when the jealous feelings come up? Even if I know they aren't rational?**

A: Jealousy is a natural human emotion and will often surprise you as you engage in new sexual adventures—so expect it and prepare for it. Jealousy can mean that you have an attachment to your partner and that you care. Jealousy, though, like with any other emotion, can be managed with some clear-headed thinking, discussion, and by asking for support from your partner.

283

Distinguishing jealousy from envy is important. Envy can arise from feelings of inadequacy. Be mindful if you are comparing yourself to others. Comparing can lead to more feelings of inadequacy. Remember the old adage, "compare and despair."

Guys need to be particularly mindful of comparing themselves to others, and it's not the old penis size comparison that men need to worry about. Men like to please and want admiration for doing a good job. Many men will spend a lot of time working on or thinking about their sexual technique and how to please their partner. Consensual non-monogamy, though, is about expanding your sexual experience with others, and means that other people have other skills and experiences, and may be able to elicit new and exciting sexual responses in your partner. There is no reason to feel envious or jealous. Men need to be mindful that this is not a competition, it is about allowing your partner to enjoy her sexuality and enjoying her enjoyment. Her sexual enjoyment with another doesn't subtract from her enjoyment with you.

A typical hot spot for couples is feeling left out. A couple should talk about how to handle this because in a group setting as it will happen from time to time. If it happens to you, we suggest that you wait for a pause in the action and then use your big boy or big girl words and say something like, "I'd like to be part of this scene." If you can't express yourself at the moment, talk about it later. A caring, sensitive partner—a must for sexual adventure—will acknowledge your feelings and make an effort to be inclusive in the future.

In swinging, more than three-quarters of women identify as bisexual or bi-curious. Often in an encounter, the women take the lead with one another. Even if you are not a bisexual woman, this informal, but typical, behavior extinguishes some of the stereotypical competition for male attention that can lead to feelings of female-to-female jealousy.

284

Sometimes, though, there are just people, behaviors, or situations that are off limits—and remember, you may not know this until you are in the middle of an encounter. You cannot anticipate every like and dislike, or every strong emotional response you may have—you are on a new adventure. If you have a strong, negative emotional response to a situation, a shared "out" signal is necessary, and a post-encounter discussion about setting boundaries is probably imperative.

And remember jealousy or other negative emotions thrive in secrecy. So talk, talk, and talk more about your experiences and feelings. Adverse feelings of jealousy shared with your partner will more often turn to sexy banter that leads to a fun erotic resolution. Don't feel guilty about telling your partner about your likes and dislikes, and that you have discovered that certain things are just off limits. Sexual adventure and expansion happen when both partners feel secure and safe. In the beginning, you may have more discussion than action. Be patient. Never push or manipulate a partner into any sexual activity. If you, especially you guys, can remember that your priority is your partner's comfort, safety, and pleasure you will be able to work through the tricky situations that come up in any new adventure.

Q: **What about privacy and coming out as a non-monogamous?**

A: Your sex life is a private matter and ultimately no one's business. Non-monogamy among consenting adults is legal. If you run into someone you know at an event, well, you now know they are, too. Discretion is the unspoken norm.

Of course, if you choose to reveal your private activities to friends, families, or co-workers, you have to be prepared for any response. But by and large, people don't care about or care to hear about your sex lives unless, of course, your friends are open.

That being said, sites get hacked and people gossip—there is a chance someone you don't want to know about your lifestyle will find out. The good news is chances are one in 10 couples you know are or have been non-monogamous, and they may well be your doctor or PTA president.

285

Q: **Who are sexually open people?**

A: Next time you are in a large crowd, take a look around. Chances are you'll be looking at one somewhere in that crowd, you just won't recognize him or her. Sexual adventurers come in all shapes, sizes, and age ranges.

There are an estimated 4 to 9 million swingers in the U.S. If you want an excellent, comprehensive, and exhaustive examination and explanation of swingers and the lifestyle, we recommend Terry Gould's book, *The Lifestyle: A Look at the Erotic Life of Swingers.*

Q: **How do I talk to my partner about non-monogamy?**

A: If you have never broached the idea of non-monogamy with your partner, we suggest you share one of our sexy stories. Smart couples, if they can, prioritize pleasure, play, and relaxation. When you introduce the topic, consider the timing. Pleasure is important, but if your spouse is preoccupied or stressed out, sex may be the last thing on their mind. So pick a time and place where your spouse is most likely to be relaxed and receptive.

Don't lead with demands; lead with expressing how you feel about it or how you are turned on by the stories. Don't be discouraged if your spouse balks or laughs at first. Although non-monogamy, or serial monogamy, is culturally acceptable for single people, it is not the norm for married couples. Sexual monogamy is the automatic default for heterosexual couples, and your spouse may have absorbed the ubiquitous Leisure-suit Larry images of swingers. Furthermore, your spouse may not really know what non-monogamy is—he or she may think it is that you are asking for permission to cheat. The idea that a couple can maintain emotional fidelity while having sex together with other couples is new—so new, that the basic concept takes a while to digest.

Ask your spouse (this is for you guys) if they have ever been sexually attracted to another person or think or fantasize about other people while you are having sex. Gently probe. Now, be prepared for their answer. Because your spouse may have been thinking about someone you know. If she tells you she sometimes thinks about banging your best friend, don't balk, even if you are awash with surprise and jealousy. Women fantasize just as much as men. Women are just socialized to keep their mouths shut about it.

286

Q: Why am I turned on by naughty people?

A: "Bad boys" and "loose women"—mysterious, prohibited, and never fully known, will almost always hold allure in our erotic imaginations. That is because the very thing that is forbidden or unattainable is the very thing that our minds want to discover and explore. Curiosity, whether sexual or intellectual, is a characteristic innate to being human. So when our natural curiosities are impeded, the force of the interest builds. And nothing has been more defined, shaped, restricted, or outright forbidden by cultural and religious forces than sex and its pleasures, especially female sexual pleasure. And therein lies the allure: what we are attracted to, but what is prohibited, often fuels excitement.

Males have an advantage, both culturally and physiologically, of recognizing when they are sexually aroused. To put it simply, they can be at "full mast," and can both feel and identify more quickly the source and experience of their sexual arousal. Their sexual development is more easily identified or known. And, needless to say, overt male heterosexual sexuality—sex for pleasure and gratification—is more widely culturally understood and accepted. I'll spare you the chapter of examples here.

A female's awareness of her sexual arousal, in contrast, may be more diffuse because the physiological cues for sexual arousal are less obvious, especially when the adolescent female is first developing. But there is more. Not only are the physical signs of arousal more obscure, steeped in a culture that attempts to deny, control, or repress female sexuality, but what the "signs" (or signifier, to borrow a term from semiotics) mean for the female lack clarity and definition. So, a female may be sexually aroused and attracted to any number of persons. But if she doesn't fully recognize her arousal—and is denied knowing and exploring the very thing that is most attractive to her—arousal becomes associated, not with the object or person, but with the experience of prohibition or subversion. The bad boy or naughty things in their many forms and manifestations are what subconsciously appeal.

In "The Flirt," Dylan, the bad boy, though attractive and exciting to Elaine, may have been a bust in bed for a myriad of reasons that I don't need to explain to most adults. But he is not a bust in Elaine's imagination because Elaine is a female creature of our culture, in which the very prohibitions placed on her attraction to his type, inadvertently amplifies her excitement.

Swinging is an interesting phenomenon, in that it can only exist in a culture that is sufficiently liberalized. This, then, begs the question: if all sexual prohibitions are removed will desire die? I'd conjecture, probably not. For one, the capacity for physical, sexual arousal is innate and strong— a biological prerogative. So is curiosity—also a natural prerogative. But moreover, the priorities that define and give meaning to our marriages and lives—raising our families, making a living, coping with struggles—place natural limits on sex and the pursuit of pleasure. There will always be obstacles to sex, helping it to remain eroticized and exciting.

288

Female sexuality needs to be nurtured, but not controlled. A liberalized and prosperous culture can contribute to ensuring that female sexual desire and pleasure will be given a safe arena for exploration, bad boys or not, and an opportunity for her to develop her own sexual voice and decide whether or not to act on her desires.

Q: **What if I can't satisfy my partner the way someone else can? That would drive me wild!**

A: Sex is not a competition. Although there are people who approach sex with a sport-like attitude, the average non-monogamous person approaches as a cooperative endeavor, with the purpose of enhancing both partner's erotic lives.

When you choose to open up, you are starting on a sexual adventure and are addressing, whether you know it or not, phenomena common to happy, loving, long-term couples. The phenomena are that your sexual patterns may have become routine and familiar. By introducing new partners in your sex life, you are adding the very qualities that fuel sexual passion—novelty, mystery, and excitement. For sexual and erotic love to burn brightly, a little space is required; inside that space is where sexual passion is rekindled. Your partner may respond with nervousness, anxiety, or just plain excitement and elation at encounters with new partners. We hope so. Enjoy it and consider it an expansion of your shared sexual territory, not an annexation by another. Remember no one person can fulfill every sexual fantasy, but a couple can share and even act out their sexual fantasies and be happier for it.

289

Q: **Once you open up, can you stop? What if I like it and my spouse decides she or he does not like it?**

A: Of course you can stop, but like deciding to open up, it may take a lot of discussion and negotiation. Like traditional dating, there can be good and bad experiences. And like any activity, non-monogamy could become tiresome for either one of the individuals. No one should ever be manipulated, pushed or coerced into accepting non-monogamy as relationship style or into any sexual activity, no matter how much one partner is into it.

We believe that swinging is primarily a couples activity, done for the benefit and pleasure of the pair—so going solo is not swinging by our definition. Solo is when a marriage or partnership is open. We believe that an open marriage or partnership may lead to a deeper or more romantic connection with a liaison simply by the nature of the activity.

Q: Are all non-monogamous people bisexual? Because I am 100 percent straight.

A: No, not all are bisexual. Swingers, though, are comfortable with same-gender nudity and the fact that persons of the same gender will be sexually aroused in close proximity. Women tend to demonstrate or are more comfortable with bisexual contact, and in the swinging world, a high percentage of women identify as bisexual or bi-curious. Bisexual men, much rarer, will either identify as such on dating websites or let you know up front. And I do have to let the nervous men know that having casual, brief sexual contact with a male—say crossing swords when you are with the same woman at the same time—does not make you gay, so get over it. In the heat of any good action, bodies move fast—you should be so lucky.

290

That being said, swinging events primarily cater to heterosexual couples. Some large resorts, or resort cities, are rainbow friendly but have separate and distinct club scenes catering to gay couples. Large resort cities also have clubs for couples interested in kink or BDSM.

Q: Who in the world has time for non-monogamy or any kind of "alternative" sex?

A: That is up to you. Sexual adventure doesn't start on a dating website, at a club, at a resort, or in an adult toy store. The sexual adventure begins with your biggest sexual organ— your mind. We hope that you are a happy couple, and we hope that you can find the time to tune into your erotic imagination and share your erotic fantasies with your partner. If sharing the stories and fantasies leads to some real-life action, we are happy for you. If not, that's ok, too. Spicing up your shared sexual life takes a few minutes when you share something new, something naughty, and maybe something or someone else that has been on your sexy, big mind. And, in our opinion, sex is more fun than golf—and it's easier to keep track of the balls.

Acknowledgments

OUR EFFORTS TO write a lively companion to sexual adventure could not have been done without the people we met as we navigated our adventures as well as the professionals who wrote about this topic before us.

We are indebted to **Curtis Bergstrand** and **Jennifer Blevins Sinski** who conducted comprehensive research on swinging and laid the groundwork for understanding who swingers are and why they seek adventure. Though we have never met him, we'd like to extend a special thanks to **Terry Gould** whose masterful, sensitive, and comprehensive book documents the history and practices of those in the lifestyle.

We so appreciate **Laila Pilgren** of the *Sex Academy Barcelona* and **Ata and Michal** of *Barcelona PolyPeople*. They work tirelessly to promote a positive, healthy, and playful approach to sex, and provide spaces for people to create authentic and meaningful relationships.

We love you **Ruben, Ellie, Georgia, Aimee, Mike, Jason and Lea, Marco** and **Margaret**. Thanks for keeping the faith that our book would be published and for making us feel at home in Barcelona. We'd like to give a special shout out to the **anonymous salesman in Vegas.**

Our literary agent, **Jessica Craig,** guided and encouraged us, and believed that this topic was not only fascinating but of particular significance to women and their sexual choices.

Thank you to **Zoe Bowethorpe** who skillfully edited many versions of our manuscript and provided valuable suggestions and insight into this hot topic. We appreciate the sharp eye and wit of our designer **Julian Luske,** and **Katrina Logie** for her tireless networking.

We are grateful to **Merideth Finn** and **Michele Weiss** of *Cue The Dog Productions* for seeing the potential for a TV series or movie in our early drafts.

Finally, we'd like to acknowledge our kind, tolerant, and understanding families and pre-adventure friends **Alan, Gene, Andre,** our special friend **A, Rob, Samantha, Debbie, Heidi, Ed, Patty,** and **Barron.** Thank you for accepting us even when we cross a boundary or two. And the real loves of our lives, our five children—**I, A, L, Z** and **S**—we love you more than you will ever know and we appreciate your efforts to pretend that our book was about dates... and other dried fruit.

294

Sources

- Bergstrand, Curtis R. & Blevins Sinski, Jennifer. *Swinging in America Love, Sex, and Marriage in the 21st Century.* Santa Barbara, CA: ABC CLIO, 2009.

- Easton, Dossie & Hardy, Janet. *Ethical Slut, third edition: A Practical Guide to Polyamory, Open Relationships and Other Freedoms in Sex and Love.* Berkeley, CA: Ten Speed Press, 2017.

- Fernandes, Edward M. "Swinging Paradigm: An Evaluation of the Marital and Sexual Satisfaction of Swingers." *Electronic Journal of Human Sexuality*, 12, 2009.

- Foucault, Michael. *History of Sexuality, Volume One, An Introduction.* New York: Vintage, 1990.

- Gould, Terry. *The Lifestyle: A Look at the Erotic Rites of Swingers.* Canada: Random House Canada, 1999.

- Herbenick, Debby. *Because It Feels Good: A Women's Guide to Sexual Pleasure and Satisfaction.* New York: Rodal, 2009.

- Jenks, R. J. "Swinging: A Replication and Test of a Theory." *The Journal of Sex Research*, 21(2), 199-205, 1985.

- Jenks, R. J. "Swinging: A Review of the Literature." *Archives of Sexual Behavior*, 27, 507-521, 1998.

- Jenks, R. J. (2001). "The Lifestyle: A Look at the Erotic Rites of Swingers." *The Journal of Sex Research*, 38(2), 171-175, 2001.

- Lloyd, Elisabeth. *The Case of the Female Orgasm: Bias in the Science of Evolution.* Cambridge, MA: Harvard University Press, 2005.

- McCarthy, Barry. *Sex Made Simple: Clinical Strategies for Sexual Issues in Therapy.* Eau Claire, WI: PESI Publishing & Media, 2015.

– Meana, Marta. "Elucidating Women's Heteosexual Desire: Definitional Challenges and Content Expansion." *The Journal of Sex Research*, 43, 104-122, 2015.

– Morin, Jack. *The Erotic Mind: Unlocking the Inner Sources of Sexual Passion and Fulfillment*. New York: HarperCollins, 1996.

– O'Neill, George and O'Neill, Nena. *Open Marriage*. New York: M. Evans and Company, Inc., 1984.

– Pavlicev, Michael and Wagner, Gunter. "Evolutionary Origin of Female Orgasm." *Journal of Experimental Zoology*, 00B, 1-12, 2016.

– Perel, Esther. *Mating in Captivity*. New York: HarperCollins, 2006.

– Rubel, Alicia N. and Bogaert, Anthony F. "Consensual Nonmonogamy: Psychological Well-Being and Relationship Quality Correlates." *The Journal of Sex Research*, 52:9, 961-982, 2015.

– Ryan, Christopher and Jetha, Cecilia. *Sex at Dawn: The Prehistoric Origins of Modern Sexuality*. New York: HarperCollins, 2010.

– Small, Meredith. *Female Choices*. Ithaca, New York: Cornell University Press, 1993.

– Taormino, Tristan. *Opening Up: A Guide to Creating and Sustaining Open Relationships*. San Francisco: Cleis, 2008.

– Walden, Kim and Lloyd, Elisabeth. "Female Sexual Arousal: Genital Anatomy and Orgasm in Intercourse." *Human Behavior*, 59(5), 780-792, 2011.

www.ingramcontent.com/pod-product-compliance
Lightning Source LLC
Chambersburg PA
CBHW070738180626
46818CB00007B/2904